DEAD WRITERS
IN REHAB

Published in 2024
by Lightning Books
Imprint of Eye Books Ltd
29A Barrow Street
Much Wenlock
Shropshire
TF13 6EN

www.lightning-books.com

ISBN: 9781785634000

First published by Unbound in 2017

Design by Mecob
Cover image by Lee Madgwick

Typeset in Sabon LT Std and Avenir LT Std

British Library Cataloguing in Publication Data
A catalogue record for this book is available from the British Library.

PAUL BASSETT DAVIES has been writing for a long time and he still hasn't finished. He writes for stage, television, radio and film, including the screenplay for the feature animation film *The Magic Roundabout*, and a film about counter-culture comic book heroes, *The Fabulous Furry Freak Brothers*, developed with their creator, comics legend Gilbert Shelton. Among his work for television and radio are his various radio plays, his own radio sitcom, and the series *At Home with the Hardys*, co-written with Jeremy Hardy, in which he also appeared. In addition, he co-wrote and produced the Sony Award-winning radio show *Do Go On* for BBC Radio 4. He has written several short stories, some of them published in his collection *The Glade and Other Stories*. His first novel, *Utter Folly*, topped the humorous fiction charts in 2012. His other novels are *Dead Writers in Rehab*, *Please Do Not Ask for Mercy as a Refusal Often Offends* and *Stone Heart Deep*. He was once the vocalist in a punk band while moonlighting from his job as a cab driver.

DEAD WRITERS IN REHAB

Paul Bassett Davies

To the memory of
Barry Warren Wasserman

I know why the caged bird sings.

But that pigeon outside my room at four in the morning? What the fuck is *his* problem?

Wait.

Outside what room? And how do I know it's four in the morning?

All I really know is that it's very dark.

The darkness persisted.

Perhaps I'd gone blind, which had happened before. Sometimes I just assumed I'd gone blind, when there was another reason why I couldn't see anything. On one occasion, several years ago, I opened my eyes to what seemed like darkness but was in fact a light so bright it was black. After a moment I realised I was lying on my back in a field looking up into the sun. Birds were singing and the meadow around me smelled sweet. I stood up carefully, checking for broken glass, and looked around. It was a lovely midsummer day somewhere in England. I was wearing a white tuxedo and a green bow tie. I appeared to be completely alone in the open, rolling countryside. Then I caught a faint bark of laughter and made out some little figures in the far distance, loading things into the back of a big truck. There must have been a road there.

I set off through wild grass that swished gently at my knees. I knew I was about to undergo a brutal transformation as my senses came to their senses. Sure enough, a thundering brandy-and-cocaine hangover, one of the meanest of the tribe, erupted inside me like an enraged alien foetus. Once the pain had settled down to an agonising throb data began to assemble itself.

I'd been at a wedding reception in the grounds of a big manor house that was presumably not far away, tucked into the undulating landscape, probably just over a slight rise to my left. There had been marquees and a stage with lighting and a PA system, which was probably what was being loaded into the truck in the distance. It was my first publisher's second wedding. He was a Canadian who'd hit the UK just in time to surf the 1980s alternative comedy boom, and help some of the performers understand they could make a lot of money from a cheap book and still be terrifically alternative. Now, having divested himself of his first wife (the word 'outgrown' was used, earnestly by him, mordantly by her), he was marrying the posh, well-connected woman he'd been living with for a while. She was a nice, sensible type, pretty in a wispy blonde English way, but not as sexy as his personal assistant, who wasn't a sensible type. She was the one he did drugs with and fucked in hotels when they went to literary festivals together. But he was an ambitious player in a fundamentally conservative industry, and when it came to getting married he made the obvious choice. The sexy assistant spent half the party in tears and the other half with me, doing coke in various places, the last of which was an elaborate temporary structure housing the women's toilets. Like everything else at this wedding reception, it was the best that money could buy and it was cleaner and more attractive than many of the flats I'd lived in. We ended up in one of the cubicles, where she decided it was time for us to fulfil the sexual promise that had always simmered between us, despite her being in love with her boss. We were just getting into it when she changed her mind and decided that one more good, loud session of hysterical crying would do the trick for her. A guy we both knew was passing the toilets and heard her. He came in and found us half-dressed, me trying to do up my clothes, hers in disarray as she sank to the ground, howling with what the guy, who'd always fancied her himself, chose to interpret as trauma caused by my unwelcome sexual advances. I didn't remember much after that, except for some shouting. In the morning, as I trudged through the field, I wondered what would happen when I got back to London. Nothing much, as it turned out. For a while I got a few more pitying looks than usual, but at that stage I was pretty much immune to anything more nuanced than a punch in the face.

Why was I now thinking about that incident from 20 years ago? I have a tendency to relate everything that happens to me to some specific disaster in the past. My third book was called *Everything Reminds Me of Something Bad*. It had been inspired by an experience I was having at the time with meat. I still have it. I always line my grill pan with tinfoil. And certain types of meat, especially lamb chops, produce a cloudy yellow fat that pools on the tin foil in a way that reminds me of how freebase cocaine – and heroin, if it's pure enough – will liquefy when you chase it down a strip of foil with a lighter under it. For two or three years after I'd given up drugs for the final time – the final time – the trigger was so powerful that I had to call my sponsor at NA, who was a sweet, long-suffering man. After a while he got used to it, and if I called him any time after six in the evening he'd pick up the phone and ask me how the lamb chops were doing.

Triggers. There's always something, even if you're not conscious of it. And now I thought I knew why the memory of that wedding reception had been playing out in my mind so vividly. Even though I was still in the dark, literally and metaphorically, I was convinced that whatever room or space or place I'd woken up in was somewhere in the countryside. That pigeon outside wasn't a pigeon. It was a dove.

From the desk of Dr Hatchjaw
Re: Patient FJ
Admission Note 1(b)

The patient FJ has emerged from the primary stage of detoxification, during which he remained asleep for most of the time, with sporadic episodes of wakefulness when he exhibited signs of confusion, melancholia, hysteria, disorientation, incoherence, anxiety, fatigue, mania, depression and incontinence. He appeared unwilling to prolong these episodes, and relapsed into unconsciousness. This may suggest a tendency to regression and womb fixation. Even at this early stage it is clear that he uses avoidance as a denial tactic. He appears docile.

We may assume that he remains ignorant of his status and whereabouts. He has not yet opened the window in his room, or the curtains, and may be unaware that the room has a window, or curtains, or that he is in a room as, at the last observation, he was found to be lying underneath his bed. This may also explain his delusion that he has lost his sight, which he has expressed during intermittent periods of verbalisation. Observation has been constant, with no intervention. The standard precautions will be taken when he emerges from his room but I am inclined to allow the patient to undergo his own orientation and to become cognisant of his circumstances without undue interference. If he exhibits any signs of trauma or aggression at any stage of the process, I will zonk him.

From the desk of Dr Bassett
Memo to Dr Hatchjaw

Wallace, thank you for patient report FJ1b. May I make a brief point? Once again I detect a tendency to over-diagnose. The fact that the patient showed some reluctance to wake up and exhibited signs of confusion, anxiety, etc., when he did, hardly justifies the inference that he wants to regress to the womb, interesting though the observation is, and doesn't necessarily imply avoidance as a tactic. The behaviours and symptoms you describe are all consistent with a very bad hangover.

Also (sorry to niggle) I feel that the use of the expression 'zonk' in a formal report is a little inappropriate. However, perhaps I'm just being old-fashioned.

Eudora

From the desk of Dr Hatchjaw
Memo to Dr Bassett

Dr Bassett, naturally I accept your rebuke concerning my report, and I note your assertion that I have a tendency to over-diagnose. I am a professional, and I strive to serve the interests of my patients and of this facility to the best of my ability. If that ability is deficient in your estimation, or if my efforts fall short of the standards which you profess to hold, I can only apologise and attempt to improve my performance. However, I cannot help feeling that your criticism is part of a strategy – conscious or otherwise – to remind me at every opportunity that, technically, you are the senior practitioner at this facility. Perhaps you are overcompensating for some insecurity you feel as a woman in a position of authority over a male colleague. Whatever the reason, I assure you I am well aware of your superior status and need no reminding.

'Zonk' was intended as a joke. Obviously it was ill-advised. I realise that I am attempting to ingratiate myself with you, and compromising my professional judgment in doing so.

NB: I would prefer you to use my title and surname in any communications. Casual use of my first name in these matters strikes me as patronising.

Dr W. Hatchjaw BA, RCPsyc, DDSB

From the desk of Dr Bassett
Memo to Dr Hatchjaw

Oh dear. What's got into you, Wallace? Sorry, Dr Hatchjaw, if you insist. Although it seems a bit silly to be using our full titles when we're just sending each other informal memos. But I seem to have offended you, and I'm sorry. However, there was no call for that crack about the high standards that I 'profess' to hold. That's not very nice.

I know the whole status issue is a bit awkward, but I do my best. As for the stuff about gender, let's not even go there. The fact is, I was simply making an observation on what you wrote in your report. I'm sure you'll do excellent work with Patient FJ, and I'm glad you're keeping a close eye on him. From what I saw of him during his admission, he looks as if he could be quite a handful! But you're always very good with that type of man, Wallace. My goodness, rather you than me!

Look, let's not get into a misunderstanding over this. If you'd like to discuss FJ, and your treatment plan, I'm more than happy to talk about it. If not, let's just have a chat anyway. Why not drop in for a cup of tea later?

Eudora

From the desk of Dr Hatchjaw
Memo to Dr Bassett

Dr Bassett, thank you for your kind offer to discuss my treatment plan for patient FJ, and your generous invitation to 'drop in for a cup of tea'. As it happens, I feel no need to discuss my patient with you at this stage, and regrettably I find myself too busy to accept the offer of tea, which holds little appeal for me, to be frank with you.

Hatchjaw

From the desk of Dr Bassett
Memo to Dr Hatchjaw

Suit yourself.

What the fuck?
Wait, sorry, I'll start again.

Patient FJ
Recovery Diary 1

On second thoughts, should this actually be diary entry number two? Only if I go back and treat that first bit I wrote as entry number one, and according to Hatchjaw I can't go back over anything I've written and change it.

Don't they realise what that means to a writer? To be unable to rewrite? I always begin a day's writing by going back over whatever I'm working on, from the beginning, and tinkering with it obsessively, then writing a bit of new stuff, which I then rewrite the next day along with everything else I've written so far. Obviously, there's a process of diminishing returns as I write less and less new stuff each day, but somehow I've still managed to finish several books, so fuck Achilles and the Tortoise he rode in on.

Do people still know about Achilles and the Tortoise? By people I mean the younger readers to whom I am appealing less and less, according to my current agent (my sixth, which isn't as bad as it sounds as one of them died while representing me, and another was jailed for assault). She says my writing is getting old-fashioned, and would claim that by tossing in things like that reference to Greek mythology I'm proving her point. Wait. Is the story of Achilles and the Tortoise from Greek mythology? I mean, I know Achilles was Greek, but maybe the story is actually a fable, from someone like Aesop, or someone later, that French one. What's his name? It's on the tip of my tongue. God, it's really annoying not having access to the internet. Not even a reference dictionary! What are they trying to do to us? And writing in longhand! It's been years since I've written anything longer than a cheque by hand. It starts to hurt even if I have to write my address on the back. But cheques aren't used any more. She's right, I am old-fashioned. Look at the way I wrote 'to whom I am appealing less and less...' back there, and how I'm indenting the paragraphs, even though Hatchjaw says nobody is ever going to read it except me, and it's just a facilitation tool in the recovery process. So at least I know where I am, even if the details are a bit puzzling, because there's only one place where they talk about things like facilitation tools in the recovery process, and that's in good old rehabilifuckingtation.

But this place doesn't seem like any rehab I've been in before. I've only gone halfway along the corridor so far, partly because I was feeling a bit sick and I got dizzy. There's a lump on my forehead, which may have been caused by trying to get out of bed when I was, in fact, underneath it. Which reminds me of something I used to say to women if I found myself staying the night and they asked me which side of the bed I preferred. 'The top,' I used to say. God, I was a funny drunk.

The other thing that made me turn back when I got halfway along the corridor was the noise coming from the room at the far end of it. There was something familiar about that sound and the voices making it that discouraged me from going any further.

I'd stopped at an intersection in the corridor, like a crossroads, with a passage stretching away on either side of me. I remained very still so that the nausea I was experiencing would think I had gone away, and leave me alone. It did, and as I slowly turned around to go back to my room I saw someone peering at me from an alcove about twenty yards along the passage to my left. As soon as he saw I'd spotted him he darted back into his hidey-hole. I thought about going to try and find him but he didn't seem to want my company, and I didn't have the energy for a confrontation with a potentially hostile stranger. He probably felt the same way about me.

It was when I got back to my room that I met Hatchjaw. He was lurking in the doorway and sprang out to introduce himself. I would describe him as a dark-haired man a little below average height, with a long face, bushy eyebrows, dandruff, and bad manners. After telling me his name he just gazed at me with a faint smile. I could see the dandruff on his shoulders even though he was wearing a white coat. I thought about the snowflakes that settled on a white bed sheet my mother once hung out to dry on a January day many years ago, even though snow had been forecast. 'Nonsense,' she said, 'these weathermen don't know what they're talking about. If it snows today I'll eat my hat.' Later, when she was making a chicken pie, she constructed a little hat out of pastry and ate it at dinner, very seriously, and my sister and I laughed until I nearly wet myself. My father tried to laugh too but it wasn't very convincing. He liked to be the one who made the jokes, and he didn't quite know what to do when anyone else did it.

I didn't say anything to Hatchjaw, because I couldn't be bothered, so we just stood there looking at each other. That's why I had time to notice so many details about him. I'm not normally very observant, or so I've been told. Mostly by a person who made it her mission in life to puncture my self-esteem, so perhaps I'm as observant as the next man. Hatchjaw finally spoke, in a surprisingly deep voice, and asked me if I had any questions. I shook my head. He nodded a few times then stepped aside. He didn't exactly usher me back into my room, he just made it clear that I could go back in there if I wanted to, so I did. When I tried to close the door Hatchjaw was still standing there. He seemed anxious to say something, so I raised a polite eyebrow. That was when he told me about the Recovery Diary and being forbidden to rewrite anything. He didn't actually say it was forbidden, but when I wake up in a strange place with an institutional atmosphere, and I meet a man in a white coat who stares at me with a sinister smile, and I notice the outline of a large syringe in his top pocket, and he says that I'm 'discouraged' from doing something, I'm inclined not to do it. Not only that, but Hatchjaw got decidedly testy when I asked a few innocent questions about his edicts.

'So,' I said, 'if I'm not allowed to do any revisions, then what I'm writing is supposed to be some kind of stream of consciousness, is that it?'

'If you like.'

'I don't exactly like it, no. I find that kind of thing a bit self-indulgent and silly, to be honest with you.'

'I expect you're right,' Hatchjaw said, 'from a literary perspective. But as I've said, this isn't intended to be a literary work. It's simply a way for you to examine and express your feelings, and to write an honest account of the behaviours that have brought you to your current situation. A kind of reckoning, let's say.'

'I see. But I'm still a bit confused. You're asking me to express my current feelings, but also to write about the past. So, is it meant to be a journal or a memoir?'

Hatchjaw sighed. 'It's up to you. It can be either, or both, or neither. I'm simply asking you to write whatever comes into your mind about your feelings, and any relevant reflections on your past that doing so may evoke.'

'Reflections or recollections?'

'Whichever you think is the more appropriate term.'

'But there's a difference, isn't there? Recollections are an attempt to recall past events that actually happened, while reflections could be more speculative.'

Hatchjaw's expression didn't change but I noticed a slight tremor in his cheek, which he seemed to be trying to control. Finally he spoke. 'If you wish to speculate about your past, and you find that process fruitful, then please do so.'

'Perhaps you're asking me to write fiction, essentially.'

'Please don't put words into my mouth.'

'No, of course not. Sorry. It's just that there's a bit of a paradox in what you're suggesting. You see, many of the behaviours, as you call them, that have contributed to my current predicament – whatever that is – are beyond the reach of my memory by their very nature, in that they invariably resulted in me getting totally shitfaced, and waking up without being able to remember a single thing I'd done.'

Hatchjaw spent a couple of moments considering this, while breathing heavily through his nose. Then he swallowed, and spoke through a thin smile that may have cost him some effort to maintain. 'I'm sure you'll resolve the paradox, Mr James. You're a very intelligent man. Shall we leave it at that?'

'Are you saying I can make it all up if I want?'

'Just write!' he snapped. 'That's what I'm saying!'

I treated him to my most boyish grin. 'Okay,' I said. 'I will.'

'Thank you.' Hatchjaw turned on his heel and strode away.

I was right about being in the country. I opened the curtains in my room and discovered it was a summer evening and I was looking out across a lawn that sloped gently down to some woods, with fields and hills visible beyond the woods, rolling gently up to the horizon in the far distance, all bathed in a clear, rosy sunset glow. All very nice. I hope I'm not paying for it, but I expect I am.

As I turned away from the window I thought I caught a glimpse of a figure at the edge of the woods. But when I turned back and scanned the treeline there was no sign of anyone. The low sunlight made it difficult to see anything, and after a minute I gave up reluctantly and turned away again.

I stopped in my tracks. I felt a sudden sense of danger. I have a pretty reliable instinct for the presence of any threat to my welfare, and it's enabled me to emerge relatively unscathed from a number of situations which I probably didn't deserve to survive at all. But right now I couldn't tell whether the danger I sensed was imminent, or if I was having a flashback to an ordeal I'd been through in the recent past. After a while the sensation faded, leaving me feeling merely unsettled and apprehensive.

Patient EH
Recovery Diary 17

In the night the pain returned and kept me awake for an hour or a little more. It passed and then I slept well and woke when I was ready. There was a chill at first light but it burned away and the day was long. These days at the end of summer linger and it is the lingering of one who should leave when love is over. It is best to finish things quickly. I get these goddamned cramps in the night and my legs are an old man's legs. You get the clarity back and it's good to see straight and feel things real and true again but part of what is true is that your legs feel like hell and your hands ache.

A new man joins us. His body is whole but he bears scars of that other battle known to each man here. And to those women who have gone to pieces in the same way, and they are made men by their scars. And some here have also wounds that are visible, caused by the ways that men fall in that battle.

This man staggers a little in his walking but he rolls with it like a sailor on the deck and he is not new to his pain. There is a woman here who is one of the good ones and she sees it all cold and clear and has no illusions about these things. She is a hell of a fine woman with a pleasant body and I hope I am getting to know her at least a little. Her duties may take her to attend to the new man and something rotten stirs in me at the thought, but the hell with it.

He sensed me watching him and then he was gone. The buck knows in his blood that the cross hairs are on him, and your finger on the trigger in that moment. I left him to find his own path. And screw him anyway if he's another British prick who thinks he's better than everyone else.

Patient HST
Recovery Diary 13

I don't buy that devious horseshit about nobody else reading this, and you know it.

You people are depraved psychic vampires. Describe my feelings? Do you seriously still think that's going to happen? I know what's behind the feeble-minded psychobabble. The lost souls howling and drivelling as they back you up against a wall, crazed by the need to *explain* themselves, frothing at the mouth, eyes skittering spastically, convinced everything will be just fine if someone will only *listen* to them. A very gross tableau. Fuck it. The situation is deteriorating…menacing vibrations…a need to hunker down and regroup here. And no inclination to gouge out my own entrails so you can read the auguries…throw the dice…

I don't know what kind of twisted game you're playing, and I never bet against the house. But I've come up with a new angle, just to break the savage, unremitting tedium of all this weirdness, and I've devised a game of my own.

It's pretty laid back...nothing ominous...no ante required, no dress code at the tables. I start the play by making a confession: I've been breaking the rules of this establishment. But you already know what I'm talking about. You want to make something of it? Hell, you've got my written confession right here. But if you try to use it as evidence against me...some kind of grim kangaroo court...it proves you're reading this. I've flushed you out, and I win. And if you don't bust me – well, maybe you're not reading it. Or maybe you are, but you don't have the balls to do anything about it. Either way it means I continue playing by my own rules – and I win again.

However, let's keep things friendly and relaxed... maintain protocol...don't give way to a shark ethic. We certainly don't want this stand-off to get brutal. But however you look at it, I have all the leverage here.

Those are the kind of odds I like.

From the desk of Dr Hatchjaw
Re: Patient FJ
Residential Note 1

The patient has emerged from his room, briefly, but did not venture as far as the end of the corridor. A Collective Encounter was in progress in Blue Annexe, and the patient seemed apprehensive as he approached it, and returned to his room. I must confess to some disappointment, as I was hoping that he would be tempted to investigate, and thus could be introduced directly into a group process which, I believe, would expedite his orientation. However, as I mentioned in my Admission Note 1(b) it is my policy to allow this patient to proceed at his own pace. Incidentally, I suggest that we use Blue Annexe more frequently during these long summer evenings. The quality of the light, shining through the azaleas outside the French windows, and bathing the room in a rich, mellow glow, creates a particularly tranquil atmosphere, and I have observed that this tends to enhance the mood of the group, and modify some of the habitual expressions of hostility.

Hatchjaw
NB: Please see the memo that follows.

From the desk of Dr Hatchjaw
Memo to Dr Bassett

Eudora, please forgive the petulant tone that I adopted in our recent exchanges. My behaviour has been infantile, and I must take responsibility for my own emotional responses. As we constantly tell our patients, I can't change you, I can only change how I feel about you. Of course, I wish you felt differently, but it's futile to argue with the truth. Please accept my apologies. I assure you that you continue to enjoy my utmost respect and esteem both personally and professionally.

Dr Wallace Hatchjaw

From the desk of Dr Bassett
Memo to Dr Hatchjaw

Wallace, thank you so much for your sweet note. You don't know how much it pains me when you become cold and distant, and how relieved I am when that icy demeanour begins to thaw. I always feel that I'm waiting for the storm to pass, and to see those big, brave eyebrows of yours lift like clouds to reveal the sunshine hiding in your eyes, which slowly warms me again as you allow it to beam forth. I like it so much better when you're happy, Wallace, and I'm glad you acknowledge that I can't be responsible for your happiness. As you know, the situation is complicated. I can't always be the way you want me to be. So, let's be friends, really good friends, and accept things the way they are for the present. But if you'd like to come for a sherry later, it might do us both good. No strings, no promises.

Eudora

From the desk of Dr Hatchjaw
Memo to Dr Bassett

Eudora, you are right, as usual. Yes, let's be grateful for the friendship we have. I note that you say 'for the present', which suggests the possibility of change. But I expect nothing, I demand nothing. Except a sherry! Which I will gladly accept. Certainly an improvement on the offer of a cup of tea, as far as I'm concerned! I look forward to it very much and I'll drop by after I've completed handover to the Night Obs unit.

Wallace

Patient FJ
Recovery Diary 2

The bastards. My friends, those bastards. And at least one bitch of a wife could be involved, almost certainly my first, as I'm pretty sure the second one wouldn't go along with something like this. Unless someone managed to convince her she'd be doing the right thing, and genuinely helping me in some unfathomable way. That's always been the trouble with Paula: she's far too trusting. But there again, she's not naïve, and people who assume her sweet nature is a sign of gullibility are making a big mistake, especially if they try to use her to hurt me. But they might have convinced her to play along, the people responsible for putting me in here, whoever they are. My friends, colleagues, rivals, enemies – all of the above, or none – this is their doing. The bastards.

Okay, I accept that both those other times, when it was all over, I could see they'd been right. I hated it at the time of course, especially the first one, when the whole concept of an *intervention* made me physically sick as they cornered me in the kitchen, in my pyjamas, and explained it to me. I was probably going to be sick anyway, given my condition, but ever since then I can't hear that word, *intervention*, without feeling the bile rising in my throat. I stood there with my back to the sink, gazing at them like some poor, dumb, bewildered badger about to be torn to pieces by a pack of slavering hounds who've somehow learned to speak a special smug, sanctimonious language all about *denial* and *responsibility* and *co-dependency*.

But they were right. It probably really did save my life. Especially the first time, when I woke up in what turned out to be The Priory. The second time was a bit different, as I knew what was happening and where I was being taken (which turned out to be a less expensive facility, because I wasn't selling so well by then, and the TV series hadn't been recommissioned, and the screenplay had been given to someone else, to be 'improved' in the way that a heretic is improved by being burned at the stake).

But that was rehab. This time the bastards have put me in a fucking nuthouse.

Why? I'm not nuts. I'm not even drunk any more. Clean and sober for five years. During which my behaviour has been exemplary, by my standards. It's been a long time since I had a fight or broke something valuable, like a Ming vase or a marriage, or caused a major embarrassment in public or told someone what I really think of them. I'm still a cunt but that's just me. In fact there's a good case for not giving up any of your bad habits, because when you do you'll discover you're just the same only now you've got nothing to blame it on. However, I gave it all up, and whatever makes me intolerable now isn't drink or drugs. And not mental disorder, either. I'm probably the sanest person I know. So what's all this about? Who has put me in here and why?

After my encounter with Hatchjaw I went back to sleep.

When I surfaced again I had no idea how long I'd slept. My mind was a blank.

I decided not to panic. I'd tried that before and it had never worked.

Slowly I began to remember a couple of things. Unfortunately it didn't help much, because the couple of things I remembered were that I knew very little about where I was except that I didn't like it, and I knew nothing at all about what the hell was going on.

I became aware that it was daylight and I was starving. I hadn't been fed, and I expect they thought it was the easiest way to lure me out of my room.

No one was loitering outside my door so I set off down the passage in the same direction as before. An easy choice, as my room is the last one in the corridor so they didn't exactly need to lay a trail of cheese. I walked past doors on either side of me that were identical to my door, all painted blue, and all closed. I reached the point where I'd turned back last time. I paused to listen for telltale sounds of confessional drivel, which is what had stopped me in my tracks on my first expedition. I didn't hear anything this time so I carried on.

The corridor led to a doorway. The door was open. I walked through into a large room, tastefully decorated, mainly in blue. Some big French windows were letting in a generous helping of daylight and fresh air. All very pleasant. But you could strap me into an orange jumpsuit and deprive me of all sensory stimuli, like some trembling peasant suspected by the CIA of harbouring unwholesome thoughts about democracy, and lead me into a room like this and whip the bag off my head, and I'd know exactly where I was. It takes more than a few coats of Dulux Blue Lagoon and some rubber tree plants to disguise an institution. There's something in the DNA of a building like this, whether it's a school, a prison or an old people's home. Bad vibes.

I looked around. I couldn't see any food but I could smell something cooking somewhere. There were three doorways out of the room, including the way I'd come in, and the French windows. A faint scent of something I recognised but couldn't name drifted in from the garden and mingled with the aroma of distant cooking. The food smelled good and I wondered which was the quickest route to its source.

I became aware of someone breathing heavily behind me. I turned to see a burly, grizzled man slumped in an armchair near the door I'd just come through. He was glaring at a woman who was sitting as far away from him as she could get while still remaining inside the room. She was about forty, with big eyes, and she looked tired. She was studiously ignoring him. The grizzled man, who had a scrubby beard and looked as though he might have mislaid a trawler somewhere nearby, turned his gaze slowly away from the woman and looked up at me. I thought for a moment there was something familiar about him, but when he spoke I could hear he was American, and I don't know any Americans who look like him – although I know a Scottish barman with similar facial hair and the same mottled, rosy complexion of someone who likes to get drunk quickly and uses spirits to do it. The American squinted up at me and shaded his eyes with his hand as if I were an enemy aircraft coming out of the sun. He growled at me:

'How is it going with you?'

'I'm rather hungry.'

'That's a good sign.'

The woman on the other side of the room gave a clearly audible snort. The American glared at her again. He seemed to lose interest in me. I heard a cough, and I noticed a person standing beside the French windows, apparently admiring the view. He turned towards me, took a few steps forward and performed a curt little bow.

'Sir, permit me to direct you to the commissary,' he said.

I stared at him. He was a short, balding man with peculiar little glasses and an immense, bushy beard. He was wearing a kind of frock coat made of corduroy, with a waistcoat to match, and a pair of chequered trousers.

He walked up to me and held out his hand.

'May I introduce myself? I'm Wilkie Collins.'

I shook his hand. 'Foster James. Pleased to meet you.'

'The pleasure is mine, sir. You are newly arrived among us, I believe?'

'Oh, yes,' I said, grinning inanely, 'fresh meat.'

He frowned and seemed about to ask me something but then his face cleared. 'Fresh meat in search of fresh meat!' he said, and laughed. He had rather a nice laugh, for a raving lunatic.

I laughed back at him politely, terrified that he might turn violent. He suddenly thrust out his arm and I sprang away from him, nearly falling over a low stool. He shot me an odd look. 'Allow me to escort you,' he said. He bent his elbow and waggled it at me. I understood what was expected of me so I took his arm like a shy debutante and allowed him to guide me to the door opposite the one I came in through. As we left the room I heard someone mutter something in which I caught only the word 'asshole'.

As the nut job who thought he was Wilkie Collins led me along another corridor and towards the smell of food, he kept up a constant stream of pseudo-Victorian chatter about 'assuaging the pangs of hunger' with 'revivifying comestibles' and 'fortifying refreshments'. I must say he did it all very well, and not just the language; his whole deportment, which was formal but chummy, seemed completely authentic, and much more convincing than most of the actors you see in films or TV adaptations of Victorian classics. He even smelled slightly musty.

After the bit about 'fortifying refreshments' he stopped abruptly. I stopped abruptly too, as my arm was still linked to his. He turned to me. 'I must tell you,' he said earnestly, 'that you shouldn't expect to find anything in the way of beverages that tend to intoxicate if taken unwisely, or, indeed, any unwholesome stimulant.'

I told him I knew far too much about this kind of place to expect to find any booze here. I was an old hand at this game, I said. For some reason he seemed very impressed by this remark. He narrowed his eyes and tilted his head back, as if taking the measure of me. After a moment he nodded sagely, patted my hand, and we set off again.

We reached what was clearly a dining room of some kind. There was a serving counter with steel shutters behind it, which were closed. The smell of cooking came from behind the shutters. I sighed.

'Another hour or so until we lunch, sir,' the little madman said, 'but fear not; help is at hand for the hungry vagabond.' He pointed to a large vending machine in the corner. We wove our way towards it between the tables and chairs that filled the room. The tables were round and each one seated four. There were about a dozen of them.

The machine contained soft drinks, chocolate bars and pre-packed rolls and sandwiches. 'Fresh every day, I can vouch for it, sir,' my new friend said. 'Quite remarkable.' He beamed at me behind his little steel-rimmed oval spectacles. His eyes were grey with tiny flecks of amber in them. I rummaged in my trouser pockets and came up with some change, but he put out his hand to stop me. 'I see you are unaware of the system in place here, sir. Permit me.' He reached into his coat pocket and produced a small, round token of some kind. It was vivid purple. He came up with another, smaller one that was green. He handed both the tokens to me. 'That should suffice for a sandwich and a cordial.'

'Thank you very much. Very kind.'

'I trust you will repay me when you've become acquainted with the system.'

'Absolutely,' I said.

He put his hand on my arm and gave me a worried look. 'I'm sorry to press the point, but I would be obliged if you do so at your earliest convenience.'

I looked at him. He was serious. This was definitely a loan. I nodded and treated him to a reassuring smile, then I got a cheese and tomato roll and a can of Diet Coke out of the machine. I unwrapped the roll and took a bite. Not bad. My companion watched with satisfaction. He bounced up and down on his toes a couple of times. His boots creaked. 'Would you care to take a stroll in the grounds?' he said. 'I'll gladly show you around.'

He watched me expectantly as I chewed another large mouthful. I swallowed it with a big, painful gulp. 'No, thanks,' I said.

He looked crestfallen. After glancing around quickly, he lowered his voice. 'As a matter of fact I believe a confidential discussion between us would be of mutual benefit. We can talk as I show you around; that will also serve to allay suspicion.'

I took a swig of Coke. He frowned at me, and I was suddenly aware I was being rude, even if he was a lunatic. The little man's formal courtesy, assumed or not, made me feel like a lout. I inclined my head briefly and placed my hand on his arm. 'That's very kind of you,' I said, 'but I'm rather tired now and I'd prefer to go back to my room. But I'll take you up on the offer another time. Thank you.'

'Very well. Can you find your own way back?'

I nodded, with my mouth full again.

So they've put me in the loony bin. I knew it wasn't a normal rehab. Some of these joints have pretty strange ideas, but the whole point is to get some kind of grasp on reality. A man who's firmly convinced he's a dead Victorian writer, and has got the whiskers to prove it, is delusional and belongs in a mental institution. Which is obviously what this place is. Which means I must have done something that made whoever put me here believe I was insane. Which is very worrying because I still can't remember a fucking thing.

It's interesting, though, that Wilkie Collins was a notorious opiate hound. Addicted to laudanum in a big way, like a lot of the Victorians, including Victoria herself, according to some people. It's certainly true that for most of the nineteenth century half the House of Commons and most of the Lords, including a lot of the bishops, were laudanum addicts, along with thousands of doctors, lawyers, teachers, governesses, and a vast, twittering army of spinsters who'd faint at the merest hint of depravity but found great relief from all manner of maidenly ailments in the little brown bottle of comforting medicine. To say nothing of the poor, if they could get it. So, if there had been such a thing as rehab in Wilkie's day he would have been a good candidate for it. I wonder if the nutter who's impersonating him here has gone to the extent of developing a real-life opiate habit. Not that I plan to ask him. What I plan to do is to get out of this place.

But what if I can't? What if whatever I did was serious enough for me to be sectioned, and detained under the Mental Health Act?

Unless it's more sinister than that. What if someone wants to get me out of the way, or punish me? An old enemy taking revenge. Christ, there are enough candidates. It could be a conspiracy, and they might have paid this place to certify me and when I try to leave I'll find I'm a prisoner. Fuck, what am I saying? That's basically the plot of a Wilkie Collins book. Get a grip. As soon as I feel a bit better I'm going to walk out of here.

Patient DP
Recovery Diary 15

Dear Diary, I feel so awfully jolly and bucked up that I may get through the whole day without bashing my head against the wall.

Will that do, kids? No, I know it won't. But a blank page is worse than an empty glass. At least you can gaze at an empty glass and imagine what might fill it. Maybe that's the idea: they set a task that gives you such a dandy headache you forget about any other pain that's making you feel sorry for yourself. It's just the kind of scurvy trick that doctors will play in their determination to help you, despite your unwavering ingratitude.

It is certainly horrible here, but I would be a fine louse to complain too much, for I am ever the optimist and

I'm sure it's doing me some good. Anyway, I had better quit crabbing about these present straits as I haven't a damn thing to say that will make them any better. Instead, as instructed, I shall try to describe my feelings. (I may have to excuse myself to go be a little sick on account of it, because you never know what you will find when you get to lifting up rocks in this way.)

Well, let's see. I'm sleeping more and crying less, and it's been several days since I've woken up screaming with hysterical laughter because I can't get a drink. Yesterday I thought about what it would be like never to have a drink again, and today I thought about the same thing without breaking into a cold sweat. I am even able to pen these few poor scraps after only a few hours' hesitation, and not have the yips come stealing over me. Progress, of a kind. I'm beginning to notice the sunshine, and the birds outside, even though they're too small to eat. That's another thing: I have an appetite. I ate a traditional breakfast today, but without the martini.

And now there is a new man. Not bad looking; maybe a little old and overweight but he has a certain something, and I know where he keeps it. I'll admit he may not be the perfect answer to the lisping prayers of an innocent maiden, but that description ceased to fit me many moons ago, and if the inevitable should by any chance happen there may be trouble and I will be in it. I know myself only too well. It's a fascinating subject but it gets a little predictable after a while.

Patient WC
Recovery Diary 16

I feel a renewed energy and confidence today, perhaps invigorated by an encounter that took place earlier, and of which I will relate more in due course.

As to my progress, I believe I am finally beginning to understand the precepts upon which this institution, and my treatment within it, are based. As I have previously recorded in this journal, I had always believed my occasional use of laudanum to be simply the most effective remedy for the gout from which I suffered. When it was first suggested to me that I was in some way dependent upon what I considered to be a purely medicinal recourse, and unable to abstain from it if I chose, I rejected the suggestion out of hand with some asperity, and, indeed, asserted that those who made it were more in need of medical attention than myself. However, that belief has been slowly changing, in the manner, and with the result, that I have described in these pages.

This report, I trust, fulfils my obligation to make a daily record of my progress, and the emotional responses which I experience in relation to it. This, at least, is still my understanding of Dr Hatchjaw's demand (reiterated by Dr Bassett, on the few occasions we have met, in the gentler, less imperative terms to be expected of her sex) to 'describe my feelings'.

And now to other matters. My encounter with a mysterious newcomer today has given impetus to my efforts to penetrate a riddle that has confounded me since my arrival in this strange place. The riddle of the place itself, and my presence in it, is of a different order, and I am convinced that the key to that mystery lies in my own hands, as I have been encouraged to believe by the medical practitioners here.

However, it is of those practitioners that I now wish to speak. Hatchjaw is clearly subordinate to Dr Bassett in professional terms, and this in itself is surprising. Hatchjaw is a learned and accomplished physician. His methods differ somewhat from those of his colleague (or superior, as I must learn to think of her) in that he tends towards a more analytic approach that presupposes a mechanical basis of psychology, while Dr Bassett seems to favour a broader, more metaphysical view. However, these differences are no greater than those that you might find between any two persons of science. Many is the time that I have observed a pair of eminent London medical men, at my very bedside, at complete loggerheads over the most rudimentary matters of diagnosis, treatment and prognosis. I have been led to the view that what I may call 'natural sympathy' is just as important – and effective – as erudition in the treatment of sickness. I believe this secret was known to our ancestors but has now been lost within the mighty precincts of our colleges and universities.

However, the mystery I find myself unable to penetrate is not the professional but the personal relationship between Bassett and Hatchjaw. It requires no particularly keen eye to detect signs of uncommon intimacy between them – deeper than that which might be expected to develop between persons who have stood in relation to each other merely as colleagues, for no matter how long. I believe there is some secret and powerful bond between these two, under whose constraints at times they submit, and at other times rebel. Their proximity appears to please and to distress them in equal measure.

Today, I thought I might be offered a clue to the mystery. As I escorted the newcomer to the dining hall, and mentioned that he should not expect to find intoxicating liquors on the premises, he said he was familiar with places like this, and used the words: '*I am an old hand at this game*'. Immediately I seized upon this. The man is clearly familiar with this kind of institution. Furthermore, he understands 'the game' well – all too well, his ironic manner seemed to imply. In that case, can he shed some light upon the strange behaviour of the two doctors towards each other? I determined to seek a confidential interview with him, and to conceal my intentions from any unwelcome observation under the pretext of showing him around the grounds (for we are observed constantly, both directly and indirectly, and our most private proceedings are known to the doctors by a means which I am at a loss to explain). However, he declined my offer. Something tells me that he knows more than he is prepared to reveal at present. I must be patient and careful. He may hold the answer to the riddle of the two doctors, even if he does not know it himself.

But an even greater mystery torments me, and I sense its malign influence pervading every corner of this enigmatic institution in a miasma of unease. Dare I hope that the newcomer will also be able to illuminate this other, more sinister question which has baffled my every attempt to penetrate it? Namely, who is the mysterious figure I have glimpsed, lurking at the edge of the grounds in the dusk, as the shadows lengthen, and whose face I have never yet seen? Even now my pulse quickens at the thought that the solution to this problem may be within my grasp.

Oh god oh fuck christ no no no no no

From the desk of Dr Hatchjaw
Patient FJ
Residential Note 2

FJ has begun orientation. The process is, of course, always unpredictable but I was hoping for a more managed contextualisation. The inevitable trauma associated with the process has been exacerbated for FJ by his chance encounter with patient PW. Unfortunately my Patient Background Report appears to be incomplete, and I was unaware that FJ was acquainted with PW. Perhaps I should have checked, but it's easy to overlook this type of information when we are dealing with such a broad spectrum.

If FJ remains in his room for longer than 24 hours, I will employ the usual methods to enhance his socialisation. I hope to have him participate in the next Collective Encounter for Latent Group 3.

PS: Please also see memo that follows.

From the desk of Dr Hatchjaw
Memo to Dr Bassett

Eudora, I just wanted to say how much I enjoyed the sherry.

Wallace X

From the desk of Dr Bassett
Memo to Dr Hatchjaw

Wallace, I'm so sorry, it's really my fault that your PBR on FJ was incomplete. I've been trying to get my head around this new data system and I've been putting all the patient background cross-referencing stuff to one side, hoping to incorporate it later. I think I'm going to have to get another assistant. And please don't think I'm bringing this up in order to make some kind of point. We'll just have to accept that this might be a delicate subject between us for a while, given what happened. But that's all in the past, and now I genuinely need some help as I am hopeless at this kind of specialised administrative work. You've always been much better at it than me. And don't for goodness sake think I'm implying you should be doing it. But please let's discuss the possibility of getting some new help, and do so like two sensible, mature adults.

Regarding Patient FJ and your proposal to employ 'the usual methods to enhance his socialisation', can you please make sure that the water is at least warm? It's positively cruel to use that thing with cold water. I'm sure you agree, but you sometimes forget.

Eudora
PS: I enjoyed the sherry very much too.

From the desk of Dr Hatchjaw
Memo to Dr Bassett

Eudora, thank you for your gracious apology but you really mustn't blame yourself. These things happen. I completely agree that you should have a new assistant. I've been waiting for you to bring it up because I've felt that if I raised the topic you might think I was being insensitive. So, I'm pleased you've broached the subject. Purely as a matter of scientific interest, do you think that by mislaying (or failing to collate) information that you must have known, on some level, was important to me, you may perhaps have been punishing me subconsciously? I speak only as a psychologist, as I'm sure you understand.

Wallace

From the desk of Dr Bassett
Memo to Dr Hatchjaw

I beg to differ. You speak not as a psychologist but as a complete bastard. Can't you leave it alone? Don't you think I've suffered enough over everything that's happened? I don't know how you can behave like this, especially after the sherry last night. I should have known better.

From the desk of Dr Hatchjaw
Memo to Dr Bassett

Eudora, I assure you that I was making a strictly scientific enquiry as a matter of professional curiosity. I didn't intend to hurt your feelings – which you claimed to have set aside with regard to me anyway. If, that is, they ever amounted to much in the first place. And since you brought it up, I have to say that you're the one who's behaving as if the sherry meant nothing. I'm afraid I can't be so clinical about these things.

Wallace

From the desk of Dr Bassett
Memo to Dr Hatchjaw

Oh, just shut up, Wallace. Stop it.

Let's just both take a deep breath and see if we can have a civilised discussion about the question of an assistant some time in the near future.

By the way, FJ appears to be having rather a tough time of it. I could hear him from my office. Still, I'm sure you've got it all under control.

Eudora

Patient FJ
Recovery Diary 3 (or 4)

I feel calm now. I should be screaming. I think I was screaming before.

They're clever, making you start this diary before you find out, because they know that when you do you're going to have to write about it just to stop yourself from going mad. Or killing yourself. But how do dead people kill themselves? Dead people like me. I'm dead. Oh Jesus, I can't believe I've just written that. I'm dead. Or I'm mad. God help me.

Mad or dead or both.

I'm back. I had to stop for a while there. Okay, let me think. Is there another explanation? What about drugs?

It's a bit early for me but you go ahead. Funny. No, but could it be some kind of hallucination or delirium? It doesn't feel like it. I've had hallucinations on acid trips and I've had very vivid opiate dreams but I knew they were dreams and hallucinations while I was having them. Maybe this is some kind of psychosis. Maybe I was right, and this is a nuthouse, and I had some kind of breakdown. I wish I could believe that. But I can't. I don't feel weird, or spaced out, I feel completely normal. Everything looks real and feels real. It is real. I'm not insane. I know mad people are convinced they're sane and all that shit but this is real and I'm not mad. I'm dead.

Fuck, I'm dead. I must be, given what just happened.

After I finished the sandwich I went back to my room. I didn't want to delay my departure much longer but I felt a bit shaky and I still couldn't remember anything. So I had a nap. When I woke up I was hungry again and it was nearly dark outside. I'd obviously missed lunch. I'd probably missed dinner too. I left my room and cursed my way along the corridor. When I got to the Blue Room I couldn't remember which doorway I'd gone through before to get to the dining area. No one was around. The French windows were closed and some table lamps were on. A smell of stale food was in the air. I decided to open the French windows. As I pushed the doors open I saw that someone was standing just outside them, facing me. He stepped into the room. I stepped back. Fuck, I said, and sat down in one of the armchairs. I was looking at a dead man.

I knew he was dead because I delivered a very moving little speech at his memorial service two years ago. I spoke with wry humour but also great tenderness. I kept the tone light but let them see the struggle I was having to control myself. Very poignant. Not a dry eye in the house. I'd always hated him.

It was my dear friend and deadly rival Patrick Warrendale, preposterously undeserving winner of the Booker prize, and prize dickhead I'd always detested, except when I was crying into my beer (red wine actually, and always very good) at his place in Notting Hill and swearing he was my best friend in the world, the whole fucking world, no really my best my truest friend the only one who's standing by me as I go through this terrible divorce, awful bankruptcy, loss of girlfriend or contract or agent or whatever, and thanks so much for letting me stay in your spare room until I can just get myself sorted and oops sorry I've just done a vomit down the side of your sofa. Don't worry, Paddy says, I'll clear it up. But haven't you got a girl, I say, a cleaner, a girl, some lovely young immigrant totty who does all that and probably shags you on the side for good measure as well you lucky bastard even though you've got a perfectly good wife who you stole from me I seem to remember, but haven't you got one of them, a girl, an au pair with a nice pair, one of them? Oh yes, he says, but I couldn't let her do that, I couldn't make Yolanda do something like that, and he means it the stupid guilt-ridden liberal bastard and he really does clean up my sick himself the bastard why is he always so good to me and why am I such a dreadful cunt.

Yes, that's how it was, I'm afraid.

Not always, though. At the beginning he was only a bit more successful than me. We were part of the same generation of writers, the same non-existent movement invented by lazy journalists (is there any other kind?) which meant that writers like me and Paddy and our gang – and we were a bit of a gang – were lumped together with sub-Nabokovian panty-sniffers and militant lesbian magical-realists, just because we were all roughly the same age. Paddy had a head start because of who his mother was, so they were all waiting to see what he'd do. Which was to come up with a few glib neologisms and write about the kind of bad behaviour that always impressed him even though he didn't have the balls to do it himself. Not seriously, anyway. He dabbled, and cultivated a hoodlum boy genius image. I always found his stuff fundamentally puerile. Even when he was fifty he was still writing like a precocious teenager trying to show off. I was the real tearaway, the one who did the overdosing and the adultery and the getting into fights and fucking everything up. He watched from the sidelines and then wrote very successful books and I know for sure that at least one of them was based on me. But he was too clever to make the mistakes for himself. Or so I thought.

He had a heart attack at fifty-three. Triple bypass. A

week out of hospital and I was at his place, fetching him tea as he lay on the sofa. I asked him why he thought it happened. Bad genes? Bad diet? Bad luck? And out of the blue he told me he'd had a massive coke habit for years. I was stunned at first but it made sense when I began to think about it. The most important thing for Paddy was to be cool. He used to join in, he was one of the lads, even one of the bad lads, but not one of the really bad lads. He used to go home early. And now we know why. All the time he was sneaking off and hoovering up the coke. Unbelievable. And weird for me to be hearing about it after all this time because I'd given it all up by then. But Paddy swore the heart attack had scared the shit out of him and he was going to stay clean. And he was back on the coke within six months and he had another coronary. His heart exploded and he dropped dead.

Everyone was very pleased. Of course we were all shocked and saddened as well, and the world had lost a great talent and we had lost a dear friend, blah blah blah – but the literary landscape suddenly felt a bit less crowded, especially the field for various book prizes. But I missed him, too. He was my friend, whatever that means.

And now he was standing there looking down at me. Hello, Jim, he said, how are you? He stuck out his hand. I didn't want to touch it. He grabbed my hand and gave it a firm shake. He was solid and real and he even smelled the same. What the fuck, I said, you're dead. Am

I? he said. And then he gave me this horrible smile. That was what did it. The smile. I jumped out of the chair and backed away and then I turned and ran, banging into the walls, and I didn't stop running until I got back here to my room and I put my head under the pillow and screamed. And now I'm writing this and I'm dead.

From the desk of Dr Hatchjaw
Memo to Dr Bassett

Dr Bassett, it has come to my attention that you have intervened in the treatment of my patient FJ. I had not yet decided upon the correct moment at which to introduce the patient to an encounter session, but you have made it virtually impossible for me to prevent him from attending the next one. You know that I plan each patient's recovery very carefully – you, yourself, have used the word meticulous – and now I find that you have undermined my strategy with regard to FJ. What makes it worse is that you appear to have done so with no thought of consulting me. I must insist that you give me an undertaking to desist from this kind of behaviour in future.

Dr W. Hatchjaw BA, RCPsyc, DDSB

Patient FJ
Recovery diary 4 (or 5)

I've met Dr Bassett.

I was alone in my room, gazing into a bottomless abyss of howling, existential horror. Pretty much an average day, even before I discovered I was dead. But everything gets boring if you do it by yourself for long enough so I decided to go and find someone else to do it with. I had a vague idea of looking for Paddy. It crossed my mind that if we were now both dead I could finally tell him what I really thought of him. I'd probably done that a few times when we were alive but I would have been too drunk to remember it afterwards and that's no fun. And I was lonely.

I'd been thinking about Paula, which I always do when

I feel lonely. Or maybe it's thinking about her that makes me feel lonely in the first place. Either way, the thought of her comes with a hollow ache of solitude, and always will. Perhaps I shouldn't have married her. Would that have changed anything? Not really. It might have changed the way I fucked it up, but not the end result. I would have lost her anyway: different route, same destination. And it was all my fault. Which is part of the loneliness I feel when I think of her: it was me alone who lost her, my decision, my choice. Out of all the paths I could have taken, I thoughtfully inspected the signpost saying This Way to Everlasting Regret and strolled nonchalantly in that direction with no comrade, guide, or tempter to lure me on. I've always been a bad influence on myself, and perfectly capable of leading myself astray without any outside interference. In this case there was no other woman in the picture for me, no other man for her, no false friends stirring the shit, no weird, dysfunctional families in the background dividing our loyalties or trying to break us up, no sudden elevation to a different social or professional sphere for one or other of us (to destroy fragile illusions of equality); none of that, none of the usual suspects, and nobody to blame but me. I threw away the best thing that ever happened to me and I did it all by myself. What a fucking genius. I shouldn't be allowed out on my own.

Enough of this.

Misery loves company, and I went to find some.

I wandered out and headed for the Blue Room. As I reached the intersection I heard the tapping of high heels and turned to see a small, tidy woman striding briskly towards me from the corridor on my left. She gave me a bright smile and thrust her hand out in front of her. 'Hello,' she said, 'I'm Eudora Bassett and you must be Mr James.' I said I was and asked her, please, to call me Foster. She smiled even more brightly, as if this was the one thing in the whole world she'd been hoping for, and we shook hands.

She looked about forty. She had short, slightly curly hair and a round face with nice lips. Her body looked round, too, but in a good way. She filled up her white coat very snugly. Well-upholstered. She reminded me of Austrian women I've known. Everything packed into a nice, firm little package that knows what it wants, and if that happens to be you, then you're in for some enthusiastic, dirty fun. God knows why I was thinking of sex. Maybe it was the cliché about sex and death and everyone wanting to fuck after a funeral. Clichéd but true, because I've had some great sex after funerals – although not my own, admittedly. Her eyes were brown and I love brown eyes. And she had a good strong handshake without making a point of it. She wasn't one of those women who grips your hand like a lumberjack to let you know what she thinks of men and especially you, you pathetic little worm. Dr Bassett and I then had the following conversation:

Her: How are you settling in, Foster?
Me: Okay, thanks, but I think I'm dead. Am I dead?
Her: What do you think?

Me: I think I must be. I've seen an old friend of mine who's dead.

Her: Did you talk to him?

Me: Yes.

Her: So, are you sure he's dead?

Me: Well, I suppose…but if he's not dead…oh, God! Does that mean I'm still alive?

Her: No, you're dead.

Me: Oh, God.

Her: In a way.

Me: What? What way? You just said I was dead!

Her: You just said your friend was dead. But then you said he was alive.

Me: Well, yes, in…in a way…

Her: That's right.

Pause.

Me: Look. Please. Just tell me what's happening. Please.

Her: I can't.

Me: Yes, you can. What is this place? Why am I here? What does it all mean?

Her: Do those questions seem familiar to you?

Pause.

Me: Okay, yes, very clever, those are the big questions that people always ask about life. I mean real life, when people are alive. Right. Fine. But…(*Pause.*). Come on. Just tell me what's going on.

Her: I'm sorry, but I can't.

Me: Okay, you're clearly in a position of authority here, and I'm not asking you to violate any sort of professional ethic, but I really need help. I feel very vulnerable right now. I feel so…I'm in a real mess. Sorry, this is a bit strange for me. I probably shouldn't say this, but to be honest I find you… no, never mind. But there's something about you that really makes me feel…that I can trust you. And I know you can help me.

Her: Keep your hands to yourself, please, Mr James.

Me: I haven't touched you!

Her: But you were thinking about it.

Me: Christ, what are you, telepathic now?

Her: I don't need to be telepathic.

Me: I suppose I'm just…craving some kind of intimacy, just the simple physical reassurance. Because of feeling so freaked out by all this. And you're an attractive woman, you know.

Her: Thank you, I'm flattered, and stop it.

Me: Okay, yes, sorry. Sorry.

Her: The point is, I'm afraid there are some things I just can't tell you.

Me: Oh, come on. Why not?

Her: Because I don't know.

Me: What do you mean you don't know?

Her: I mean there are some things I don't know. Don't look at me like that. Listen, Foster, we hold communal meetings which are very useful, very supportive. Small groups in which we share our experiences. I expect Dr Hatchjaw has told you about them.

Me: No. But I heard one. Shit, I knew that was what it was.

Her: Look, I know you must be feeling very upset at

69

the moment, but you'll feel better soon, even if that seems hard to believe right now. Go to the meeting. And now if you'll excuse me I must run. Goodbye, Foster, I'll see you again soon.'

She shook hands with me again, and flashed me another smile, which revealed a tiny fleck of lipstick on one of her teeth, and then she was tapitty-tap-tapping away along the corridor. I waited until she turned another corner but she didn't look back. Nice legs.

So that was Dr Bassett. And she said I was dead. And so is everyone else here, possibly including her and Hatchjaw. So the little nutcase who thinks he's Wilkie Collins actually is Wilkie Collins. And now I know why I thought I recognised the grumpy geezer with the beard. It's Hemingway. And a few minutes ago a tall man wearing sunglasses and a hat loped past my window, and he definitely looks familiar. It'll come to me. I'm also pretty sure I recognise the quiet little woman with the big eyes. And I can easily find out who she is,because we're all in this together and we're all dead. What fun.

Actually, it could be fun, in a horrible, post-mortem way. The quiet woman hardly looked at me but there was something about her, and something that passed between us, that tells me she's up for it. The lurking beast is stirring yet again. And the great thing is that I can try anything. What's the worst that can happen? It's already happened. I'm dead. We're all dead.

In a way. Bassett said I'm dead 'in a way'. Does that mean

there's a hope I may still be alive? Or perhaps dead but eligible for resurrection? I don't think so. I think she means I'm in a process, not a state. I'm dead, but that's not the end of the matter. It can't be, otherwise I wouldn't be in this place, whatever this place is. And the best chance I've got of finding out is going to the 'communal meeting'. And I know what that means. It means the dreary, balls-aching orgy of solipsistic navel-gazing, petulant resentment, impotent rage, whimpering guilt, denial, and lachrymose self-pity that is the wonderful healing miracle of group fucking therapy.

Patient EH
Recovery Diary 18

I feel hollow sick inside and I am a damned fool.

From my doorway I heard the staccato pattering of her high-heeled shoes and my blood quickened. I felt the energy and the courage to break through the thing that stood between us and although I was her patient by God I would talk to her as a man.

I wanted to talk to her about places we could be together and the fun we would have. I would make her understand I would not drink and I was all through with that. She is a woman you can talk to and I have some stories I have told to no one, and I wanted very much to tell them to her but now I will never tell them.

When I came out of my room she was in my line of sight. She had stopped and was speaking with the new British man. I knew he had accosted her in the way that men like him will accost a woman and bring them trouble, although they may not see it at first because the man ingratiates himself in a way that women like. There was a nauseating unction in his voice and he looked at her as one who considers the utility of a thing to him, and it is the way a worthless man or a pimp regards a woman.

I stepped back into my room without thinking what I did, or why I retreated. And when I had a grip on myself I knew I had been in a funk and gone all to pieces and that is about as bad as it can be for a man.

It is all gone now.

That lousy bastard. I will know him anywhere. The hell with him. The utter complete hell with him.

From the desk of Dr Bassett
Memo to Dr Hatchjaw

Wallace, I'm truly sorry. I bumped into FJ in the corridor. I could hardly ignore him, could I? He was very persistent and there were certain questions I couldn't answer, as usual, and so it seemed quite natural to refer to Group as a way of giving him some hope of further enlightenment. I seemed to recall that you had already decided to get him into Group anyway, and looking back over your Patient Notes I see that you did, in fact, say as much. However, I understand that strictly speaking you should be the one to keep a patient informed of these things. Once again, I'm sorry. To be quite honest I really don't see why you have to get so upset about it but I'll try not to do it again and, as you ask, to act with more consideration in the future.

With apologies, Eudora

Transcript

Latent Group 3
Collective Encounter 05; Blue Annexe

Present:
Dr WH – Facilitator
Patients: DP, EH, FJ, HST, PW, STC, WC

Dr WH: Hello, everyone, and just before we begin
          sharing I'd like us to welcome a new member
          to our group. This is Foster.
OMNES: Inaudible muttering.
Dr WH: Foster, would you like to say anything?
FJ: No.
Dr WH: Very well. Who would like to share
          something?
PW: I'd just like to say it's lovely to see you, Jim.

DP:	Why do you call him Jim?
PW:	Oh, sorry. Confidentiality. Have I blown it, Jim? I mean, Foster. Sorry.
FJ:	I don't care.
Dr WH:	Wait, if there is, in fact, a confidentiality issue here, Patrick, please don't say anything else for a moment. Foster? Are you comfortable with this?
FJ:	Look, I don't give a fuck. He calls me Jim because my real name is James Foster. I changed it because I thought Foster James sounded better for a writer. All right?
OMNES:	Indecipherable with some chuckles.
DP:	Nothing wrong with changing your name. Hell, I changed my name.
EH:	That's because you were a kike.
DP:	I'm still a kike, Ernie, it was just my name that converted.
STC:	Kike? What is that?
EH:	A kike, my friend, is a yid. You know what that is, Sam?
STC:	So, a disparaging reference to members of the Hebrew faith?
FJ:	My God – are you Coleridge?
STC:	Your servant, sir.
FJ:	Fuck me!
EH:	He won't, but Dottie probably will. She'll fuck anyone.
Dr WH:	Sorry, but—
DP:	I didn't fuck you, did I, Ernie?
WC:	If I may I interject here—

EH: You didn't fuck me because I wouldn't let you. God knows you tried.

DP: Why would I want to fuck a miserable, self-pitying bore like—

Dr WH: Stop! Is this really a fruitful way to spend this session?

OMNES: Yes.

EH: See, doc? They all want to hear the fun.

Dr WH: Nonetheless, it's not the best use of our time.

EH: You keep telling us we should use these powwows to help our personal growth. Well, Jesus, I can feel myself growing by the inch when I tell that bitch what I think of her.

DP: Growing by the inch, Ernie? That'll double the size of your cock, anyway.

EH: You've never seen my cock. Not for want of trying.

DP: I didn't have to see it, its minuscule size was the talk of the town.

Dr WH: Please, I really feel—

PW: Overruled, Doctor. We all want to hear this. We're writers, remember.

Dr WH: But surely...

WC: I must confess I find it diverting, although I am thrown into confusion by the participation of a lady in the discussion of a topic of this nature.

EH: (sotto) Jesus Christ.

STC: I find, Mr Collins, that often a lady's

	sensibilities in reference to the act of copulation may be far more robust than we gentlemen suspect. So, let us hear more of who fucked whom, or not.
Dr WH:	Look, the wish of the majority is an important principle, but—
PW:	Wait, we have an abstention. What about you, Hunter?

(Silence.)

STC:	Hunter?
WC:	I believe he's asleep.
PW:	Those fucking shades.
STC:	I was acquainted with a man in Bristol who wore tinted spectacles in order to deceive his wife that he was attending to her improving discourse while all the time was adrift in the bosom of Morpheus. Ha ha!
EH:	Okay. This is for the record. I never wanted to fuck Dorothy Parker.
DP:	And she never wanted to fuck you.
EH:	What about all those reviews? You called me 'the first American artist'.
DP:	I was probably drunk.
EH:	You were in love with me.
DP:	No, I admired you as an artist, a writer and a dipsomaniac, but I never loved you. You were too full of yourself, Ernie, too full of shit – which amounts to the same thing. And always obsessed with death. All those fucking bullfights.
EH:	You ran away from that one I took you to.

	You started crying.
DP:	You think I'm ashamed of that? Just because your idea of a swell time is to kill everything in sight, that doesn't make you a man, Ernie, in fact it just proves you're still a little boy. My God, everyone, here's a guy who liked killing things so much that when he couldn't think of anything else to kill, he killed himself!
EH:	At least I made a good job of it! Not like those phoney suicide stunts you were always staging. You think any of us were fooled?
DP:	I was in pain, you idiot, but you wouldn't know what that feels like because you never felt any pain, you only caused it.
EH:	Your bank balance was in pain! Sheila Graham told me when you couldn't pay the bill at the Lowell that time, you ordered an ambulance before you took the pills, so they'd see you being carried out on a stretcher, and lay off you.
DP:	That's not true, you bastard!
EH:	It was a standing joke, Dottie, just like you.
Dr WH:	Right, that's enough.
FJ:	Yes, you're clearly upsetting her.
EH:	You stupid limey prick, she can turn that on any time she wants. She's just buying some time while she thinks up her next lame crack.
DP:	Why do you assume everyone is as much of a louse as you are, Ernie?

EH:	Hell, Dottie, that outraged virtue routine is tired.
FJ:	Look, I really think you should just let her—
EH:	Let her what? You don't realise how long this fucking performance can go on for, even without the sauce.
Dr WH:	I'm going to suggest we take a break—
FJ:	You're an arsehole, you know that? A real arsehole.
EH:	An 'arsehole'? Jesus, you fucking Brits can't even deliver a good insult.
FJ:	Can't you see you're being very unkind to her?
EH:	Oh, she'll fuck you now for sure. A real knight in shining armour.
FJ:	Why don't you shut up?
EH:	Why don't you make me shut up?
DP:	All right, boys, I'm very flattered, but break it up at the back of the class.
Dr WH:	Yes, sit down please, Ernest.
WC:	Indeed, perhaps we should all pause for a moment's reflection. May I pr—
PW:	Hey, sit down, Jim. He's not worth it. Well, he is worth it, I suppose, given that he's Ernest Hemingway but—
Dr WH:	Yes, please sit down, both of you.
FJ:	Fuck off, I'm not going to sit down and let this dickhead hit me.
Dr WH:	Sit down both of you!
EH:	I'm a dickhead?
FJ:	Yes, a dickhead. God, to think I used to like

your stuff.

STC: But Mr Hemingway's pugnacious posture is congruent with the attitudes expressed in his literary efforts, which you profess to so admire.

EH: You want some too?

FJ: Leave him alone, you moron! He's not even insulting you!

EH: You want to call me a moron? Put them up. Come on.

Dr WH: Stop it!

FJ: Fuck that Queensbury rules shit.

Dr WH: No, I really must—

EH: Owww! Ahh, ahh, ahh – he kicked me in the balls!

FJ: Damn right I did. Not a bad shot, was it, Paddy?

PW: Look out!

FJ: Wha— Ah! Ah. Ahhhhhh.

DP: That was a low trick, Ernie!

EH: At least I didn't go for his balls! Your hero can still fuck you, unless he's a queer like most of these Brits!

PW: You shit, Hemingway, he wasn't even looking!

EH: You want some too? Come here!

Dr WH: No, no, I can't let you—

EH: Let go of me you fucking quack!

(Sounds of a general fracas, then Dr Bassett enters the room.)

Dr EB: What is the meaning of this! Oh my God,

	Wallace, are you all right?
PW:	He's fine, it's Jim who got punched in the face!
EH:	He kicked me in the balls!
Dr EB:	Mr Hemingway, let go of Dr Hatchjaw!
EH:	If you look carefully, sister, you'll find that he's the one who's holding on to me.
Dr EB:	Wallace, what are you doing?
Dr WH:	Preventing further violence.
Dr EB:	I see. Yes, very good. I believe you may release Mr Hemingway now.
Dr WH:	Mr Hemingway, I am merely attempting to prevent you, as clearly the most skilled pugilist present, from inflicting any further damage. May I release you without further danger to anyone?
EH:	Okay, Doc, it's all over.
Dr WH:	Very well.
EH:	Thanks.
Dr EB:	Will you all please leave? No! One at a time. That's better. We'll look into this later when tempers have cooled. Foster, perhaps someone should look at that eye.
FJ:	It's okay.
PW:	Don't worry. I've seen him take a few punches. He'll live.
Dr EB:	But perhaps you'll take him to his room?
PW:	No problem. Come on, Jim.
Dr WH:	Ernest, I hope I didn't—
EH:	No, no. But that's quite a grip you have there, Doc. Do you use weights?

Dr WH:	Well, I—
Dr EB:	Mr Hemingway, will you kindly leave now?
EH:	Sure. We'll talk about it later, Doc.
Dr EB:	You, too, Hunter.
Dr WH:	I think he's still...Hunter? (Very loud) Mr Thompson!
HST:	(*Quietly*) Back off, man. I'm awake.

TRANSCRIPT ENDS

Patient FJ
Recovery Diary 5 (let's just say it's 5 anyway, and stop splitting hairs)

I was staring into the mirror and admiring the black eye that Ernest Hemingway gave me when I realised something very strange.

Wait, I've got to do the bit about how I'm feeling first. In all the lively confusion as the therapy session broke up, Hatchjaw still managed to remind me about the discipline I have to follow in this diary: before writing anything else, express your feelings, reflect on your progress, etc. I still don't like Hatchjaw but he can handle himself in a fight. God, that was fun. I've been to a few recovery meetings where fights have broken out – having started many of them myself – and it always restores my faith in human nature.

Okay, how do I feel? I feel serene. It's not just the usual calm that descends on me after a good fight, or the satisfaction of being punched in the face by a very good writer. It's something else. The part of my brain that should be gibbering with terror as it tries to process what the fuck is going on here seems to have shut down. It reminds me of something that used to happen to me when I was about twelve, in bed waiting to go to sleep. I would suddenly be overwhelmed with dread. My mind would try to jump out of itself, like a terrified horse tethered to a tree in a forest fire, as I apprehended the full enormity of the following information:

Time is endless. The universe is infinite. I am going to die.

I would try to imagine what it would feel like to be dead. Try to understand the endlessness of time and space, knowing I would never reach the limits of a limitless void. I would become more and more horrified by the inescapable facts of eternity, infinity and death, willing them not to be true, and despairing because I knew they couldn't not be true. And then, slowly, a wonderful serenity would begin to spread like rich, warm syrup flowing through a system of pipes inside me. *There is nothing I can do. Surrender.*

I began to associate all this with the idea of God. I became convinced that what I was experiencing, after the tempest of discombobulation, was 'the peace which passeth all understanding'. After about a year I seemed to grow out of these attacks, although this cycle of feelings – terror followed by tranquillity – continued to recur in various circumstances, often involving the threat of violence or the promise of sex. And that's what it feels like now. Whatever's happening, there's nothing I can do, so why worry? Once again, I am filled with that familiar transcendent peace. But I really want a drink.

I always want a drink after a fight. And in the old days, if I'd been hurt I always used it as an excuse for an opiate binge, too. I'd justify taking some codeine, or morphine, or heroin on the eminently reasonable grounds that I was in pain and therefore entitled to a painkiller. After a few years in the recovery game you can handle the sudden cravings because you can go into your drill, but rationalisation is the bitch. So that's how I feel, since you asked. I want a drink and I want some opiates and I'm not going to get any so I may as well stop wanting them. And now I come to think of it, writing all this makes it a bit easier not to want what I thought I wanted, so maybe all this works. Thanks, Doc.

Anyway, I was gazing at my black eye when I realised I'm younger than I used to be. I look pretty good. I've never thought of myself as being particularly vain, which is probably a very vain thing to say, but I've been told I'm quite handsome by women who've been fond of me, and I've never had much of a problem attracting them. Mind you, I've found that women don't really care about how men look, or about how I look, anyway.

Of course, once they get hold of you they try to make you look presentable, especially if they marry you. They can't help doing that, and who can blame them. Other women are constantly judging them on the degree of control they can exert over their mate. But when it's only about sexual attraction I'm always amazed by what women will tolerate in a man if they want to fuck him. They don't seem to mind if you're drunk and they often don't even care if you're dirty and you stink. I think women get far more carried away by sex than men do. They become crazed with lust. Men tend to be a bit more fastidious and I can think of times when I've been getting down to some oral sex and I've been compelled by deficient feminine personal hygiene to reverse and head north again in a hurry, licking a hasty nipple on the way and making my excuses by moaning that I'm about to explode. But if a woman really wants to have sex with you she'll tear off your vomit-stained clothes, ignore the skid marks in your underpants as she rolls them down your grubby thighs, and attack a seriously unwashed cock like a starving refugee with a lamb kebab, before shoving it inside herself and squirming all over you without the slightest concern about where you might have been and when you last saw a bar of soap. Amazing. Of course, if they don't want to fuck you it makes no difference if you look like a Greek god and you're drenched in the rarest fragrances of the world's most accomplished *parfumiers*, they still won't fuck you. But they're capable of doing the most senseless things just to be with men they want, and if the men are despicable vermin it just seems to drive them to even more irrational extremes. Perhaps the difference is that a man will happily screw a woman who may be mad, bad, or dangerous if she's sufficiently alluring but he rarely makes the mistake of loving her, whereas women will allow love or desire to blind them completely to a man's true character, and pay for their mistake in terrible and tragic ways.

All this was swilling around my brain as I leered at myself in the mirror, entranced by my virile good looks. I appeared to be about forty. Maybe forty-two. Then it struck me that everyone else I've seen is relatively young. I mean they're younger than they were when they died. I think Coleridge died in his early sixties, and he looks about thirty. Dorothy Parker doesn't look quite as old as I thought she was when I first saw her; I think she's about thirty-five. Paddy looks only a few years younger than he did when I last saw him alive but it's a definite improvement. It's hard to tell with Hemingway. When I first saw him he looked about fifty. But in the meeting today he seemed younger, more like forty.

But I think I get it. Hemingway wrote *For Whom the Bell Tolls* when he was about forty, and sometimes I think that was his best book. But sometimes I prefer *The Old Man and the Sea* which he wrote when he was past fifty. Then I get infuriated by all the mythical, pseudo-religious crap in it and go back to liking the books about war and the way the characters seem to tell the truth without making a big fuss about it. Yes, I tell myself, that's how I'd be. Terse. Laconic. A manly reticence concealing a fine soul. Grace under pressure and all that. So maybe I'm seeing all these writers at the age when they did their best work, and the only reason Hemingway seems to fluctuate is because I can't make up my mind about when that was. It's not a problem with the rest of them: everyone knows Dorothy Parker was at her peak when she was between thirty and forty and that Coleridge declined after his twenties. Wilkie Collins looks about the age he must have been when *The Moonstone* was published. Furthermore, I'm now certain the guy who was asleep (or pretending to be) in the group therapy session is Hunter S. Thompson. Fuck knows what he looks like under those shades and the hat, but I'll bet he's the young maniac who wrote *Fear and Loathing in Las Vegas* and not the raddled old hack of his later years. He never wrote anything much good after about 1975, and the stuff he came up with in the last fifteen years of his life was mostly awful. However, while he may have lost it as a writer, he remained an exemplary drunk until his dying day and beyond, when they sent his ashes up in a rocket in accordance with his will. He might be good company.

Meanwhile, the person admiring me from the mirror is exactly the age I was when I was at the top of my game, although I didn't know it then.

This black eye is getting really painful. The adrenaline from the fight is draining away now that its job is done. The adrenal glands are amazing little buggers. Most of the time they just lie there, curled up on top of your kidneys. But as soon as they get a stress message from the cortex, they spring into action and squirt out the hormones like a pair of Jack Russell terriers waking up and pissing all over the place, yapping and snarling at anyone who tries to stop them. Bless the adrenal glands. Probably my favourite glands, apart from the testicles.

I'm going to lie down. That fight took it out of me. Interesting that when Dr Bassett burst in, her first concern was for Hatchjaw. There's something going on there but I don't think it's going on very smoothly right now. My guess is that those two have been in each other's pants at some point but an obstacle has derailed love's young dream. I know the signs only too well. Passion still smouldering but severe frost in the air. It could go either way: let the fire go out and freeze to death or stoke it back up to a merry blaze, strip off, tumble to the sheepskin rug in front of the fireplace and rut like stoats. We'll see.

It's dusk. I was about to close the curtains when I saw a movement among the trees on the far side of the lawn. Someone was standing there, gazing at the house in the sunset, and just as I caught sight of them they flitted back into the woods. I'm pretty sure it's the same person I glimpsed at this time yesterday, when exactly the same thing happened. Whoever it is I hope they've got a sweater on. It's been a lovely day but it can get pretty chilly in the evenings. Especially in the woods.

Oh God, that's what I used to say to Paula. 'It can get chilly in the evenings.' And she'd smile and shake her head, as if I were being silly and overprotective, and I'd have to persuade her to take some warmer clothes, especially if we were going on one of the expeditions into the countryside she loved. 'So English,' she'd say. And she would end up taking one of her pretty little cardigans that were completely useless. Then later we'd be sitting outside a pub, and as the late summer shadows lengthened she would shiver, and say, 'You were right, darling,' and I would drape the thin material around her delicate little shoulders and pull her towards me, and she would nestle herself against me, and say, 'You're always right.' Then she would kiss me.

Oh God.

I'll just have a cigarette before bed. Some things never change: everyone smokes in rehab. Although I can see Hatchjaw disapproves. He frowns every time someone lights up, and he does that prissy coughing that non-smokers do around smokers, especially non-smokers who used to smoke. But I think Bassett is a smoker. I caught the familiar scent of nicotine masked by mint as she brushed past me, full of anxiety for Hatchjaw. She's a fine woman, that one. I hope he knows how lucky he is. Probably not. We never do.

Patient STC
Recovery Diary 15

Still I roll, a wretched, rudderless wreck, but the motion is less violent, no longer the unceasing storm-tossed torment of earlier days, and there are periods of calmer weather in which I have some small respite from the aching in my limbs, with an indescribable restlessness, that makes action to any available purpose, almost impossible. I note with interest that a sudden stimulus – such as the pugilistic outbreak that brought our late gathering to a premature end – has the power to drive from my mind, at least for a time, the drear reflections upon which it is customarily fixed, and to draw my attention to external phenomena, and even to excite my interest. This is to be considered an improvement in my health. Of pain I have enough, but that is indeed to me, a mere trifle.

Of this contest or *tournament* between two of our number I wish to write further and I am inspired to do so in verse. Herewith:

> *In Therapy did Hemingway*
> *His rights uphold pugnaciously:*
> *When 'Jim', the newcomer, decried*
> *The calumnies that Ernest tried*
> *To heap on Dorothy.*
> *On this the outraged damsel fair,*
> *Of glittering eye and raven hair,*
> *Did scorn the warriors who strove*
> *With flailing fists their troth to prove,*
> *And there upon the ground they tussled large*
> *When Lo! the healing sages of this lair*
> *Cried 'Cease! Desist!', and of their sternest charge*
> *Defiance these two knights would never dare.*
> *But oh! that deep...*

I was obliged to leave off my verses to attend to a visitor, and now I find my train of thought impossible to recover. I strove to ignore the tapping at my door, and the importunate cries of this person (whom I cannot name because of the clandestine nature of our transaction) but, with no small disregard for my privacy and feelings, he simply entered my room – unfortunately the lock on my door is worn down and functions but poorly – and demanded what he was owed. I had no choice but to admit him and proceed with our agreement. A plague on the person, and poor lock.

Patient HST
Recovery Diary 14

I know what you people want. But I can endure the terrible raving and jabbering in the endless meetings, and the clumsy, groping mindfuck tactics in the counselling sessions, and you can read every word I write in this so-called personal account, but it won't tell you a goddamn thing you don't already know. You won't break me. I know who you are.

And I know that you know that I know. Let's not try to fool each other. I can keep the others guessing but not you. They don't know whether I'm asleep behind my shades with my hat pulled down, or whether I'm just faking it so I don't have to watch my own soul slide into a rancid sinkhole of festering self-pity like a fly being gulped down by a hideous sucking wound, but you people can see it all.

The first thing I check when I walk into a casino is the cameras, and I give the pit bosses a friendly wave, telling them I know they're watching me...but maybe they should pay attention to the big blonde who's acting drunk and falling out of her dress to distract them from the shifty little rat-like guy who's with her, because *he's* the one who's trying to scam them. Me, I know the game is rigged.

So where do we go from here, *amigos*? You have no fucking idea who you are dealing with. If you knew some of the sick, drooling zombies I've spent time with in a purely *recreational* capacity, never mind a professional career that's led me to consort with baying political wolverines who would happily rip my throat out if they thought they could get a vote or a bribe out of it, you'd know I'm not going to lie down and let you get ugly with me. Christ, I've seen off better opposition than you over a bottle of tequila, a handful of uppers and a few games of Russian roulette in the desert, whiling away the time on a cold, clear night, waiting for a drop from an unregistered Cessna with no lights and a teenage Colombian pilot flying solo for the first time.

As for the fight in the meeting, a jerking corpse could throw a better punch than the new guy. Hemingway might just last a few seconds with one of the smaller West Coast Angels if the Angel was blind drunk and crippled on mescaline but he'd have to cut out all the 'put yer dooks up' bullshit. However, I have to admit it woke me up there for a while. And you, Hatchjaw. That was a nice armlock you put on Hemingway. Speaking as someone who's been stomped by professionals, I'd want you on my side if it ever happens again. But bring a gun. I know I will, if I can...

Make me an offer. Tell me what I have to do to extricate myself from this demented Mongolian clusterfuck and get out of here, and I'll tell you what I'm prepared to reveal of my mission. I know you bastards will read this, so don't fuck around. Get in touch. Use code if you want. Use semaphore. Just give me a sign, sweet Jesus, give me a sign.

From the desk of Dr Bassett
Memo to Dr Hatchjaw

Wallace, I hope you're all right. I knew the group was volatile but I had no idea they would become uncontrollable. Should we review our security arrangements? It would be easy enough to have one or more of the orderlies in attendance at CEs, although it would be a shame to do anything that might inhibit the patients' confidence or discourage frank expression. We don't want them to feel they're under guard, but at the same time I certainly don't want to risk you getting hurt again. It's a fine line, isn't it? Let me know your thoughts about this. Meanwhile, I trust you're recovering from any injury you may have sustained and any shock you may have suffered.

Eudora

From the desk of Dr Hatchjaw
Memo to Dr Bassett

Thank you for your concern, but I assure you that I sustained no injury at all, nor am I suffering from shock. There was a minor expression of physical hostility between two of the patients but I quelled it calmly and effectively. Far from being 'uncontrollable', the situation was entirely under my control. I was obliged to restrain EH and was able to do so by deploying certain skills in which I am fully trained. I thought you were aware of my experience in this capacity, but you must have forgotten for some reason. I am perfectly capable of looking after myself and of controlling the CEs for which I am responsible.

Hatchjaw

From the desk of Dr Bassett
Memo to Dr Hatchjaw

Sorry, sorry, sorry. I wasn't trying to suggest that you aren't capable of handling any situation that might arise. And I was actually very impressed by the way you were dealing so effectively with EH, who was very fierce and angry. I think you established complete dominance, which was clearly required. And I do remember you telling me about – and demonstrating – your prowess in the martial skills you refer to. I remember the occasion very well. Happy days. I was simply concerned that if the situation arises again, and you have to deal with it in the same very decisive way, it might distract you from what you are even better at, which is giving the full benefit of your insight and judgment to the patients, in your capacity as a healer and counsellor.

Eudora

From the desk of Dr Hatchjaw
Memo to Dr Bassett

Please don't patronise me. I'm not a child, Eudora. But as we're on the subject, I note that your attempts to infantilise me are consistent with the tone of your previous memo, the motive for which, conscious or unconscious, was emasculation. I wonder why you feel driven to do this?

Hatchjaw

From the desk of Dr Bassett
Memo to Dr Hatchjaw

Oh Christ, I can't seem to say the right thing at all.
Well, you're probably right, Wallace, and there may be
unconscious drives which prompt me to adopt a tone
which you will find offensive for whatever reason.
You're very acute about that kind of thing, and I expect
I'm conflicted. But my conscious motives are simple: I
just don't want you to be hurt. I know that you can take
care of yourself, as you say, but I can't help wanting to
take care of you, too. I can't pretend I don't feel that
way about you. Why not come by later for a sherry? It
might make us both feel better.

Eudora

Patient FJ
Recovery Diary 6

There's been an interesting development. It can be summed up in one word: contraband.

Someone is bringing stuff in. Naturally, I'm excited. I'm also disappointed. Most rehab veterans will have experienced this contradiction. You're excited by the possibility that what you crave is available on the premises. And you're disappointed because you're excited. Grappling with this conundrum exposes you to a secondary contradiction, between the shame of acknowledging that you've got no willpower, and the relief of giving up the struggle to pretend you have. And once you admit you'll relapse at the drop of a hat, you invariably start looking for someone's hat to knock off.

I found out about the contraband after breakfast, while I was on a reconnaissance expedition. I'd decided to escape. I didn't know if I could, or even if there was anywhere to escape to, but I was determined to find out. However, in order to leave I needed to know where to start from. I still had only the vaguest conception of the house and its relation to the surrounding countryside. I didn't want to abscond in the wrong direction and discover, for example, that the rolling landscape beyond the woods rolled on to infinity, or that the woods themselves were patrolled by werewolves.

No, the best plan was to locate *the front door*. An entrance is also a potential exit. Where there's an entrance there must be a way to arrive at it, and thus a route by which to flee from it. And people arriving at an entrance must be coming from somewhere, which suggests a possible destination for the escapee. QED.

I set off with the intention of walking all the way around the outside of the house.

But I soon discovered that the building seemed to possess innumerable wings, extensions and architectural excrescences, alternating with shadowy alcoves, sudden recesses and unnecessary colonnades. Every time I assumed I'd negotiated one of these protrusions or indentations, and expected to find myself walking parallel to the main wall of the house again, I'd realise that I wasn't quite where I thought I'd be. Basically, the place had far too many corners. I was reminded of Amsterdam, where you think the streets are at right angles to each other, and that the city is laid out in a grid, like New York. But it isn't: the streets radiate out from Dam Square, and the city blocks aren't squares but pentagons, and you get hopelessly lost. This is even more likely to happen if you've visited one of the city's coffee shops and ingested a couple of hash cookies.

After a while I began to notice features of the building which I was pretty sure I'd passed before. I suspected I'd completely lost my bearings and was now heading back the way I'd come. I stopped and gazed around. Just then something landed at my feet. It was a scrunched-up ball of paper. I picked it up and smoothed it out, to find that it was a note, written in ink. The hand was small and neat, with a decidedly antiquated appearance and style. With some effort I deciphered it, and read the following:

> *Dear Sir,*
>
> *Be so good as to oblige me with Tinct. Op. to the usual amount. I am, at present, confined to my room by an attack of Rheumatism, but on my very first Excursion, I will call on you and settle this, with what other favors I have yet to account for. I would desire you to act, in this Matter, with despatch.*
>
> *Destroy this instantly.*

The note was unsigned but I knew without any doubt that it had been written by Coleridge. I experienced a sudden sensation of lightness. I was holding in my hands something freshly written by the man himself. His words, inches from my nose, made me giddy. They had a far more powerful impact on me than Hemingway's fist in my face.

I looked up, hoping to see Coleridge's delicately pudgy features peering from one of the windows. I noticed that the building appeared to have grown another storey since I'd last inspected it. Perhaps it was just a feature of this particular part of the house: a garret, an attic, or even an ill-advised loft conversion. Whatever the explanation, windows on at least five floors now loomed above me, but none of them framed the face I was looking for, or any face at all. None of them even appeared to be open.

Had Coleridge simply tossed the note down in the hope that someone would find it, without much caring who it was, like a message in a bottle cast overboard by a despairing mariner? Or was it intended for a particular recipient, of whose punctuality Coleridge was so confident that he hadn't bothered to make sure it was collected? I looked around furtively. Had someone been approaching, and spotted me, and was now hiding around a corner? If so, they had plenty to choose from.

I waited, trying to be very still. Perhaps I would catch a glimpse of someone peeping from their hiding place, or hear the squeak of a window being opened above me. Eventually I became very aware of my own breathing. I sensed I was alone. I was pretty sure that even Coleridge was no longer near the place from which he'd thrown the note.

I examined it again. Despite being scrawled hurriedly by

an itchy dope fiend its literary style was unmistakeable. It was strewn with the commas that Coleridge employed so profligately in all his prose, like handfuls of tiny, desiccated worms he'd tipped onto the page, which slithered among the words to shrivel and curl wherever they came to rest. The tone was both peremptory and wheedling, complete with the kind of superfluous detail that's a hallmark of the practised but desperate liar. An addict, in other words.

As I turned the note over in my hands I found myself thinking about how I could use it. No, I should be more honest: I didn't 'find myself thinking' about how I could use it, as if I'd stumbled across some venal, cogitating stranger; my thoughts had turned in that direction as soon as the initial flush of awestruck gratitude had passed, after about two seconds. And why not? You don't forget about yourself just because you're a devoted admirer of someone else. And while I didn't yet know how, I was convinced I could turn Coleridge's note to my advantage.

From the desk of Dr Hatchjaw
Memo to Dr Bassett

Eudora, thank you for the sherry last night. It was most enjoyable. In view of the current situation I wonder if I could rely on your goodwill to allow me to broach a rather sensitive subject? I refer to the issue of smoking. I know we've discussed this previously without being able to agree, but I feel we should discourage it more forcefully. We have a duty to treat and ameliorate the addictive behaviour of our patients. Should we not therefore discourage addiction to tobacco? I make no mention of your own habit, which I note you haven't given up. However, that is your own business, although I feel it sets a bad example to the patients, who cannot fail to be aware of it despite your attempts to conceal it. So, can we discuss this again, please?

Wallace

PS: Do you feel we can move on from just having sherry? I'd be very pleased to have dinner again, as we used to. I miss those dinners very much.

From the desk of Dr Bassett
Memo to Dr Hatchjaw

Unbelievable! How can you? I shouldn't even have to ask that. I should know by now that you're quite capable of something like this. Just when I begin to feel I can trust you again, and enjoy sherry with you, you try to take advantage of me. Is that all it is to you? A way of making me drop my defences so you can control me? And what's even worse, you're trying to use me as a means to control everyone else as well! Let the bloody patients smoke if they want to! And I'm not just saying that because of my own 'habit' as you so charmingly call it. I'm saying it because you still can't seem to grasp the distinction between healing people and punishing them.

I feel really hurt. I just don't understand how you can be so heartless. All the time you were just thinking about how to get your own way and win some stupid argument.

As for the suggestion that we could move on to having dinner, I feel insulted that you even ask. Sometimes I really don't understand you at all. What I mistook for a fragile reawakening of intimacy turns out to have been, for you, simply a means to an end.

By the way, I want to nail down this question of getting a new assistant. I want you to stop being evasive and face what we need to do. And while we're on the subject, I think I saw someone lurking around at the edge of the woods yesterday at dusk. If it's who I think it might be, do you know anything about it? This could be serious. Much more serious than your silly ideas about smoking. We need to talk. Seriously, very soon.

From the desk of Dr Hatchjaw
Memo to Dr Bassett

Eudora, I promise you I wasn't attempting to take advantage of you. I simply thought that as we appeared to be getting along so much better, in view of the sherry, perhaps we would be able to look at the smoking question again, because it's something I truly care about. I know you think I'm being controlling, but I just hate to see you doing anything that can harm you.

Yes, I've seen someone lurking around, too. If it's who you think it might be, and who I suspect it is, I assure you it's nothing to do with me. I'm just as worried as you are. We'd better talk about all this as soon as possible. I can't do anything until much later. I'm busy with individual counselling all day. Among others I'm seeing HST and I'm concerned that his paranoia isn't responding to treatment.

I'm sorry that you say you feel hurt. I feel hurt, too. You're accusing me of things that are clearly projections of your own conflicts. You're not really thinking rationally about all this, and about my motives. I assure you that the reawakening of intimacy between us was genuine, as far as I'm concerned. And that's precisely why I raised the smoking issue. It's because of the trust and intimacy I felt growing again between us that I felt confident we might be able to discuss things objectively. If you think about it, you'll see I'm right. We're going to have to address – and resolve – the smoking issue sooner or later.

From the desk of Dr Bassett
Memo to Dr Hatchjaw

Oh, Wallace, I don't know. I don't know if this is ever going to work.

I was touched to see that you tried to express your feelings simply and clearly for once, and dropped the formal (and to be honest, rather pompous) tone that you usually adopt in your memos when you're upset, and just tried to speak from the heart. But even then you still can't resist having a go at me, can you? Telling me I'm projecting my own conflicts, and that I'm not being rational. And that if I think about it, I'll see you're right. Is that always going to be the most important thing to you – being right? You know what they say about people who would rather be right than happy.

You must know that nothing you say will make me give up smoking if I don't want to. I would have thought you'd have learned that by now, as you're so clever.

We'll have to get together as soon as we can to talk about the other development. It would be a disaster if one of the patients encountered our unwelcome visitor.

From the desk of Dr Hatchjaw
Notification of Extraordinary Meeting

A very important matter has come to my attention. I have reason to believe that at least one of my patients is involved in an attempt to obtain contraband. My suspicions are supported by certain documentary evidence that has come into my possession. There is deception afoot, regarding both the contraband itself and its possible origin.

Accordingly I have summoned an Extraordinary Meeting of my Latent Group 3, to which the patient in question belongs. I believe the quickest way to get to the truth of this matter, and the most effective means to resolve it, is to confront the patient in a group context and to encourage full disclosure.

I will report any developments after the meeting, which will take place as soon as I am able to arrange it.

Hatchjaw
NB: Please see the memo that follows.

From the desk of Dr Hatchjaw
Memo to Dr Bassett

Eudora, I'll reply to your last memo in due course, but the matter I allude to above is urgent. And before you start thinking of telling me to be careful, and not to let things get out of hand, or put myself at any risk, or whatever other fears about my safety (touching but unfounded) you may feel an impulse to express, permit me to thank you in advance for your concerns and to assure you that I am confident of my ability to keep everything under control.

Yours in haste,
Wallace

Patient FJ
Recovery Diary 7

Oh God, I don't know what to do.

Indecision. Is that an emotion? It feels like one to me. It certainly strikes without warning or reason. On some days I wake up in the morning (or thereabouts) and spring out of bed with a sense of purpose that makes every decision feel preordained and effortless, like graceful steps in a well-rehearsed dance, and on some days I stand motionless at my bedside for half an hour trying to decide which trousers to wear.

Am I doing the right thing?
  Since finding Coleridge's note I'd changed my mind about what to do with it at least three times. At first I thought I could use it to help me achieve my purpose.

But what is my purpose? I'm not even sure I want to escape now, let alone discover any more about this place, and what my real condition is. Perhaps I should just wait, and see what happens. But wouldn't that be the same, in the example I just gave, as standing by my bed and waiting for a pair of trousers to stroll out of the wardrobe?

Actually, I think I'm beginning to see a glimmer of light, although at the moment it's just illuminating the problem rather than revealing an answer. But the more I think about a small but significant encounter I've just had, the more insight I'm getting into the state of my own feelings, even if I still don't know what to do about them.

Eventually I'd found my way back to the French windows of the Blue Room and gone inside, glad to find it unoccupied. I sat down in one of the armchairs and tried to empty my mind, with a vague idea that if I stopped struggling to make a decision, and opened myself up to a more intuitive process, perhaps I could align myself with some underlying mystical current in the universe that would carry me to a place where everything fitted together harmoniously and all destinies were already decided. All that crap. Nauseating, really. And even more so as it worked, in a way.

I heard voices and opened my eyes to see two people coming into the room from the direction of the canteen, one of whom was either William Burroughs or some relatively blameless old codger – a late-flowering minor poet, perhaps – onto whom I was projecting the aura of decrepit but fastidious depravity that Burroughs seemed to have been born with. He was conversing with a stocky woman I didn't quite recognise. They barely noticed me, and after we'd nodded to each other they sat themselves down in a couple of chairs on the other side of the room, continuing their conversation.

I slapped my thighs lightly and began to push myself up from my chair in a conclusive sort of way, as if I'd been on the point of leaving anyway. I didn't want them to think they were driving me out, although they were. Just as I was leaning forward in order to get to my feet I overheard the elderly gent saying the word 'asphyxiated' and I sank back into the chair.

Of course, anyone might use that word, in the most innocent of contexts, but it was the loving precision with which he enunciated it, in a voice both dry and sibilant, that convinced me the speaker was, in fact, Burroughs. His reliably horrible thoughts on almost any subject would be worth hearing.

I shuffled forward in my seat, at the same time turning my head towards the French windows so it would seem, if anyone noticed, that I'd caught sight of something outside that fascinated me: a dear little bird hopping about, perhaps, or a gruesome murder being committed. The manoeuvre enabled me to eavesdrop more effectively on the couple's conversation.

The woman gave a throaty chuckle and said, 'In this place? You're speaking metaphorically, I hope?'

'Yes, unfortunately. There are no boys here, anyway.'

'Thank God. There was quite enough of that in Paris, from what I hear of your shenanigans there. And in

Africa.'

'And you care about them deeply, I'm sure,' Burroughs said with a note of sarcasm.

'Let's just say I care about them.'

'Me too, in my own eccentric little way. They were grateful for the cash, and you can't say I treated anyone badly. Anyhow, I genuinely liked them. I like these darker types, you know.'

The woman leaned forward and patted his knee. 'You like all types, Bill,' she said. 'You bestow your bounty without prejudice, which is admirable.'

'I can't bestow any bounty here. Only my seed, which I scatter like Onan.'

'Spilled is the word, I believe.'

'Spilled?' Burroughs said.

'Yes, that's the word that's used in the Bible. In mine, anyhow. Onan spilled his seed.'

'Oh, I think I can pump it out with a little more vigour than that, even now.'

At this, the stocky woman laughed uproariously. She seemed to be enjoying the conversation immensely. With Burroughs it was harder to tell. I got the impression he was having great fun, but in a very understated way. It was as if he were withholding his relish, as the result of a thoughtful calculation about how much of it to reveal. Perhaps that strong impression of control was part of what made him rather mesmeric.

The woman finished laughing. 'Well, if you're feeling stifled, as you say—'

Burroughs cut her off. 'Asphyxiated is what I said.' This time he elongated the word comically on a hissing expulsion of breath, as though pretending to suffocate.

The woman widened her eyes in mock horror. 'Don't expire on me, Bill.'

'I won't, but I'm bored.'

'Maybe this little intrigue of yours will divert you, and restore your legendary zest for life. We don't want you suffering from ennui.'

'Oh, maybe it will stimulate us,' Burroughs said, languidly. 'Betrayal has its gratifications. Especially if there's only a slender risk of being found out.'

'I thought you liked being denounced.'

'No, that's more in your line, isn't it?'

The woman gave a little shudder. 'Only in love. Not in other ways.'

'I understand. I'm sorry I mentioned it; that was indelicate of me.'

'No matter,' she said briskly. 'But will you really not be found out?'

'I doubt it. I'm not even in the same group. And I have a feeling that what I've discovered is not rare, by any means. I may even have competitors, who are as eager as I am to put a smallish cat among the pigeons.'

'Good. I look forward to hearing about what happens,' the woman said, leaning back in her chair, 'and I must say it all sounds rather delicious.'

'I hope so. A morsel to amuse the palate, at any rate. The question is, should I interrogate my conscience for a little longer before I—'

He broke off, noticing an abrupt change in the woman's expression. She was glaring across the room, and when he followed her gaze he saw that what she was glaring at was me. She had noticed that I was now eavesdropping shamelessly, with no attempt to conceal my interest.

Burroughs turned and fixed me with a pale stare. Slowly he dropped his eyelids and then opened them again. The reptilian effect was surely deliberate; he even allowed the tip of his tongue to appear between his thin, bloodless lips.

Time to go. The way they were looking at me made it clear that it was a bit late to stroll over, introduce myself, and laugh it all off. I stood up quickly.

As I walked away I wondered if the woman was Gertrude Stein, although the only substance abuse I associated with her was her fondness for sharing a little hash with Alice Toklas, which seemed too mild a weakness to make her eligible for the company she was currently keeping.

I made my way out via the door that would lead me back to my room, mulling over the possible nature of the 'intrigue' I'd just heard being discussed, and whether it could be anything similar to the one I'd been thinking of instigating myself.

I'd only taken a few steps along the corridor when someone emerged from a passageway on my right and nearly collided with me. He was a thin, haughty-looking man whose narrow face was framed by a colossal, curled wig that flowed down over his shoulders and was the crowning glory of an extremely complicated and gorgeous seventeenth-century costume. He backed away from me slowly, glancing ostentatiously at his buckled shoes, as if to check that I hadn't contaminated their gleaming surface by the slightest contact, then made me a bow so elaborate that it was clearly intended to convey contempt rather than courtesy. He waved a heavily scented handkerchief in my general direction, muttered, 'Rochester,' and sauntered across the intersection, taking his time to get out of my way.

So, the Earl of Rochester is here. But why? I almost called after him, 'What are you in for, mate?' but as I watched him mincing away, displaying his perfectly formed calves, and somehow expressing both arrogance and sensuality in the merest swing of his hips, it came to me. Sex addiction. Of course. He was a well-known rake, as notorious for his conduct as for his poems, which were pretty filthy, in a refined sort of way. As I waved away the choking cloud of lavender in which he'd engulfed me, I wondered whether perhaps Byron was here, or Catherine the Great. She was a terrific writer, which would justify her presence on literary grounds, although her renowned sexual appetite may have been exaggerated. Still, the encounter set my mind working in a particular direction, and put a spring in my step as I walked back to my room.

The fact is, I'm feeling very randy. I don't know when I last had sex, but even if it was fairly recently before my arrival here, that doesn't make any difference. You often emerge from detox with a raging horn, and now I'm up for any possibility of an erotic encounter. Especially with Dorothy Parker. There's something about her, and I'm pretty sure she's giving me the glad eye. Or giving it back, as I was probably making my admiration for her fairly obvious when I stood up for her against Hemingway. God, those two have got some issues. I don't know if they've ever been lovers, but they fight like champion divorcees. She's got the sharper tongue, but he's got the crueller streak. And I can tell she struggles not to show how much he can hurt her. That's pretty typical. I'm willing to bet that if one of them should ever be left crying after their bruising encounters it's not the bastard with the beard. And if that's true, and I were to offer a comforting shoulder upon which to do the crying, I've got a strong suspicion I wouldn't be shown the door. Not for half an hour or so, anyway.

I may be dead but at least I'm incorrigible.

So, that's another reason to stay here for a while, rather than try to bring my escape plan to a fruition that may prove premature and possibly disastrous. The balance sheet currently reads as follows:

<u>Possible consequences of staying here</u>:
Shelter,
sustenance,
sex,
continued blissful ignorance of what's happening.

<u>Possible consequences of running away</u>:
Pain,
fear,
madness,
dreadful confirmation of fundamental nothingness.

That seems pretty persuasive. And yet...I don't know. And it still doesn't answer the questions raised by Coleridge's note. I'm back where I started: am I doing the right thing?

Okay, everything has changed. Hatchjaw just knocked at my door.

Transcript

Latent Group 3
Extraordinary Collective Encounter; Blue Annexe

Present:
Dr WH – Facilitator
Patients: DP, EH, FJ, HST, PW, STC, WC

Dr WH: Welcome, everyone. Let me begin by thanking all of you for attending this session at such short notice.

EH: Let's hope it's worth it, Doc.

Dr WH: I assure you that I've called this meeting for a very good reason.

EH: Like what?

Dr WH: *(Pause)* I believe that at least one of you knows or suspects the reason. And I'd like to give that person a chance to broach the matter. So, does anyone have anything they'd like to share?

(*A long silence*)

WC: It seems you will have to enlighten us, Doctor.

Dr WH: Look, there has been a serious breach of our rules. If the person involved would take the initiative to speak, and begin the process of assuming responsibility for their actions, I believe they could find this whole experience constructive. Perhaps even empowering.

PW: Personally I don't know if I can handle being any more empowered. I mean, how bloody empowered do you want us to be?

DP: I'm not even sure I know what that means.

PW: You see, Hatchjaw? It could be dangerous. What if it gets out of hand and we become super-empowered? We might develop extraordinary abilities.

DP: You mean like Superman, and the Batman?

PW: Exactly. But as I don't really believe humans can develop superpowers, my superpower would have to be irony.

Dr WH: Patrick, I'm sorry, but this is not a time to be flippant.

EH: Yes, button it, why don't you?

FJ: Shut up, Hemingway. He was just making a joke.

EH: You could have fooled me. And don't tell me

	to shut up, unless you're ready for round two, you prick.
Dr WH:	That's enough! I will not permit this session to degenerate into another brawl. I won't hesitate to use whatever means are necessary to prevent it.
EH:	You're in fine shape, Doc, but you think you can take on all of us?
Dr WH:	I don't have to rely on martial arts. I have other methods at my disposal.
(*Silence*)	
WC:	Intriguing. Will you tell us more?
Dr WH:	No. And if no one is prepared to broach the subject of this meeting I shall do so myself.
PW:	Okay, enough suspense. That's our gig. What's the subject?
Dr WH:	In a word, contraband.
OMNES:	*General expressions of surprise, interest and consternation.*
Dr WH:	Quiet, please. Now you can see how serious it is, I hope. So, will someone please do the right thing, and speak out?
(*Silence*)	
Dr WH:	Very well. (*Pause*) I have in my hand a piece of paper—
FJ:	Stop.
PW:	What's up?
FJ:	I just meant…let's not do this.
DP:	What's on your mind, Jim? You want to talk about it?
FJ:	Thank you, Dorothy, but I'd prefer not to.

STC: I agree with Mr James. This strikes me as an unnecessary procedure, and one that could have unpleasant consequences.

HST: Fuck that, let's find out what we have here.

PW: Hello, Hunter! I see you're awake for once.

HST: No shit I'm awake. A serious breach of the rules? Incriminating letters? Contraband? What we have here, my friends, is a story. Read on, MacDoc, and damned be him who first cries Hold! Enough!

EH: Glory be, Mr Sunglasses knows a Shakespeare quote.

HT: I've read a few books, Papa. Even one of yours, although I didn't finish it.

EH: Screw you.

WC: With respect, Mr Hemingway, we are all entitled to our opinions of each other's work, as literary men.

DP: And women.

WC: My dear lady, I do apologise. Forgive me, I implore you.

EH: Forgive you? She'll fuck you if you keep laying that stuff on.

FJ: Why don't you just—

PW: Whoa! Down, Jim.

Dr WH: Aha! No you don't! I'll have that back, thank you!

(*Inaudible; momentary general confusion*)

PW: Holy hell, what was all that about?

Dr WH: Why don't you tell them, Mr Coleridge?

STC: I...I merely wished to peruse the note.

Dr WH:	And is that why you tried to snatch it from me?
STC:	I did no such thing. I simply leaned over and attempted to…borrow it.
Dr WH:	Mr Coleridge. Sam. Please. There's no point. Just speak out.
(*Silence*)	
Dr WH:	You leave me no choice. I will read the note, which was given to me by someone who shall remain nameless but whom I consider to have acted entirely properly and responsibly. The note reads as follows—
FJ:	Excuse me, but do you really have to do this?
Dr WH:	I'm afraid so, Foster.
PW:	Jim, why don't you want him to read the letter?
WC:	Come along, let us hear the contents of this mysterious missive.
FJ:	No, let's not.
HST:	What's the problem, man? Are you mixed up in this?
EH:	Now, that wouldn't surprise me.
DP:	Perhaps he just doesn't like the way this is turning into a goddamned circus show.
EH:	If it's a circus, bring on the clowns! Read the note, for God's sake!
PW:	Wait, if this is going to hurt anyone maybe we shouldn't read it.
HST:	Everything hurts somebody. Read the goddam thing!

WC: Gentlemen, show some restraint! We are behaving like a mob!

EH: What the hell, Collins? You were baying for it just a moment ago.

WC: I most certainly was not 'baying' for it.

EH: Yes, you were. What's up, have you just realised it's going to incriminate you as well?

WC: I demand that you withdraw that implication!

Dr WH: Enough! Wait, where are you going, Mrs Parker?

DP: I've had enough of this. I'm sick to my stomach.

EH: Hey, sit down, you!

PW: What's the problem, Dorothy? Are you involved in this?

DP: I'm not, and I'm leaving. Have fun, boys.

HST: Fuck that! Stop her, Hatchjaw.

WC: Yes, surely she can't be permitted to do that?

EH: Too late. She's gone. Good riddance to the bitch.

FJ: Now, that is totally unnecessary!

EH: Are you starting that shit again?

Dr WH: Stop! Settle down! If Mrs Parker wishes to leave she is free to do so. Please control yourselves, the rest of you. I will now read the note. This is what it says:

          'Dear Sir, if it be in your possession, could you favour me with half a scruple of the

Acetate Morphii, equal in strength to Laudanum. It has mortified me that I have been obliged to disappoint you, and must still defer it for a few days, not doubting that by, or before, this day week I shall be able to settle it.

PS: I entreat you, be careful not to have any note delivered to me unless I am alone and passing your door.'

(Silence)

(A low whistle; source unidentified)

EH: Now it's all coming out!

STC: Damn you.

EH: Are you talking to me?

STC: Damn you all!

Dr WH: Please understand, Samuel, I had no choice.

STC: No choice but to expose me? To betray me?

FJ: Oh Christ, I can't take any more of this.

EH: Where do you think you're going, Ivanhoe?

(Sounds of movement; chairs, etc.)

FJ: Get out of my way, you oaf.

Dr WH: Sit down! Everyone!

WC: Let him pass, Mr Hemingway. We are not gaolers, I hope.

EH: Take your hands off me, Collins, or I'll rip that beard off your fat face and ram it down your goddamned throat.

Dr WH: I'm warning you! Everyone, do as I say! Sit down!

PW: Yes, come on, break it up…

EH: Get away from me, you limey faggot! Look,

	your friend's sneaking out!
HST:	Hey, cool it, people...
PW:	Get off me, Thompson!
WC:	Unhand me!
PW:	Who hit me? Fuck you!
STC:	Damn you all!
Dr WH:	Right, that's it! I warned you!

(Sound of powerful gushing water.)

OMNES: *(Shouts, screams, general exclamations.)*

(Sounds of bodies falling, slipping in water, colliding with furniture, walls, each other.)

TRANSCRIPT ENDS

Patient FJ
Recovery Diary 8

I'm a bit wet. But nowhere near as wet as the others must be, except for Dorothy, who had the good sense to get out of there before Hatchjaw turned on that hose. Or water cannon, to be more accurate, given the pressure that walloped into Coleridge, Collins, Hemingway, Thompson, and poor old Paddy. It knocked them on their backsides almost instantly and sent them slithering into the corners of the room, from which I was just escaping as the mayhem erupted and so I only suffered limited collateral spray. I'm very glad I didn't feel the full force of that thing, and I'm sure the others are now sincerely regretting that they did. To be fair to Hatchjaw, he did warn us he wasn't going to take any shit, but I don't think anyone expected him to go full-scale riot police.

Come to think of it, I've seen a few of those hoses in various locations around the place, coiled behind weird cylindrical wall fixtures. It's an interesting approach to maintaining a serene therapeutic environment and I can certainly attest to its effectiveness in preventing the inmates from getting too frisky.

In addition to feeling damp I feel thoroughly demoralised. Worse, actually: I feel utterly disgusted, with myself and everyone else. Once again, we've confirmed the bitter truth that addicts can't be trusted, and we've done it with a triumphantly sordid display of every quality that makes us such irredeemable fuck-ups.

I'd decided, eventually, not to give the note I'd found to Hatchjaw, or to confront Coleridge with it, which had been the other possibility I'd considered. Both plans were half-baked, and I'm not sure what I hoped to gain by them. Did I intend to blackmail Coleridge, and force him to share whatever narcotics he was obtaining? Or ingratiate myself with Hatchjaw, and use the note as leverage to make him divulge the truth about this place? I don't know, and in the end I did neither. Instead I pressed the note between the pages of this journal, intending to keep it safe and preserve it for my eyes only. That's what I told myself, anyway, although there's every likelihood I would have ended up trying to use it to my advantage if the right opportunity presented itself.

When Hatchjaw produced the note in the meeting I initially assumed it was the one I'd hidden, and that he'd got hold of it somehow. They seem to know what we're doing all the time, and it's crossed my mind that the whole place is riddled with surveillance devices, although I haven't found any in my room. Yet.

I realised almost at once that it wasn't the note I'd found. The thick, yellowing paper was similar but it was slightly larger than the one I'd picked up, and appeared to have been torn more haphazardly from its original home, perhaps an old notebook of some kind. And when Hatchjaw began to read, of course, it became clear it was a different note. Someone had given it to him, he said. But it wasn't me. Which meant that at least one other person in our happy little family is as despicable and conniving as me, and had deliberately shopped Coleridge. I had a strong suspicion it was Burroughs, and handing over the note was part of the intrigue he'd mentioned, but I understood, with a growing feeling of repugnance, that almost any of us was capable of such a betrayal.

Why was I surprised? In retrospect I guess I shouldn't have been. But having found myself in such exalted company I simply assumed I was the most selfish and unsavoury person in the group. The lowliest worm in the apple. Thinking about it now I realise I often make that assumption, regardless of the status and quality of the company I'm keeping. Never mind, an eternity in therapy will probably sort out my self-esteem issues, but it won't change how I feel about what happened today.

I find the whole thing unbearably sad. It's ridiculous that I still have any illusions about writers and their bad behaviour, but seeing people like Hemingway, Coleridge and Collins at their worst and weakest is simply terrible. It nearly broke my heart when Coleridge got caught by Hatchjaw trying to swipe the note, and he started blustering and wheedling like...I don't know. Like a fucking junkie, that's what. All of them. All of us. No better than the most feral crackhead in a rat-infested squat, feebly summoning the last remaining strength in his wasted muscles to stab his best friend in the groin over some pitiful gratification.

I just found myself in a kind of reverie, reflecting on the past. Perhaps I wanted solace, and I'd cut my mind adrift in the hope that it would snag on memories of happier times. A balm for my revulsion. And now I'm feeling melancholy. This always happens. At first it's pleasant to relax in a warm bath of retrospection but if you loiter for too long sadness starts to chill the water.

Melancholy is always about nostalgia, for me. A wistful longing for what can never be recaptured. How sweet those precious bygone days, how sublime those feelings, how magical that moment. And now? All gone. And all bogus. I'm regretting the loss of what I never had in the first place. When the magical moment is actually happening I'm usually waiting for it to be over so I can reminisce about how magical it was.

As I stand on the shore gazing at a glorious sunset with my arm around a lovely woman, and I experience the transcendent joy of it, I'm also thinking about the sand in my socks. And when you look back on those moments, and you're pierced by poignant longing, it's not because you'll never experience that moment again, it's because you never experienced it properly in the first place.

I think that's why ghosts are so gloomy. They're not pissed off about being dead, they're just nostalgic. They're searching for something they remember as being special but they'll never find it. It must get frustrating, and that's probably why some of them like to go around scaring people. I'd certainly be tempted to do that, especially to certain people. My ex-wives would go to bed with the fucking lights on, I'll tell you that.

That's not true. I wouldn't want to scare Paula. I wouldn't really want to scare either of them. In any case, an encounter with Felicity would be more likely to give the ghost a nasty turn. Nothing scared her and she certainly never needed me to protect her. Or do anything for her. Even when I put up shelves or fixed the car, or other things I was quite proud of, I invariably got the impression she didn't think it was a big deal, and could have done it just as well herself. Naturally, she wanted me to get that impression, and all the other ideas of my general uselessness she managed to convey in all those subtle, infuriating ways that she always denied so innocently whenever I accused her of doing it.

But Paula often seemed genuinely helpless, even if she was sometimes exaggerating to make me feel good because she knew I was worried about our age difference.

No, I certainly wouldn't want to scare her. I never wanted to see her afraid, and I very rarely did. She tended to be fearful of things that might happen, rather than things that actually did happen. She fretted about the possibility of being caught up in a war, or the threat of impending environmental disaster, but she was extremely brave when confronted with the risk of actual, immediate danger.

One day we came home to find we'd been burgled. While I stood paralysed in the doorway, fighting down a rising tide of panic, terrified that intruders might still be in the house, and racking my brains for the whereabouts of anything that could be used as a weapon, she pushed past me and marched around, flinging open every door, yelling bloodcurdling oaths and curses in Italian, daring the *ladri maladetti* to show their poxy faces. Half an hour later she was curled up on the sofa with my arms around her, crying like a child because they'd broken a ghastly little glass swan that had belonged to her grandmother. I honestly believe that if, at that moment, one of the thieves had emerged from some unlikely hiding place, I would have torn him apart with my bare hands, ripped his slippery, still-beating heart from his chest, and eaten it in front of her.

Christ, I miss her.

So, if I was a ghost and I could get out of here I wouldn't dream of scaring Paula. I'd just go and apologise to her. I'd tell her I was sorry I let her fall in love with me, and she deserved better. Which she did, despite her anguished protestations that I was the only one she wanted. She may even have believed that. And maybe she was right, and I had a problem accepting unconditional love – from her, or from Felicity (fat chance of that) or my parents (even less chance) or from Uncle Tom Cobley and all.

Paula had a touching faith in that kind of thing: all the insights that therapy is so good at providing. She insisted that if only I could learn to love myself I would be able to accept love from her, and all that bollocks. Even if it were true, it's still bollocks. Insight is all very interesting but it doesn't change anything. All the insight in the world wouldn't have stopped me poisoning the love she offered me. That's just who I was.

I wish I'd ended it sooner, before our life together turned into one long, continual misunderstanding. It was like a relationship between pen pals in reverse: we began in the same place, knowing everything about each other, and by the end we were in different worlds with nothing in common but an imperfect grasp of the other's language. I should have simply left, and let her get on with her life and find someone else, instead of hanging around and making both of us miserable just because it suited me.

Then maybe that memory of watching the sunset on the beach with my arm around her little waist and her little hand tugging gently at the curls on the back of my neck would be perfect, even with the sand in my socks.

I just wrote, 'If I could get out of here.' What the fuck is the matter with me? Apart from being dead, obviously. If that's even true. But dead or alive, I still haven't made any really serious effort to find out if I can leave this place, and what will happen if I do. I'd made up my mind I was going to, but then I found the note from Coleridge and got distracted. Or rather I distracted myself. I deployed all my usual cunning tactics to defeat my sense of purpose: speculation, indecision, procrastination, bullshit, drama, and trying to be far too clever for my own good.

But the events of the last few hours have settled it. Whatever happens to me if I try to leave, it can't be any worse than the shame and misery I'll experience if I spend any more time witnessing the utter degradation of people I once admired more than anyone else in the world. A horrible circus show, as Dorothy said. There was definitely something about the way she looked at me just as she left the room. The glance she threw in my direction. Shit, what am I doing? That's the last thing I should be thinking about. But I'm glad she missed the water cannon, all the same.

I'll leave now, definitely. True, I don't know where I'm going or how I can get there. I'm not even completely sure *why* I want to go. But somewhere in my mind a crazy idea is cavorting: that somehow I can go and make everything all right. All the things I got wrong, with everyone: my family, my friends, my colleagues, rivals, enemies, wives and lovers. Especially Paula.

I know I'm being unwise. To the old saying, 'if it ain't broke, don't fix it,' I would always add: even if it is broke, don't fix it, you'll only make it worse.

But I'm willing to take the risk. Everything I just wrote about wanting to apologise to Paula is a lie, because I'm not sorry I let her fall in love with me. I wanted her to love me, and just because I didn't know what to do about it doesn't change that. I still want her to love me, even if I still don't know what to do about it. But I want her so badly. Just to see her would be enough. Just to see her smile one more time.

Thinking about Paula again I just had the strangest flash of memory, of being with her and being very afraid. Nothing to do with the kind of cowardice and courage I was talking about earlier, after we'd been burgled: this was something else, and of a different order of magnitude. Just for a moment I experienced an exceptionally vivid sense of us being together as something truly catastrophic and horrible was happening. Not the disaster of our relationship, something else. But what? I don't know. It's gone.

And so am I. I'm out of here.

Patient WSB
Recovery Diary 666

A feeling of the brain being hollowed out from the inside.

Recognisable as the work of disembodied telepaths – entities evolved beyond the corporeal, feeding on pure need – who locate their prey by sensing every tremor in the prehensile filaments of hunger secreted by users, blindly seeking the network. Easiest to find a victim in a group, where connections are being made constantly... dense webs, pulsing with waves of vibration. 'Wherever two or three are gathered together in thy name,' the defrocked priest intones over the dropper as he inserts it delicately in the wound, trying not to drool.

The predators take a tip from baboons, mandrills and other vicious simians, and attack the weakest member of the congregation. They immobilise the victim with a type of delicious nerve gas then reach down through the corpus callosum with ectoplasmic fingers and palpate the hypothalamus.

'Ah, Jayzus, we got a nice plump specimen here,' the leader of the troupe informs his acolytes, squeezing gently.

The whole team gets to work, a spectral machine greased with invisible but pungent juices of the higher insect lusts, and begins the delicate business of drainage.

But while the gland is being milked it itches like hell. The victim has no way to get inside and scratch it, short of unscrewing the head from the neck-pipe. A tricky operation at the best of times, especially the replacement procedure. Very poor success rate. And even if it succeeds the risk of infection is unacceptably high. The telepaths themselves are rank with intuitive contagion, and then the patient gets in there with dirty fingernails. Before the head is even back in place a process of insectile parthenogenesis has already commenced. Millions of tiny parasitic eggs hatch out and disgorge squirming larvae that feast on the synapses and dendrites, replicating their functions and taking control of them for their own purposes until the discrete parts of the brain no longer work together. It's every man for himself in there. Eventually the brain itself is nothing but a thin distended membrane which bursts when it's no longer able to contain the swollen mass of ghostly maggots.

Otherwise pretty good, thanks.

News travels fast among the dead. We have our own frequencies.

There's too much blue paint in this place and it adds to the feeling we're underwater here. A museum of the drowned, each one adrift at the bottom of a different ocean. White bones picked clean but still maintaining a functional skeletal integrity as we stroll doggedly along the seabed, waiting for instructions. Movement is slow but sound waves travel unmolested and we pick up on recent developments with no trouble.

It seems there was an eventful therapy session. Interrogation, denunciation, confession – I used to know types who got their kicks from witnessing that scene and would pay good money for it. Bribe the gaoler to be smuggled into the torture chamber and watch from a dark corner, jacking off discreetly. It's not the pain that turns them on but the inevitability...the satisfaction of a cycle always playing out in the same way, the only variation being the precise moment when the suspect breaks. This creates just enough uncertainty to provide a thrill, without upsetting the whole apple cart.

Am I to blame? There was no real secret about the contraband. What somebody did was offer written evidence to a shadow archive, adding a little substance to the miasma of speculation that drifts through this place. We should treat that scribbled note as a kind of amulet: an archaeological find that confirms in solid form a symbol system rife with magic, taboos and curses. And I didn't write the note, after all. But was I the one who left it where someone was going to find it? Can I even remember?

The past is a foreign country.

'There is a problem with your visa, señor,' the agent hisses through narrow lips that are nearly closed beneath his pencil mustache and unblinking lids, to prevent his tongue from flickering out and giving the game away. Then he slithers quickly across the customs house leaving a telltale trail of slime. The reptiles maintain their cover story only casually. You're not going anywhere unless you can slip them enough bills or some other type of currency, depending on their deviant tastes.

How can I revisit my crimes when I don't even know if I committed them? You'd think my memory would hold up for a couple of days but the fog is rolling in back there. One good jolt of C in the mainline would blow it all away and leave my recent history pin-sharp and gleaming, but that's out of the question, naturally.

Betrayal, like selling, is more of a habit than using. And we're all still sick in here, whatever else we are. But you can get used to anything, and it's incorrect to assume that death will be the final cure.

I feel an urge to sever one thing from another, to slice and cut. Maybe I'll swipe a blunt knife from the cafeteria. Minor surgery on a few pages of this notebook. Reconstructive origami. To help with the transition back to animal life, if that is what this is. Sanity in death, perhaps. Addicts are drearily sane. And while the factual memory of an addict may be quite accurate and extensive, his emotional memory may be scanty.

I no longer have The Sickness, but a memory lingers on, of not caring to remember, even if the facts are not in dispute. The old familiar song.

FADEOUT TO MAMBO MUSIC

Patient DP
Recovery Diary 16

I'd been waiting to lay him, and now I was laying in wait for him.

One way or another we were going to end up in bed together, damn it. It had been in the cards ever since we first set eyes on each other and, predictably, after Jim defended me in my maidenly distress and took a punch for me, my drawers were ready to hit the deck whenever he wanted to whistle. When it began to seem that he wasn't going to get around to it I decided to take matters into my own hands, unsteady as they may have been. There are times when you have to spell these things out for men, especially if they've been thrown off the track by bewildering signs of intelligence in a woman. I decided that this was one such occasion and drastic measures were called for, on the principle that if you're calling for measures, friends, make mine drastic every time.

Aside from anything else, I'd had enough of the hideous loneliness that afflicted me. But there are worse things than loneliness, and one of the prettiest is to be at the mercy of an impulse of the heart, to say nothing of any other organs.

Truth to tell, I wasn't feeling nearly so insouciant as I may be making myself sound. The prospect of making my feelings known and being turned down is always enough to scare a certain commodity out of me. And I didn't have recourse to any Dutch courage, that useful nourishment I habitually employ to summon up the nerves of steel for which I am a legend among my social circle of well-known cowards.

I knew where Jim's room was, and that he had to go through the Blue Room to get anywhere worth going. Well, I sat there grimly all morning, holding a book in front of my nose, like a besotted cheerleader pretending to be absorbed by the trophy case while she watches the door of the jocks' locker room. He showed up at around eleven, and he looked like he was in a hurry. In fact he looked like he wasn't even going to notice me as he stalked through the room with knitted brow and hasty step, so I decided to take diversionary action. Just before he passed me I stood up, dropped my book, and bent down to pick it up so he nearly collided with my ass – which I left there long enough to be sure he noticed it, for better or worse – then I straightened up and turned, and assumed my most convincing feather-headed tizzy, and blushed shamelessly. He looked at me thoughtfully, and after a moment he gave me a nice smile. In return I exposed the work of New York's cheapest orthodontists. He didn't run away so I considered we were making fine progress, and at least I wasn't making an awful pest of myself.

'Sorry,' he said, in the British way of apologising for things they haven't done, and lurched in a couple of different directions. At best it was a half-hearted attempt to get past me, and it died at birth – from neglect, to judge by the effort he put into it – then he just stood and looked at me. I asked him where he was going.

'I'm not quite sure, to be honest,' he said.

'Just a case of wanderlust?'

That provoked a flicker of something. 'Perhaps,' he agreed. 'At any rate, I thought I'd try to get away from here. Although I don't really know why, when I come to think about it.'

'Maybe,' I said, 'you've got an urge to seek solace in travel.'

He laughed a little. 'Solace. Yes, that's probably what I'm after.' He paused for a moment, then leaned towards me, dropping his voice as he gazed into my eyes. 'How about you?'

He clearly thought he was handling this damned smoothly, but he was about as subtle as a battleship changing course.

'Aren't we all?' I chortled merrily.

That got another thoughtful look from him. He was doing too much thinking for my liking, and my apprehension was only increased by the doubtful look

147

he now cast around the room, eyeing the various doorways in a dangerous way.

As his gaze returned to mine I smiled brightly and began to get all a-bustle with my book and my bag, and tugging at my clothes in the general manner of someone firmly set upon imminent departure themselves. 'Well,' I said, 'if you're really in a hurry, please don't let me detain you.'

'No, not at all,' he said with some haste, and I knew the tide had turned.

I tapped my book against my thigh. 'How come?'

'Well, I get the impression we've got plenty of time. Here, I mean. In this place. Unless you know something about it that suggests otherwise?'

I shook my head sadly, but not too sadly. 'Beats me.'

'Yes, all very mysterious. But I suppose there's no real need to be in a massive hurry to leave.' He paused. 'What do you think?'

I could see he'd lost interest in the doors, windows, or other means of egress, and I took my own sweet time in replying. 'There could be reasons to linger awhile,' I said.

He leaned in and gave me that soupy, narrow-eyed look again, like Valentino trying to find his glasses. 'Yes, I'd like to think so. I'd like to think so very much.'

'Don't think too hard,' I said. 'It can hold things up.'

'*Carpe diem*, you mean?'

'That's the spirit, team. And when I *carpe* a *diem* it stays *carped*.'

'That sounds like a call to action.'

'It does, doesn't it?'

We confronted each other with a clear and level gaze for a moment, making sure we both knew exactly what the other had in mind, and that it was the same thing. Then I turned my back on him and walked in the direction of my room, swinging my rump encouragingly like a railroad signalman waving the lamp that leads the stranded passengers to salvation. He was right behind me all the way.

Around 20 minutes later we were both feeling pretty happy about what we'd just achieved, and there were encouraging signs that we might achieve it again. The house was beginning to fill up nicely for another performance. Just as we seemed to be approaching curtain-up and the orchestra was clearing its throat we heard someone yelling right outside the door. I was fairly sure that what was being yelled was, 'Fire!' and equally sure that the voice yelling it belonged to a certain E. Hemingway. My immediate thought was that the rotten bastard knew that Jim was in my room, and what we were doing in there, and it was his idea of fun to make us come tearing out of there in a state of disarray. It would be just like him. A lot of men who write for a living seem to have a decidedly juvenile sense of humor. But then Jim raised his nose from its nest in my snowy bosom and sniffed. Like many men of his age it doesn't seem to have occurred to him to trim the undergrowth that tends to flourish in the nostrils at his time of life. But despite the lavish foliage, his nose seemed to work better than mine did, which isn't surprising. I've always had a lousy sense of smell, which has been a distinct advantage in some of the hotel rooms I've frequented. I should have been more grateful for my sinus trouble as a girl. I reflected on this as Jim took another deep snootful of the atmosphere. Then he leaped from the bed. 'Fuck,' he declared, 'something's burning.'

The efficiency with which he got most of his clothes on makes me suspect he's beaten a hasty retreat from more than one boudoir in his time and I noticed he'd employed the trick of tying his shoes together so he could sling them around his neck in a crisis. I've had some practice in the art of hasty post-coital enrobing too, and we were both out the door in a matter of seconds. Then all hell broke loose.

I guess I'm lucky to be alive. Now, there's an expression I can't recall springing unprompted to my lips on too many occasions in the recent past.

Patient FJ
Recovery Diary 9

Feelings: elation, relief, pride, sore throat.

Of all the motives I've had for leaving a woman's bedroom in a hurry, the outbreak of fire hasn't been one of them until now. The unexpected homecoming of a husband, partner or offspring have been the most common reasons. Sometimes it's been because I've had a pressing appointment of a similar nature elsewhere, and sometimes I've simply legged it because of shame, disgust, or remorse.

There have been a few freakish occurrences to enliven the predictable litany. Once it was because a bat flew in the window. I was visiting an old flame who lived in a very nice country house owned by the man she'd sensibly married instead of me. I'd phoned her and told her that I found myself in her neighbourhood, which was perfectly true as I'd driven forty miles out of my way to get there, once I'd established that her husband was away by phoning his office and pretending to be someone else. It was early spring and I arrived for a late lunch which we had outside with a bottle of wine. We went inside and had another bottle and then went to bed, where we were serenaded by trilling birdsong through the open window as we fucked our brains out. As dusk fell, and I wondered if it would be gentlemanly to stay the night, something clattered onto the windowsill and fell to the floor, where it flopped around spasmodically. I got out of bed and nearly stepped on it. It was a bat. Bats have always horrified me. I hate the way they're both furry and skeletal, with their sharp little teeth and wizened, simian faces, like airborne goblins. That deep, visceral loathing now propelled me to the farthest corner of the room where I staggered around trying to get my trousers on, trembling and whimpering. All the time, Joanna was shouting at me from the bed, with the sheets pulled up to her chin, saying that bats can't take off from the ground and have to be launched from a height, so all I had to do was pick it up and fling it out of the window. She may as well have asked me to pick it up and bite its head off. She was still shouting implausible instructions at me as I hopped from the room and pogoed down the stairs.

I thought about getting in touch a few months later to apologise, find out how it had turned out, and perhaps raise the possibility of another pleasant afternoon workout, but I thought the chances of the latter were slim and I didn't get around to it.

I'm reliably informed that a bat won't kill you, even a vampire bat, although I don't propose to ever give one the opportunity. But a fire will kill you and it can be cruel. People walk from burning buildings claiming to feel fine, and expire many days later from burns that doctors can't do anything about except ease the pain of them as they watch you die. It happened to a friend of mine, and I didn't want it to happen to me, or to Dottie, and when I smelled smoke and heard the yelling I made damn sure we both left her room in a hurry.

As we lurched out I saw a bank of smoke drifting rapidly towards us from the far end of the corridor, where it led into a part of the building I hadn't visited. I grabbed Dorothy's hand and dragged her in the opposite direction. Almost at once the smoke overtook us, like a river that had burst its banks. After a few steps I stumbled on something and pitched forward, losing my hold on Dottie. Just as I was regaining my balance I felt myself being grabbed around the ankle. I looked over my shoulder and saw Hemingway crouched behind me. At first I thought he was trying to fight me again but then I saw that his face was grey and he was having trouble breathing. I hauled him to his feet, put his arm around my shoulders to hold him upright, then looked back for Dottie. She was on her knees and I thought she'd fallen too but she was bending over a dim shape within the roiling smoke, which I'd tripped over, and it was a woman's body.

Dottie looked up at me and Hemingway and yelled, 'It's Colette!'

Just then the woman stirred and began to raise herself up and I saw the familiar shrub of wild, curly hair and a smeared bloom of dark lipstick. I staggered towards them, entwined with Hemingway, but Dorothy shouted, 'No, get him out of here, I'll help her!' Colette was now on her feet. She really was a tiny woman, like a midget or a doll. I could see that Dottie would have no trouble with her.

I turned and lumbered along the corridor, dragging Hemingway with me into the Blue Room. He seemed to be recovering. He slid his arm off my shoulders and grasped me around the waist, then he took a few shuffling steps forward, as if he was trying to dance with me. I extricated myself from his embrace and turned to look at him. He was breathing heavily but apart from that he seemed in reasonable shape. I waited for him to thank me but he didn't. He looked me up and down, nodded curtly and clapped me on the shoulder. 'Let's get out of here,' he said. I looked back and saw Dottie emerging from the corridor behind us, trotting along with Colette. A few other people were bunched up with them. The smoke was now a solid wall that filled the corridor, pressing up behind them.

As Hemingway and I got to the French windows half a dozen other people appeared, from the direction of the dining room, and there was a momentary bottleneck as everyone tried to get out at once. A couple of people stepped back to ease the pressure and eventually we all spilled out onto the lawn in a relatively orderly fashion.

We turned to look back at the house. Smoke was now filling the Blue Room. Flickers of fire were spurting from a ground floor window about 15 yards away to our right. The window next to it shattered and we all flinched. At that moment tiny flames sprang up all around the French windows we'd just emerged from, as if the frame were draped in a string of Christmas lights that had suddenly been turned on. The flames grew bigger and joined up and then the whole window frame was ablaze. There was a series of loud cracking sounds in quick succession. After that we could hear a voice coming from somewhere inside the building.

'Help!' it shouted. It was a woman's voice.

Patient HST
Recovery Diary 15

Nothing like fear to clear the sinuses.

You know where I was when the fire started. And what
I was doing. Maybe you've known all along, and you
wanted to see how long they'd keep getting high on a
placebo. Purely in the interests of research, of course.
You stone-cold bastards.

Talking of which, Hatchjaw, you were pretty frosty
from what I heard. I came late to the party because of
what happened just before, when my important business
meeting was interrupted. My first instinct if there's any
danger of being busted is to run like hell, and when I
heard someone yelling down at us from the window
I sprinted for the corner of the building. But when I

turned to check on the little guy, he was still standing there. He was fumbling around in his beard, where his glasses were tangled up. I didn't want to leave him there to answer any awkward questions, so I ran back and hissed at him to get moving. The fool just stood there with his mouth open. I grabbed his shoulder and spun him around. He backed away, lumbering into the flowerbed that ran alongside the wall of the house. I tried to get hold of him again...and that was when he dropped what I'd just sold him, and the tabs fell out of the box and rolled all over the damn flowerbed.

Now I had a problem...either I had to help him find the tabs, or tell him what they really were and admit I'd been ripping him off. So I dropped to my knees, scrabbled around between the plants, and got most of the pills back into the box. When I stood up he made a grab for it. We did a crazy little dance for a while, lurching around in the shrubbery as I tried to hustle him away and he tried to get his hands on the goods, clucking and gobbling like an angry turkey. I told him to stop fucking around, and shoved the tabs in the top pocket of his coat. That calmed him down, and he let me push him along the flowerbed and around the corner of the building, where we flattened ourselves against the wall, waiting to see if anyone came after us. I stood there, sweating...hyper-tense...wondering if Collins was ever going to figure out what was really in those tabs. Maybe he wouldn't, because if you've paid to get high you definitely want to believe it's happening, and you'll blindly ignore a whole heap of evidence that it's not.

Hell, when I was a kid how many times did I toke happily on a joint of oregano, or fuck knows what else, and convince myself it was working? The power of denial is awesome.

I smelled the smoke just before I heard the familiar sound of tightly-packed human beings losing their shit. I know what can happen when you hear that sound. When Altamont went bad I wasn't near enough to the stage to get involved, and a few years later I missed The Who concert that turned into a lethal stampede, but I was at some gigs in the sixties and seventies when things got ugly, especially when the Angels discovered the joys of acid, and I know the vibe. I froze for a nanosecond, then my reserves of adrenalin kicked in and I figured that standing against the wall of a house that appeared to be on fire was not the best place to be. I pulled the little guy away from the wall and started skirting across the lawn, edging around the side of the building from a safe distance. I adopted a low, crouching lope...trying to keep it casual...but ready to run if some terrible retribution looked like coming down...twisted, vengeful shit...I was ready for anything.

When I got a view around the corner the first thing I saw was a body flying through the air. What fresh insanity was this? I wasn't seeing someone who was leaping for safety, I was seeing someone being thrown out the window. I've spent enough time around people who were unconscious to recognise the condition in a human body, and this one was definitely unconscious. A tense scenario…fire, breaking glass, an airborne figure exiting a premises by the quickest route…it was just like old times.

That was you tossing your lover out the window, Hatchjaw, you incurable romantic. And you're not the only one. As you were defenestrating your girlfriend, the new guy, Foster, or whatever he calls himself, was trying to get back inside the building, searching for the object of his affection and responding to the age-old yodelling of lustful hormones. The goddam human comedy never stops, does it? And I predict further entertainment. Pretty soon Foster is going to find out just how much of a shitstorm he's bringing down on himself by making an enemy of Hemingway. That fucking clown is dangerous.

Real gone, my friends.

Damnedest thing but I just saw someone at the edge of the woods again, only for a second, but it freaked me out even more than last time. I swear I recognise that oversized maniac. I haven't seen him for years but I'm not likely to forget him.

Patient FJ
Recovery Diary 10

After all the excitement had subsided I found myself baffled by the following question:

If I'm dead, why do I feel so alive?

The more I thought about it the more baffled I was. My perplexity seemed like an active, malignant force intent on testing my mental faculties to destruction. I started to feel quite scared of it. Eventually I managed to unclench the mental fist I was making for myself, and calm my nerves by refusing to think about anything at all.

I'm faithfully describing this process because Hatchjaw asked me to keep my diary observations up to date, and I respect him. This is a relatively new development, as until recently I thought he was a dick. Even after the impressive way he subdued Hemingway in the encounter session I still thought he was a dick, I just thought he was a more dangerous dick than I'd suspected. But I feel different about him now, for two reasons.

Firstly, because he rushed into a burning building to rescue the woman he loves. And secondly, he gave me something new to think about that has made me reconsider everything I believed about myself. It's a pity I've had to wait until I'm dead before I got a life-changing insight, but you can't have everything.

So, right now I'm feeling grateful and a little awestruck. Here's what happened.

When I heard the woman's voice calling for help from inside the house I thought it was Dorothy. I don't know why. I'd seen her just a moment before and she was right behind me, guiding Colette into the Blue Room. But she was among a knot of people, and I was worried she might become trapped in a bottleneck like the one I'd just emerged from. It had been a bit hairy for a few seconds, and there was a moment, as we crammed into that doorway, when I felt the panic stirring inside each of us like nervous birds on a wire, and if just one of us had allowed their fear to take flight everyone might have lost it.

I don't know who stepped back to ease the pressure, but I'm grateful to them for keeping cool. I would have stepped back myself had I not been anxious to stay close to Hemingway, who was coughing like a tractor engine on a cold morning. I tried to manoeuvre myself into a position behind him, to drive him gently forward, but he didn't want to be driven. It's possible we added an extra couple of seconds to the evacuation as a result. With that experience fresh in my mind I could easily imagine that something similar had happened to Dottie, and that she was trapped in the fire.

This idea seemed to spring up in my guts rather than my mind and my reaction was visceral. A powerful force propelled me forward. At the same moment Hatchjaw knocked me hard on the shoulder as he ran past me towards the French windows. Without hesitating he leaped through the ring of flames and into the house. I regained my balance, launched myself after him, and nearly had my arm dislocated. Someone was holding me by the wrist. It was Paddy. As I tried to pull away from him I felt my other arm being gripped. I turned and saw Dorothy. She said something to me that I didn't hear because of a roaring noise in my ears. Her eyes were shining, but that could have been the reflection of the flames. I turned and looked dumbly at the doorway through which Hatchjaw had just disappeared. All around me people were taking little steps towards the house and then stepping back, shaking their heads at each other. Hemingway barged in front of us and began performing his own version of this futile minuet, crouching down like a rugby player about to join a scrum, shuffling forward, flinching, and then shuffling back, cursing violently.

A window on the first floor flew open and a huge cloud of smoke billowed out. Hatchjaw appeared, waving away the smoke and coughing. He yelled something down to us and gesticulated wildly. Everyone looked up at him with open mouths. Nobody seemed to be thinking very clearly. I was still trying to process the fact that the voice we'd heard from inside the burning building wasn't Dottie's, and my mind was groping towards the realisation of whose it was, and why that explained Hatchjaw's recklessness, when Paddy let go of my wrist, sprang forward, and whirled around to face everyone.

'We've got to catch her!' he screamed at us. He'd grasped what Hatchjaw wanted.

We looked up again. Hatchjaw stepped back from the window and reappeared an instant later supporting Eudora Bassett. He had one arm around her waist and was trying to keep her upright as he batted the smoke away with his other hand. He heaved her to the window and got behind her, propping her up against the ledge. I positioned myself beside Paddy, who was now directly below the window. We were joined by Dottie and Hemingway and a couple of others. Coleridge nudged against me, muttering something as he gazed up at the window with a weird, rapturous expression. We all raised our arms instinctively, and then all realised at once that this was a useless gesture. Hatchjaw was of the same opinion. We heard him yelling, 'No, no, no!' as he frantically swept his free hand around in a clutching gesture. Paddy grabbed my wrist again, and I understood. Hatchjaw wanted us to form a net or cradle with our arms. We lurched around, banging into each other as we tried to grip each other's forearms. After a few seconds we'd managed to form ourselves into a kind of ragged human hammock. Hatchjaw shouted, 'Ready?' and without waiting for a reply he launched Dr Bassett out into space.

We were too close to the building. Dr Bassett flew head first from the window with terrific momentum, like a diver at the start of a race trying to cover as much distance as possible before she hits the water. We began a frenzied, crablike shuffle away from the building, attempting to maintain the knot we'd locked ourselves into. We were still moving when Dr Bassett's body thumped into our intertwined arms. We all staggered, clutching at each other as we tried to keep the cradle intact, and took a couple of involuntary galloping steps backwards, then the whole edifice toppled over.

Slowly and carefully we extricated ourselves from the collapsed, multi-limbed creature we'd created, trying all the time to ease Dr Bassett's inert body to the ground as gently as we could. Her skirt had ridden up and was exposing her underwear, which I was pretty sure was silk. I saw that she wore stockings. She'd struck me as the type. I sincerely hoped she'd be all right. I reached towards the hem of her skirt, to pull it down, but Dottie got there first and rearranged it. Someone kicked me in the back, quite hard, and I looked up to see a large black woman looming over us. I hadn't seen her before. She had a big, round face set in an expression of ferocious concentration. She swooped down on Dr Bassett, displacing the rest of us by jabbing at us with her elbows and prodding us out of the way with her boots. Very swiftly she checked Bassett's pulse and breathing. She seemed to know what she was doing.

Just as the newcomer raised Bassett carefully into a sitting position there was a terrific thud from behind us, followed by a sharp scream.

We looked around to see that Hatchjaw had jumped out of the window. He rolled around on the gravel path, clutching his right ankle. He scrabbled onto the grass and raised himself painfully to his hands and knees. He began to crawl towards Dr Bassett, gritting his teeth and suppressing a yelp each time he moved. Even the fierce black woman seemed awed by his determination and didn't try to stop him from hauling himself into position alongside Bassett. He leaned himself against the black woman's ample shoulder and gasped out:

'Is she all right?'

'She'll live,' the black woman said.

Dr Bassett opened her eyes and saw Hatchjaw gazing at her. The look that passed between them told me everything I needed to know.

After that a number of things happened, including my first meal in the community dining room, where someone who I thought was Christopher Marlowe, but later discovered to be Dr John Dee, doled out some very passable stew from a huge, steaming tureen. The rules about the tokens were suspended in consideration of the recent emergency. As well as the residents I'd already met, there were about thirty other people crammed in there, but I didn't notice very much about them.

I sat at a table with Dottie, Paddy and a swarthy man who smiled politely at us but didn't seem inclined to speak. I was ravenous and utterly exhausted. As I finished eating, Hatchjaw appeared. His ankle was bandaged and he was limping heavily. He informed us that Dr Bassett was recovering. Everyone cheered, and Hatchjaw scowled furiously. He gave a gruff announcement about an investigation into the cause of the fire. I believe I actually fell asleep for a couple of seconds at that point, and when Paddy nudged me in the ribs Hatchjaw had gone. I hauled myself to my feet and plodded back to my room, where I lay down and sparked out.

Patient EH
Recovery Diary 19

A man can never thank you enough for saving his life. His gratitude is like the blood pumping from a doomed animal, and he hates you for it. And you detest him in your turn because he makes you desire it, this pouring out of his life and still it is not enough.

You save a man from his death by fire, and the shame of knowing what he owes you is intolerable to him. That is how it is with men and the business between them unless one of them is an ungrateful British prick.

Or he is crazy. There is no saying what such a man will do, or neglect to do. I recalled that in the room with the others where we fought he was reckless in the manner of one who runs with the bulls and does not wish to outrun them, but turns and taunts them with his mortality, and then you know he is a madman.

As we stood outside the building a window burst, and then the sound of timber cracking, like a shell followed by a fusillade, and then a cry struggled through the smoke and it was a woman's voice. The voice tugged at me and I moved without thinking but my limbs were heavy from the effort of taking that man from the flames. There was disorder in the crowd of fearful people who milled in my path and by the time I fought my way through I was on the wrong side of them, moving away from the house. I turned and stood my ground, choking from the smoke still in my lungs. I saw the figure of a man, plunging back into the house through the blazing frame of the French windows, like a black circus dog that leaps through the hoop without knowing why the command stirs him to act.

It was Hatchjaw, and others ran after him, three or four, a woman among them. They called to him and one of them rushed forward and was pulled back by the others. It was the ingrate madman, and I had taken him from the flames although he was my adversary, for that is how a man can live with himself in spite of everything. In his madness he was trying to follow Hatchjaw, or perhaps he wished him harm, there is no knowing, but the others held him back. Among their number was Dorothy and she pulled his arm and clung to him, heedless as always of everything except her own ugly desire.

Hatchjaw came to the window and when I understood

what he wanted us to do I made my way to join the group that gathered below him. When he moved aside I saw Eudora and a spasm of pain gripped at my heart and I was too late to help them catch her. They bungled it and she lay on the ground and they crowded around her with little sense of what they should do. I saw the British fool try to put his filthy paws on her and I rushed forward to strike him but the big negress pushed him aside and took control of everything that needed to be done. Her actions and her manner told me she had seen combat and she was competent to attend to anyone who was wounded.

Still the anger churned in me and I could not trust myself to go near that man with the killing urge in my blood. I turned away and I saw her at the edge of the forest.

She was watching the fire. Standing just inside the treeline as before. But this time she reckoned without the flames which allowed me to see her plainly by their light, and to be certain it was her. I could even see her notebook swagging down the pocket of her pants in the front. She would never wear a skirt if she had a good reason to dress like a man. There was the usual hardness in her eyes but admiration too. Once, she said, 'I like it when you have something bigger than yourself to think about, Scrooby.' I think she was the only one who truly knew me and I'll give the bitch her due.

I returned her steady gaze. She smiled and maybe there was mockery in it, and then she turned and she was gone.

Patient FJ
Recovery Diary 11

I was woken up by someone knocking at my door. It
was Hatchjaw. He came in and sat down on the bed. He
seemed to be glowing with health and vitality. I wanted
to ask him something before I forgot, so I did.

'Who was that rather formidable black woman?'

'Mary Seacole,' he said.

I remembered her history. She'd gone out to the
Crimea in the wake of Florence Nightingale and had
been an extraordinary nurse, caring for innumerable
wretched soldiers on all sides of that stupid, pointless
conflict, and inspiring great love and loyalty in everyone
who got to know her. A remarkable woman. Nightingale
got the glory, and Mary faced a lot of prejudice and
obstruction from the establishment, but she overcame it.
She wrote a memoir, and it's a terrific book, written with

the kind of honesty and directness that more conventionally accomplished writers struggle to achieve all their lives. So, that was her claim to literary fame. But why was she in rehab?

'What's her poison?' I asked Hatchjaw.

He shook his head. 'I'm not at liberty to divulge that.'

'Let me guess. Laudanum?'

'Sorry, but patient confidentiality prohibits me from discussing her with you.'

'Was it booze? She doesn't look like a boozer.'

Hatchjaw paused for a moment then said, 'It was probably ether.'

Interesting. One of the few drugs I haven't tried. But if it gave the poor woman some comfort and happiness, good luck to her.

'Probably?' I said.

Hatchjaw smiled. 'She may not have had a problem with ether. Or anything else, for that matter. She may be faking.'

'Why?'

'I'm beginning to suspect she's only here for the company. Mary wasn't accepted socially in her lifetime. And people sometimes seek treatment for complex reasons, and with hidden motives, as I'm sure you're aware.'

I certainly was. I knew several people, for example, who attended AA and NA meetings simply in order to meet producers, agents and publishers. This practice was particularly widespread in Los Angeles and the more fashionable parts of London. These people had to exaggerate their modest (or non-existent) indulgences, and claim to be in the grip of powerful and debilitating addictions. Often they got carried away, especially the actors, and constructed a series of lurid fictional melodramas into which their depravity had supposedly plunged them. These inventions became increasingly susceptible to being exposed as they grew wilder and more improbable. The fakers encountered other problems, too. Sometimes they'd be in a restaurant, enjoying the single glass of wine to which they were accustomed, when they'd be accosted by a fellow member of AA, and have to pretend they'd just fallen off the wagon. This lie then required them to appear at the next meeting to deliver a tearful confession, and pledge their renewed determination to fight the good fight all over again, one day at a time. All this could get exhausting for them, and the stress of maintaining such elaborate deceptions frequently drove them to drink or drugs, and they became genuine victims of the addictions which, in the beginning, they'd merely been feigning.

I turned to Hatchjaw. 'So, if Mary Seacole is here simply because she wants to be, and doesn't have any addiction issues, does that apply to some of the others too?'

He leaned back against the wall and drew his legs up, making himself comfortable on my bed. 'Possibly,' he said, regarding me owlishly. 'Yes, I'd have to say the policy seems to be one of self-selection.'

Aha, I thought. That could explain why I'd seen some other patients whose presence I couldn't account for. There was Colette, for a start. I knew she'd led a colourful life and kept exotic company, and she'd probably enjoyed a glass or two of absinthe in her time, but she was a famously disciplined writer and I'd never heard of her being addicted to anything. Except, perhaps, exotic company itself. And maybe sex, although you got the impression it was simply a matter of enjoying it a lot, rather than there being anything particularly compulsive about her numerous affairs with both men and women. But you could see why this place might attract her. The company was varied and volatile, and most of the patients would be prone to the reckless neediness that was characteristic of addicts, and which would make them good prospects to be seduced without too much effort or fuss. There were also half a dozen orderlies around the place, all beefy young men, and I imagined she'd be happy to take them to bed.

My sighting of Gertrude Stein could also be verified by the open-door admissions policy. She was just a friendly pothead in search of congenial company, and she found it here, among people who shared her relaxed attitude to the conventions that must have made early-twentieth-century life quite challenging for a strapping lesbian who wrote peculiar poetry. Good luck to her.

And then there was the striking young man with red hair and an alabaster complexion I'd spotted in the canteen earlier. I could now confirm my suspicion that it was Thomas Chatterton. He probably wouldn't have had time to develop any serious addictions in the short span of his lonely, dismal life before he ended it with a breakfast of arsenic and opium. By all accounts he'd hoped his writing would bring him fame, and with it the money to support his mother and sister, and he was cruelly disappointed. But he managed to produce enough extraordinary work, including his medieval forgeries, to prove to later generations that he'd possessed some kind of genius, before his nature conspired with his circumstances to make his brief existence intolerable.

But he looked happy now. If in life he'd craved the respect of his literary peers he was finally in the right place, and getting it in spades. When I saw him in the canteen he'd been nattering cheerfully with Coleridge, the pair of them alternately whispering with their heads together and leaning back to roar with laughter. Coleridge had always idolised Chatterton, and even though young Thomas died two years before Sam was born he could now bask in the admiration of his successor, unfettered by the tedious constraints of linear time. Moving to the afterlife transforms one's social circle, opening up all kinds of opportunities to make new friends and, in my case, fornicate with them. As I started speculating on other possible benefits of the transition from life to death I was disappointed to realise I hadn't experienced the much-trumpeted moment when your entire life flashes before your eyes, which would at least have given me the satisfaction of finally remembering all my fucking passwords.

While I was musing on all this, and the perpetual struggle between the nobility of the spirit and the weakness of the flesh, I'd almost forgotten about Hatchjaw. Now he patted me on the knee in a very chummy way and I looked up to see him gazing at me earnestly from beneath his shaggy eyebrows.

'How are you holding up?' he said.

'Actually, I'm feeling pretty good, and I wanted to ask you about that. I mean, right now I feel invigorated. Full of life. Right?'

Hatchjaw nodded. 'Right. It was exciting, wasn't it?'

'Don't dick me around. What I'm saying is that I feel full of life, and yet I'm dead. So for Christ's sake, tell me what this is all about.'

Hatchjaw frowned. 'Sorry, but I can't.'

I pulled back my fist and I might have hit him if a couple of thoughts hadn't flashed through my mind. One was that it's never a good idea to hit your doctor. The other was that Hatchjaw had proved he knew how to take care of himself by the way he'd dealt with Hemingway, who'd given me a black eye not too long ago, and I try to make it a rule not to get beaten up more than once a week. I slapped my palm down on the bed beside me, then put my head in my hands and stared at the floor.

When I finally raised my head Hatchjaw was still looking at me. I spread my hands and appealed to him. 'Nothing? Are you telling me you don't know any more than I do?'

'We have to accept,' he said slowly, 'that we will never know everything, or even a fraction of all there is to know, and our thirst for comprehensive explanations, and absolute meanings causes us more distress than almost anything else.'

'Don't give me that crap,' I said. 'We're programmed to seek meaning, and quite right, too. The effort to construct a narrative from the chaos is behind everything creative in the human spirit. What do you want us to do, just switch our minds off and accept everything without trying to understand anything? Like animals?'

'No, no, no. Not at all. I'm just saying – and I know you've heard this plenty of times before – that we're always looking in the wrong direction. Looking out there for the big explanation, when we really have to start in here.' He placed his hand on his breast.

'Fucking right I've heard it before.' I turned away and went into a sulk. It's true: I've heard all the angles, delivered by every practitioner on the therapeutic spectrum, from the cheerful behaviourists via the ponderous Jungians to the mystical babblers, plus a few that were off the map entirely, and if Hatchjaw was drifting in that direction I didn't like it.

The bed creaked beneath me. Hatchjaw stood up and went to the window. 'All right,' he said, 'let's think about something else. I noticed you were trying to get back into the building when it was on fire. Why did you want to do that?'

'I don't know. Maybe for the same reason that you did?'

Hatchjaw smiled again. He had a nice smile and it made him look quite handsome in a craggy kind of way. 'Extraordinary, isn't it?' he said. 'Love. It really is just as crazy as they say.'

'I don't think I'm in love with her,' I said. 'I've only just met her.'

'But it doesn't matter, does it?'

A familiar pang of yearning clutched at my heart. I

was thinking about the first time I saw Paula. She was poised, lost in thought, at the top of the steps outside a house in Maida Vale where there was a party. As I walked up the steps she turned and looked at me. Then the front door opened and a braying fool emerged and flung his arms around her. After a moment Paula extricated herself gracefully from the host's embrace and squeezed past him, by which time I was close enough for him to lurch at me and move in for the clumsy hug that men exchange when they've know each other long enough, even if they despise each other. Paula always denied she'd seen me on the steps, and claimed that she'd first noticed me in the party, but I remember the moment with absolute clarity. It was when I fell in love with her.

It was different with Felicity. It was the same process, in a way, but in slow motion. And we fell out of love in agonisingly slow motion, too. But that doesn't change what you felt, when you felt it.

'No,' I replied to Hatchjaw, 'it doesn't matter. Something…stirs you. And that's it.'

'And it's not just lust, is it? It feels like something higher than that. Something good and noble.'

'Maybe. I think it's foolish to deny the possibility of those things, anyway.'

'And yet…' Hatchjaw gazed out of the window. 'We always fuck it up.'

'We do. Sometimes it takes real dedication but we always find a way.' I stared at Hatchjaw's back. I thought about all the people who had ever turned away from me. Unable to bear it. I thought about the nightmarish stasis that gripped me and Felicity for the last two years of our marriage. The chilly politeness with which we tormented each other was far, far worse than fighting would have been. We could have broken through it if we'd fought, or fucked. But we were scared to fight each other, and she didn't want to have sex because she thought we'd lost our intimacy, and I thought we'd lost our intimacy because we weren't having sex.

I sighed. 'None of it should matter to us any more,' I said to Hatchjaw's back, 'but it does, doesn't it?'

Hatchjaw grabbed a small chair that stood beside the window and whirled it around to face me, dragging it forward so our knees were touching when he sat down on it. He peered into my face with a peculiar kind of excitement. Merriment, perhaps. 'I think you're a hero,' he said.

I laughed. 'Really? What about you, then? You actually rescued your maiden.'

'I'm not really talking about that. I'm talking about your addictions. What you go through.'

'What's heroic about that? It's the opposite of heroic. It's pathetic. I know I'm meant to believe addiction is a disease, and I'm not to blame, and all that shit, but no matter how often I hear that I simply can't buy it. Not entirely. I know I'm helpless, I accept that bit. But I don't think I'm blameless.'

'I don't think you are, either.'

I raised my eyebrows. That was a bit off-message, from a therapist.

'But that's the point,' Hatchjaw continued. 'I believe

you want to redeem yourself. You want to do what's right. And it's very, very difficult for you to do what's right. But you're convinced you have a better self, and I think your drinking, and all the other things, I think it's all part of the struggle to find your better self. To find it and rescue it. But you can't find it in everyday life, in normal reality – for whatever reason, let's not worry about all the 'Mummy-didn't-give-me-a-rubber-ducky' explanations – and so you go searching for it in other places. You seek your better self in other lands. The magic realms. The alcoholic worlds, the drugged dimensions. I understand that, James. I understand that quest and I think it's admirable. In fact, it's heroic.'

I started to say something but I couldn't. I let out a long, shuddering breath and I began to cry. I allowed the tears to flood down my cheeks and make my clothes wet. I wept without thinking about anything or feeling anything particular. I just wept. It didn't seem to have much to do with me, although it was quite relaxing. It lasted about a minute and then it stopped. Hatchjaw produced some tissues from somewhere and handed them to me, then got up and strolled to the window again. I blew my nose.

'Tell me,' Hatchjaw said, 'out of all the theories and explanations about addiction that you must have heard, what's the most convincing to you?'

'I'm not sure any more. Something about what you've just said seems to have had a strange effect on me. So I may have to change my mind.'

'No bad thing. Okay, but up until just now. What framework has given you the most insight, or resonated with you most strongly?'

'The one about inconsolability. You know?'

Hatchjaw nodded. 'Carry on.'

'The idea that some people are simply born with a sense of loss. Of regret for something. And the drinking, or the addiction or whatever, it's all about that pain. Not that addicts are trying to console themselves, because you can't fill that hole, it's bottomless. It's something else. You're trying to take your mind off the fact – the knowledge, the absolute certainty – that nothing can make you happy. It's a way of dealing with that hopelessness. The addiction doesn't console you, but it dulls the pain of inconsolability.'

'Very well put. A good story, well told. I'm not dismissing it by saying that, by the way. It's as good as any other story, and better than most. And there's nothing wrong with the fact that it's a story, either. They're all stories. As you said, we're programmed to understand the world through stories. And of course, for a writer that's even more true. For many writers, narrative is the drug of choice.'

'What about the story you just told me? About being a hero.'

'That's just a story, too. But you liked that story, didn't you?'

'I did. It made me cry.'

'Exactly. And if one particular story moves you more than others, and appeals to you, and throws fresh light on what it means to be human, and speaks to something deep in your heart, well, that's a good story, right?'

'It's terrific. How does it end?'

Hatchjaw laughed. His laugh was delightful: rich and unforced, and it surprised me. I also noticed he had no fillings in his teeth. I was sure they were his own, too, because they were quite discoloured, and you wouldn't go to the trouble of getting stained false teeth. I started to laugh, too. We both seemed to be pretty happy.

Hatchjaw walked to the door and opened it without bothering to answer my question. He stood in the doorway, smiling at me. 'Keep up the good work, James. Sorry, I'm calling you James, but I haven't asked if you'd still prefer to be called Foster.'

'I don't mind. Call me Jim if you like.'

'All right. Jim. It was good to talk to you.'

'You too...'

'Wallace. That's my first name.'

I nodded slowly. 'Okay, Wallace. Thanks.'

'I hope what I was saying made some kind of sense to you.'

'Absolutely. God, yes. As I said, it's really given me something to think about.'

'Good. It's just that I'm on some pretty powerful painkillers at the moment.'

I laughed again. 'Go for it, Wallace.'

He raised a hand in farewell and closed the door gently behind him.

I lay back on the bed. I felt okay. I decided not to think about anything for while. I found it surprisingly easy. As I began to doze off, I had one of those creepy hallucinations you sometimes get just before you go to sleep. I felt something sticky in my hand, and when I looked at it I saw I was clutching the fabric of a dress Paula used to wear. Then I realised I was dreaming, and woke up just long enough to feel a sense of calamity before I sank into real sleep.

From the desk of Dr Bassett
To Dr Hatchjaw

Wallace, what can I say? I owe you my life. Everything else seems so trivial beside that fact. Our arguments are so silly. It's as if the fire was a warning to us, to get over ourselves and focus on what's truly important. Perhaps we'll always feel conflicted and confused but we shouldn't be uncertain: the fire has banished those feelings. For me, anyway. I expect there will always be challenges for us to face, if we're together. But facing challenges is what makes it all worthwhile, don't you think? I'm still recovering and I'm a bit feeble, but I thought I'd let you know how I'm feeling right now.

Eudora

From the desk of Dr Hatchjaw
To Dr Bassett

My dearest Eudora,

Thank you so very much for being so frank. I was thrilled to read what you wrote. I'm still thrilled. I feel very proud to think I might deserve you. But let's not worry too much about the future, let's just be thankful for what we've got. Don't concern yourself about anything. Just rest, relax and get well.

I agree with you about the fire. It was a wake-up call to both of us. As for what caused it, I've gone ahead and arranged for an inquiry, as a matter of routine procedure. I don't want to worry you, so please don't fret about this at the moment, but we may have to face a couple of unpleasant possibilities. One is that the fire was started deliberately, and if that turns out to be the case, I have a feeling that we'll find it has something to do with the person we've both seen lurking about at the edge of the woods, rather than any of the patients. If, on the other hand, the fire was accidental, then we can't rule out the possibility that a cigarette may have started it. It wouldn't be the first time, after all. But, as I said, don't worry about all this for now. Just get well.

Wallace

From the desk of Dr Bassett
To Dr Hatchjaw

Dear God, what's the matter with you? When you say 'it wouldn't be the first time,' are you referring to what happened with your tie? Which, let me remind you, got a hole burned in it, or what you insisted on calling a hole even though it was little more than a scorch, when my cigarette fell out of the ashtray and landed on our clothes, which were on the floor BECAUSE of what WE and that means YOU as well as me, Wallace, were doing at the time, and the memory of which you ruined for ever by going on and on about your stupid fucking tie afterwards? Because if you are, you're even more petty and vindictive than I ever imagined. In fact I think there's something wrong with you, frankly.

From the desk of Dr Hatchjaw
To Dr Bassett

Dear Eudora, once again we have misunderstood each other. For some reason you seem to think I'm accusing you of being responsible for the fire, when all I wanted to say was that we must be open to all possibilities so that no avenue of inquiry is closed to the forthcoming investigation. However, you've taken my comments as a personal attack, which is most unfortunate.

Please unlock your door. Or if you won't let me in, or come out, at least talk to me through the door. It's clear that we need to discuss this.

I'll wait outside your room whenever I have a spare moment. Unfortunately I will be substantially preoccupied with our special visitor, who is arriving shortly to assist with the investigation. But whenever I can get away, I'll be outside your room.

Wallace

Patient PW
Recovery Diary 12

I am feeling abraded, bilious, cynocephalic, and disgruntled.

And I'm worried about Jim. I care about him despite everything, or because of everything. And I know he cares about me, much as he'd like to deny it. Both of us have found it difficult to deal with being each other's best friend. Or worst friend, which amounts to the same thing much of the time. What would have happened if we'd devoted as much energy to cultivating our friendship as we did to sabotaging it? We certainly wouldn't have had as much fun.

I once sent him a postcard from Venice with a photo of a hideously ugly old woman on the front, squinting malevolently into what must have been a very early camera in the middle of the nineteenth century. I think it was intended to illustrate traditional peasant costume from the region. Jim and I always sent each other postcards from foreign cities, and made it a rule to find pictures that were as dissonant as possible with the image most tourists would associate with the site. Jim and I had been through one of our recurrent bouts of hostility and I wanted to re-establish relations without appearing to concede anything. On the back of the postcard I wrote:

I'm your friend but you are sometimes your own worst enemy.

And, as your friend, any enemy of yours is an enemy of mine.

And that's why I'm your enemy, my friend.

That's still a fair summary of how I feel about Jim. Nothing much has changed, and death doesn't seem to have improved him. He's still the same staggeringly solipsistic bastard he always was. I love him, of course, and he's still good company. Of all the selfish, drunken, literary ruffians I've known, I'd probably pick him to spend the afterlife with, given the choice.

I wonder what he'll make of the most recent development.

Patient FJ
Recovery Diary 12

Feeling: pissed off. Really, really pissed off.

I mean, give me a fucking break. Sherlock fucking Holmes?

Just when I thought I was beginning to make some kind of sense of what's happening to me, it all falls apart. I'm not claiming that I'd arrived at any remotely rational explanation, but at least I thought I'd understood the rules. I thought, Okay, I'm dead (or something similar) and so is everyone else here, and what we all have in common is that we're all writers, and we've all got (or had) substance abuse issues. Fine. Yes, it's stark raving mad, but there appeared to be parameters to the insanity. There was a paradigm of sorts, and part of it was that we may be dead, but we are all real people. But Sherlock Holmes IS NOT A REAL PERSON. And neither is Doctor fucking Watson.

The Adventure of the Singular Sanatorium
by Dr John Watson

It was with a weary step that I followed my old friend Sherlock Holmes as he strode ahead of me along a curving drive flanked by tall evergreens. The high iron gates, outside which our cab had stopped, were a quarter of a mile behind us. I couldn't recall, precisely, why the driver refused to enter the grounds. I had fallen asleep in the train, and my mind was still clouded by strange dreams in which I had seemed to revisit certain episodes from my service in the late Afghani war. Despite the afternoon sunlight I shuddered as I tried to shake them from my memory and clear my head.

The dark trees gave way to rolling lawns, and I saw that our destination was a large, rambling mansion. Its date was indefinable and it appeared to have been enlarged and altered in various ways at different times over many years.

A short, dark-haired figure wearing a white coat trotted down some stone steps in front of the building and came to meet us. He introduced himself as Dr Hatchjaw, and confirmed that it was he who had summoned the great detective for a purpose Holmes had not, as yet, seen fit to reveal to me, save to declare that the case might prove sufficiently interesting to rouse him from one of the periodic fits of torpor into which he had been plunged for several weeks. I saw that Holmes was now regarding the man with a keen eye; a certain quickening in his manner – which no one but myself would have noticed – told me that something about the doctor had provoked his intense interest.

Hatchjaw appeared to be in his middle years, active and fit, and his grey eyes gleamed with intelligence beneath exceptionally shaggy brows. As he led us up the steps, Holmes caught my eye and gave me a curt nod: this was my cue to engage Hatchjaw in conversation so that my companion could observe him surreptitiously. Accordingly, when Holmes paused at the top of the steps and turned, as if to admire the view, I asked Hatchjaw about his medical training and practice. He informed me that he now practised as a specialist in nervous disorders, and that many of his patients suffered from the consequences of addiction to drugs, including morphine and cocaine. I glanced at Holmes to see how he took this reference to habits with which he is, unfortunately, only too familiar, and from indulgence in which I have frequently tried to dissuade him. Holmes merely gave me a bland smile, and turned to our host.

'Dr Hatchjaw,' said Holmes, 'I wonder if I might be permitted to look around the grounds before going inside?'

Hatchjaw frowned. 'If you wish. But shouldn't you inspect the scene of the fire immediately, while any clues are still fresh? Fingerprints and suchlike that may deteriorate as time passes?'

Holmes smiled. 'I see that you have heard something of my methods. However, I propose to entrust a preliminary examination of the scene to Dr Watson.' With this, Holmes produced his magnifying lens, and handed it to me with a flourish.

I must confess I was surprised. Never before had Holmes asked me to undertake something of this kind, and I was at a loss what to make of it. But my surprise was as nothing compared to my astonishment when Holmes swept off his deerstalker hat and clapped it on my own head. As I tried to recover my composure Holmes took a step back, regarded me with a twinkle in his eye, and nodded approvingly. 'Very good, Watson,' he said, 'you know what to do.' He turned to Hatchjaw. 'Dr Watson is eminently capable of discovering any clues. And I assure you that I shall not be wasting my time, or yours, if you permit me to take a stroll, and perhaps to speak to any patients I may encounter.' Holmes performed a perfunctory bow, and without waiting for an answer he turned, descended the stone steps, and sauntered away.

Hatchjaw's manner when he turned to me courteous enough, but I could see he was disappointed to lose the chance of witnessing the celebrated investigator at work. I gave him what I hoped was a reassuring smile. 'Shall we go inside?' I asked.

Signs of the recent fire were apparent from the moment we stepped through the doors. A sour tang of charred wood hung in the air, and visible tokens of damage became increasingly evident as I followed Hatchjaw across a wide hallway and up a flight of stairs. From a few remarks he threw over his shoulder I was able to piece together the circumstances of the fire. He alluded casually to the fact that he had rescued a colleague from the flames, but when I pressed him for more details he didn't reply. We were now on the landing at the top of the stairs, and I noticed that the walls and floors were damp. It was only then that it occurred to me to ask Hatchjaw how the fire was extinguished.

'Sprinklers,' he replied.

Seeing my confusion, he described an ingenious hydraulic system of water jets, which had effectively quenched the flames. When I expressed my surprise he told me that such a system was not unusual, but that this house was equipped with a type that was particularly powerful and effective, which had prevented the conflagration from causing more damage.

By this time we had made our way into a large, open room on the far side of the landing. It was blackened by soot, with signs of severe damage. Hatchjaw turned to face me and raised his unkempt eyebrows enquiringly.

Having been fortunate enough to observe Sherlock Holmes at work during a period of many years, and in many different circumstances, I had learned something of his methods. I presented an impassive countenance to Hatchjaw before turning away and gazing slowly around the room. I observed that the glass in all the windows was missing, but all the frames – which were of a sash-weight design – were closed, save one, which was raised by a foot or more. I walked to this window and examined it. I noticed that the floor below it was covered with ashy fragments of material. I got down on my knees – with some stiffness – and inspected them using Holmes's lens, which revealed them to be made of patterned cotton. As my eye roved over them I glimpsed a flat, metallic object that was almost concealed beneath the charred scraps. Very carefully I extracted it and examined it under the glass. It had been twisted out of shape by the intense heat, but it was unmistakeably an ashtray.

I got to my feet. 'Tell me, Dr Hatchjaw,' I said, 'was this a smoking room, and do you believe it to have been the seat of the fire?'

Hatchjaw's eyebrows shot up like a pair of startled caterpillars and his lugubrious features were transformed by a smile that gave him an appealingly boyish air.

'Yes!' he exclaimed, 'although it wasn't a designated smoking area, but it was certainly used as one.'

'By the patients?'

Hatchjaw paused for a moment before he replied. 'Yes,' he said, 'patients…and some of the staff. One of the staff, really. Although I don't want to…' He trailed off. Something was clearly troubling him. But he shook it off, and strode to join me at the window, his energy rekindled by the curiosity with which he questioned me:

'What are your conclusions, Dr Watson? What do you deduce?'

'I note that this window must have been open,' I replied, trying to imitate Holmes's manner, 'and I surmise that an ashtray was balanced on the window sill. In all probability someone was smoking a cigar or cigarette here when they were distracted, possibly by whatever activity is signified by the footprints in the flowerbed immediately below the window, which, you will observe, indicate at least two sets of feet, running to and fro.'

I pointed out of the window at the flowerbed which had, indeed, been disturbed by what looked like footprints. I confess that I may have overstated my deductive prowess with regard to this conclusion, although something had certainly disordered the earth below the window. 'The cigar or cigarette,' I continued, 'was dangerously close to the cotton curtains, and a light breeze would have sufficed to bring them into contact with it, causing the fire.'

Hatchjaw nodded slowly, lost in thought. After a moment he emerged from his reverie and shot me a keen look. 'What now?' he asked.

I racked my brain, and tried think what Holmes would do. Then it came to me. 'I shall need to question the patients, if you agree, Dr Hatchjaw.'

'Of course, ' he said, as if he expected as much. 'And anyone else?'

'Indeed,' I said, taken aback for a moment. 'I will need to question everyone who was on the premises. But I'll start with the patients, if I may.'

Hatchjaw nodded. Some of his exuberance had left him. I noted that he appeared to be subject to abrupt changes of mood. 'Yes, yes,' he muttered, 'we can go this way. Please follow me.'

He led me out of the room through a door opposite the one by which we had entered, and I found myself following him along a corridor, lined on one side by windows looking out on to the garden, and on the other by dark oak doors. After a few paces Hatchjaw stopped and I nearly bumped into him. He turned to me with a troubled expression, and spoke in a low voice.

'This is the window,' he said, indicating a charred frame beside him, 'from which I was able to…assist my colleague to safety. Having ensured, of course, that people in the garden were ready to catch her.'

I glanced out of the window at the drop. It was not inconsiderable. 'And where is your colleague now, Dr Hatchjaw?' I asked. 'Would it be possible to speak to her?'

He knitted his tangled brows and dropped his voice even further. 'This room,' he said, indicating a door on the other side of the corridor, 'belongs to my colleague, Dr Bassett. Well, I say my colleague, but she is technically my superior at this establishment.' He broke off and stood in silence, gazing at the door.

'But what do you suggest?' I asked, matching his subdued tone. 'Shall I speak to her before questioning the patients, or not?'

'The thing is,' he said, 'Dr Bassett has been somewhat…' Again he trailed off. He took a deep breath, and was about to resume, when the door was flung open.

A female figure almost sprang out of the room and confronted us. She was short, like Hatchjaw, and not unattractive, or perhaps it would be more accurate to call her vivacious, as her figure and features displayed energy and charm rather than conventional beauty. She looked me up and down with a decidedly critical gaze, which she then transferred to Hatchjaw. She regarded him haughtily and her eyes glittered with suppressed passion.

'For God's sake, Wallace,' she hissed, 'what the hell are you playing at?'

'Nothing to worry about, Eudora, just part of the investigation I told you about,' Hatchjaw said, in a voice that was clearly intended to soothe her but seemed to have the opposite effect.

The little woman glanced at me again. 'I suppose you're going to tell me,' she said to Hatchjaw, 'that this is Sherlock bloody Holmes!'

As I attempted to overcome my shock I recalled that I was wearing Holmes's deerstalker hat and still holding his glass in my hand.

'No, no, Eudora,' said Hatchjaw, amiably, 'this is Dr Watson.'

I thought she would strike him. Rarely have I seen such naked fury in a woman's expression. She seemed to swell with outrage for a moment, then she turned on her heel, shot back into her room, and slammed the door behind her with such force that it shook the frame.

Hatchjaw stared in silence at the closed door, as if he were waiting for her to emerge again. Finally he tore his gaze away and looked at me. 'Perhaps we should talk to the patients first,' he said.

At that moment a flash of movement from the garden caught my eye. I thought I saw a figure at the edge of the woods that bordered the lawn on this side of the house.

Hatchjaw saw me start in surprise. 'What?' he cried, peering out of the window, 'who did you see?'

'I thought I saw a man at the edge of the woods there.'

'A man? Are you sure? What did he look like?'

'I don't know. I didn't see him for long enough.'

Hatchjaw continued to gaze at the treeline. 'Several people have seen someone out there at odd times recently,' he said. 'Perhaps you can help us find out who it is.'

'I'll do my best. That is to say, Mr Holmes and I will do our best.'

Hatchjaw nodded. 'Fine. I'll take you to the Blue Room. I expect we'll find some of the patients there.'

With that he set off once more, and I followed him, wondering all the while what Holmes was doing at that moment. For I had not been entirely honest with Dr Hatchjaw. In truth, although I had glimpsed the figure in the trees only very briefly, I was sure I recognised him. And if I was right, we were all in mortal danger. But Holmes more than any of us.

Patient HST
Recovery Diary 19

Madness, madness...but interesting madness.

When I looked up from the bench I figured there was something familiar about the man standing in front of me. He was tall, about my height, but with better posture. He looked down his long, hawk-like nose at me and he seemed like an arrogant fuck but I have no problem with that...and he got my attention, even though he encountered me at a point when I was reluctant to engage with anyone representing the human race.

I was sitting in a remote part of the garden because I wanted to be alone. I was picking up menacing vibrations from everywhere... I needed to keep out of the way of whatever hellish scenes were playing out in the aftermath of the fire. I was also mulling over the situation with Collins and Coleridge, and the dumb shit I was pulling. It was force of habit, pure and simple. There wasn't even any money in it for me. All I was getting out of it was a bunch of plastic tokens, and I was dishonouring the noble profession of dope dealer by selling drugs under false pretences. Let's call it selling, anyway, even though the damn tokens were now mounting up under my bed faster than I could use them. Collins and Coleridge were opium hounds, and I should have respected their taste and discrimination. God bless the poppy, and the peace it brings the troubled spirit and the weary body. Instead I was exploiting their pitiful gullibility. Meanwhile I was drinking around thirty cups of coffee a day, because it was one of the few things on offer in exchange for the tokens that I could tolerate. Fine coffee, as it happens, but there's only so much coffee a man can drink before he feels the need to crawl out of his skin and eat a handful of downers, and I had reached that point, but I didn't have the downers.

I wasn't feeling good about myself, so when a shadow hit my face and I looked up from under my hat to find a tall, thin stranger blocking my sun I took it as a personal insult. And he was wearing a cape, which is a garment I've always associated with hippies, and just one of the many reasons I always hated them.

'Yes?' I snarled.

'May I take this opportunity of finding you alone,' he said, 'to ask you where you were when the recent fire broke out?'

'Who wants to know?'

He stuck his hand out. 'My name is Sherlock Holmes.'

He was crazy. I liked him. I shook his hand, which seemed to give him a big kick. He kept pumping away, looking down at my hand as if he needed to weigh it before selling it to someone. He finally gave it back and stood there inspecting me lazily. I nodded at the bench beside me. He sat down and leaned back, squinting into the sun and crossing his ankles. 'Thank you,' he said.

I waited for him to say something else but he didn't. So I said, 'Why do you want to know where I was when the fire broke out?'

He sat up sharply and turned to face me, giving me an intense, beady stare. Maybe it was meant to freak me out, and it might have done if I hadn't dealt with too many cops, spooks, litigators and seedy, mean-minded freelance investigators in my time to be worried by one of them eyeballing me, whether he wanted to call himself Sherlock Holmes, J. Edgar Hoover, or Genghis Khan.

'Whom do I have the honour of addressing, sir?' he said.

'Dr Gonzo,' I said. No point revealing my real name to anyone professing to be on the side of the law, even if he was batshit crazy.

He raised an eyebrow. 'A medical man?'

'Not exactly.'

'But with some experience of medicines and drugs, I take it?'

'Oh, yes. You could say that.'

He nodded and pursed his lips. 'Then I believe you are the man I want,' he said.

'Want for what?'

'To confirm something for me, if you would be so good. I believe that shortly before the fire broke out you were engaged in conversation with a fellow patient in the garden on the side of the house adjacent to this, in other words, the eastern side. The transaction that you were conducting with this gentleman can only be described as nefarious.'

I lowered my shades and stared at him. 'How the fuck—' I began, but he held up his hand and twitched his nostrils at me.

'Permit me,' he said, 'to continue. Something – or someone – interrupted your intercourse with the gentleman, and you left the scene hurriedly, only to return almost immediately in order to collect your companion, fearing that if he was apprehended he might disclose the nature of your business with him. It was then that the commodity which was the object of that business became scattered in the flowerbed, from where you strove to retrieve it as quickly as you were able, before making off once more. Am I correct in what I have said?'

'Holy shit.'

'I will take that as an affirmation. I fancy I have surprised you.'

I didn't say anything to that. He knew he had surprised me, and I wasn't going to give him any more satisfaction. I just stared at him grimly, wondering how dangerous he could be to me. But fuck it, how dangerous could *anyone* be to me, given my situation?

He made a noise somewhere between a bark and a laugh. 'Ha. Forgive me. It is not my intention to mystify you. The explanation for my knowledge of your proceedings is relatively simple. Most of what I know was divulged to me just a few moments ago by your collaborator. Or should I refer to him as your victim?'

'Who, Collins? You talked to him?'

'Indeed.'

'And he ratted me out? Just like that?'

He narrowed his eyes. 'If you're asking me whether he betrayed you, I can tell you that he did not. Not by his own lights, anyway. He told me no more than he had to.'

'Like what?'

'Simply that certain facts I had deduced were correct. I won't bore you with the details of how I arrived at my conclusions; suffice it to say that he admitted he was addicted to opium, that he has not conquered his addiction, that he has been purchasing supplies of what he believed to be that substance clandestinely, and that he has been the victim of a deception on that head. Of course, like all addicts, he is in many ways a willing party to that deception, which he has practised upon himself just as much as anyone else has. Regarding the recent events surrounding the fire, I got the whole story out of him: how he met his supplier at an appointed time and place; how their transaction was interrupted by someone who may have seen them in the act, how the supposedly precious drug was scattered in the confusion of the moment, and how he and his companion retrieved it and then fled the scene. However, he stoutly refused to name the other party in this affair. His loyalty was remarkable, even after he learned that the person he trusted had been playing him false for so long.'

He'd been telling me all this in an offhand way, leaning back with his long, elegant legs crossed and his arm draped over the back of the bench. Now he turned to face me, and at the same time his hand gripped my shoulder. I didn't like that, but his bony fingers were powerful...and I didn't feel like finding out what it would take to dislodge them. He gave me the beady eye again. 'Do you deny that you were the man who was with Mr Collins?'

'No,' I said. 'You got me. But I'd like to know how you figured it out, if Collins didn't tell you.'

He let go of my shoulder and gave me a thin smile that you could easily mistake for a sneer if you wanted to make something of it. 'Very simple. Your shoes still bear a few traces of mud, in which there is the impression of a small hydrangea leaf, of a type that I have seen, so far, only in that particular flowerbed. In addition, when I examined your hand I observed dirt under your fingernails. When you admitted to me that you have a knowledge of drugs, I felt certain that your were my man. And now, as you don't deny the deception that you've practised on Collins, will you allow me to ask you one or two questions about it?'

I shrugged. 'Shoot.'

'What is the substance that you have been passing off as opium?'

'It's a mixture of soap and wax.'

'Wax?'

'They have candles in the eating area. You can light them for the evening meal if you want to have a romantic dinner with another dead person.'

Sherlock Holmes – I was ready to believe it was him – frowned. 'Then Mr Collins was not smoking the substance, or he would have discovered the deception at once.'

'That was the beauty of it. I knew he wouldn't try to smoke it. Too much hassle, too much drug paraphernalia. He knew what to do with it. There's more than one way to ingest a small pellet of opium. Or what you think is opium.'

Just for a moment he seemed to lose his cool. Then he gave a little cough. 'Just so. The mucous membrane of the rectum is particularly suited to absorb the drug in its raw state. Thus Mr Collins would not examine it too closely. I presume you used some kind of colouring mixed with the soap and wax?'

I grinned at him. 'Sure. From the same place it was going to end up. Which disguised the smell of the soap and gave it a little pungency, too.'

He tilted his head back, flared his nostrils, and looked at me through half-closed eyes. I got the feeling he had a low opinion of me. But he just gave a sigh and leaned back on the bench again. He produced a nice-looking silver case and flipped it open.

'Cigarette?' he said.

I took one of the oval-shaped cigarettes...Turkish, expensive looking...and we both lit up using my Zippo. He asked to see it, and as he was inspecting it he said, 'I have no reason to judge you, Dr Gonzo. I leave that to your own conscience, which you seem to think is clear. So be it.' As he turned the lighter over in his hands, giving it a pretty close inspection, he continued casually, 'But if you're the kind of man I take you for, who seems to have a tight grip upon himself and isn't rattled easily, I don't understand why you feared detection so much when your little game was interrupted. That puzzles me.'

'I don't like being busted as a matter of principle. And I definitely didn't want to be busted by the good lady doctor. I like Bassett.'

'Ha!' he shouted, and sprang up from the bench.

'Jesus,' I said, 'don't do that. You made me jump like a motherfucker.'

He threw his cigarette on the ground. 'So, it was Dr Bassett at the window? I suspected as much. Very good, the picture is complete.'.

'Shit, didn't Collins tell you that? I thought you already knew.'

'That is what I wished you to think.'

He gave me that smile again. The twisted bastard had fooled me. Pretending to be shocked by the thought of the fake opium going up someone's asshole...relaxing with a cigarette...what was the matter with me? It was the kind of tactic every dumb cop learns about on their first week in the job: put the suspect at ease, make him think you like him, he's impressed you...the interrogation is over, relax with a cigarette...man to man...all standard procedure.

Holmes began to pace up and down in front of me. 'I was confused at first,' he said, as if he was talking to himself, 'because in my conversations with the other patients they have referred to Dr Bassett calling from the window when the fire had already taken hold. But that was a different window. Yes, I see it all.' He whirled around to face me. 'Thank you, Dr Gonzo, you have been most helpful.' I thought he was about to walk away but he seemed to change his mind. He sat down again, leaned towards me, and spoke in a low voice. 'I must ask you one more question, and I beg you to keep your eyes fixed upon mine as I do so, no matter how much my question may surprise you. For the last few minutes a figure has been observing us from the woods, about two hundred yards away. No! Don't look. Just tell me if you have been aware of this presence before, and if so, tell me whether you know who it is.'

'Shit!' I said, 'so you've seen him too?'

'You know him? Quickly, tell me who it is.'

'It's a crazy motherfucker who used to be my attorney,' I blurted out. 'Christ knows what he's planning. The twisted bastard is capable of any kind of hideous violence.'

Holmes narrowed his eyes and looked at me for a while longer, then he nodded curtly and got up from the bench. He gave me a little bow.

'Thank you once again, Doctor. Good day.'

He turned on his heel and stalked away. It wasn't until later that I found out he'd walked off with my lighter.

Patient WC
Recovery Diary 18

Remarkable! Quite remarkable.

How fitting that new methods of criminal investigation, which I have written about, and urged upon a reluctant public and police force, are the very procedures that have led to the discovery of my own dark secret! Should I say my downfall? I think not, for the light that has been thrown upon my predicament by the deductive powers of Mr Holmes may prove to be my salvation. And how gratifying that this gentleman could almost be the product of my own pen, were it not that his penetration far surpasses the inventive powers of any merely literary intellect. My own creations in this line pale into insignificance by comparison, although I believe I can congratulate myself, in a small way, for my foresight if nothing else.

'But, wait!' I seem to hear my worthy physicians cry, 'what of your feelings, man?' Very good. I am sensible of my obligations, especially as it was through the agency of Dr Hatchjaw that Mr Holmes was brought upon the scene, and to him, too, I owe a debt of gratitude. My feelings, then, are sanguine – even elevated. I have gained an insight into the workings of my own mind which I hope will prove invaluable if I can put it to good use. The key to my recovery is now in my own hands, as the doctors here, in their different ways, have been trying to tell me all along. However, true enlightenment is achieved only through experience, and I believe I have now had such an experience, and I am elated by my prospects.

As to the instrument of that enlightenment, I encountered him in the garden. I was making my way back to the scene of my recent dealings with Mr Thompson. I will no longer refer to him as Dr Thompson, as I have been disabused of my notion that he possesses any medical qualifications whatever. But I am getting ahead of myself.

I was revisiting that part of the garden with the intention of retrieving any pellets of opium (as I then believed them to be) that we had failed to gather up when our tryst was interrupted. As I approached the flowerbed I scanned the upstairs windows as casually as I could to make sure no one was watching, having learned my lesson about the risk of observation from that quarter. Seeing no one at the windows I then cast my eyes around the grounds on that side of the house. Remembering the shadowy figure I had, on several occasions, seen fleetingly at the edge of the woods I paid particular attention to the treeline. Satisfied that I was unobserved I strolled closer to the flowerbed. Taking care to remain on the grass I bent down to look at the shrubs and the soil beneath them. Unfortunately my spectacles slipped from my nose and landed on one of the plants. As I was retrieving them I heard a voice, close beside me:

'Fine specimens, are they not?'

I stood up hastily, fumbling with my spectacles. A tall, angular man with a sallow complexion and an aquiline nose was standing beside me, gazing keenly at the shrubs. His sudden appearance unnerved me, as I had been sure no one was nearby only a moment before.

'Forgive me,' The gentleman said, 'I didn't mean to startle you. Allow me to introduce myself. My name is Sherlock Holmes.'

'Wilkie Collins, at your service, sir.'

'Are you interested in macrophylla, Mr Collins?'

I looked at him enquiringly, still unsettled by his sudden appearance. 'Excuse me,' I began, 'but I don't think I understand what—'

'Macrophylla is the name of this species of hydrangea. Also commonly known as mopheads, for reasons that are obvious from their appearance.'

'Oh, I see. Fascinating. But I am no expert. I was merely admiring the blooms.'

'Not for the first time, evidently.'

'I beg your pardon?'

'Despite the fact that you have not stepped into the shrubbery itself, a petal from one of the plants is lodged in a fold at the bottom of your right trouser leg,' said Sherlock Holmes, 'and there are traces of mud on your boots, which, by the way, appear to match one of the sets of footprints that are visible in the flowerbed.'

I tried to conceal my consternation. 'Why, yes,' I stuttered, 'as it happens I was here yesterday – admiring the plants, and...so on.'

'And did you perhaps mislay something, and have now returned to search for it?'

'Certainly not,' I said. 'I mislaid nothing, as far as I know. And I must say that I resent being questioned in this way.'

'I'm sorry, Mr Collins,' he said, in a gentler tone, 'but it is my job to ask questions. I have been engaged in a professional capacity to conduct an investigation here.'

'And what have I to do with this investigation?' I asked, aware, even as I spoke, that my voice was betraying symptoms of anxiety.

'I have formed the belief that someone here is concealing a secret.'

I felt myself quail under his penetrating gaze. 'What kind of secret?' I asked.

He looked at me in silence for a moment, then turned his eyes to the house, and the blackened window frames above us. 'I am here to investigate the recent fire,' he said, 'and I must discover whether anyone is concealing information about its cause.'

'Do you mean that someone started the fire

deliberately?' I asked, with a degree of relief that, whatever his answer, my conscience was clear on that score.

'Not necessarily. But even if it was accidental, certain facts are being withheld from me, and I believe you may be able to help me unearth them.'

'What makes you think that?'

'Would you care to take a stroll with me, Mr Collins?'

So it was that I found myself walking among the trees with Mr Sherlock Holmes. On a couple of previous occasions I had gone a little way into the woods that surrounded the house, but I had never felt the urge to penetrate them very deeply. The woodland appeared to be the same whichever way one went, becoming neither denser or thinner, and may have extended for several miles in every direction for all I could see. Mr Holmes, too, didn't seem inclined to go very far beyond the treeline, and we kept the house in sight as we skirted around it, picking our way through the undergrowth.

Having walked for several minutes in silence, he finally spoke. 'May I ask you, Mr Collins, what you were doing when the fire broke out?'

I cleared my throat nervously. 'Certainly. I was enjoying a walk.'

'Alone?'

'That is correct.'

'And your walk took you to the flowerbeds we have just left?'

'It's possible,' I replied after a moment's hesitation,

'that it may have done.'

'And you still insist that you were alone?'

'I do.'

We walked on in silence again. Holmes was a few paces ahead of me when he stopped abruptly and peered closely at a tree beside him. In a swift movement he plucked something from the wrinkled folds of its bark and held it up to the light. I saw that it was an insect of some kind. To my astonishment Holmes popped it into his mouth, chewed with relish, and swallowed it. Then he turned to face me.

'I'm afraid I don't believe you, Mr Collins,' he said amiably.

I was so taken aback, both by his accusation, and the extraordinary spectacle I had just witnessed, that I was unable to say a word.

'Come, come,' Holmes continued, 'let us stop playing games. I know that you were there, and I also know you were engaged in some kind of business of which you're heartily ashamed. I believe it concerns the treatment you are receiving here for your addiction to opium, and the dissimulation you are practising with regard to it.'

What he said staggered me, quite literally, and I believe I swayed on the spot.

'Here, Mr Collins,' said Holmes quickly, 'come and sit down.' He was standing beside an old fallen tree trunk that had come to rest in such a way that it formed a kind of natural bench. He sat down on it and beckoned for me to do the same. I sank down beside him with my thoughts in turmoil. The only thing of which I was certain was the futility of trying to conceal anything from this remarkable man. When I was able to speak I said, 'How do you know all this?'

'My reasoning is simple. This establishment is devoted to the cure of addictions. In your case I judge the drug to be opium. The treatment, as I understand it, involves no coercion but depends upon the co-operation of the patient. Is that correct?'

I nodded my head, transfixed by him.

'Very good. Now, follow my reasoning. In this place I see a man who clearly has a guilty conscience. His manner is furtive and he displays a fear of being observed. I suspect that he is struggling against a powerful compulsion to act in a way that he knows to be dishonourable. What could this powerful compulsion be? Why, nothing other than the addiction that has brought him here in the first place. When I see him searching, covertly, for something he appears to have lost in a place that shows signs of disturbance by two sets of footprints, moving hastily and erratically, I surmise that he is being supplied with the drug clandestinely, by an accomplice, with whom some kind of altercation has taken place. Furthermore, I conclude that he has retrieved the missing drug and it is even now about his person. Aha!'

I found my wrist suddenly clamped in his iron grip. I looked down to see that my hand had strayed involuntarily to the breast pocket of my coat.

'Exactly as before,' said Holmes, releasing my wrist. 'The very same action. Do you recall, Mr Collins, that earlier in our conversation I said I believed someone here was concealing a secret?'

'Yes, I do.'

'At that moment you patted the pocket of your coat, in an unconscious action that you have just now repeated.' He leaned back, observing me with amusement. 'It's a common trick,' he continued, 'and one that's frequently employed by pickpockets. You may notice that sometimes in a crowded public place someone will begin to talk loudly about how dangerous the area is, and say that everyone should be on their guard against thieves. The speaker is, of course, the accomplice of pickpockets who at that very moment are noting the way that every gentleman present will invariably touch the place where his watch or purse is kept. We can't help doing this unless we train ourselves to be aware of the compulsion, and to resist it. I simply employed a similar psychological technique. And now, perhaps you would be so good as to let me see what is in the breast pocket of your coat?'

Here I must pause. I thought I had absorbed the shock of what Holmes then revealed to me, but as I come to write about it I find myself astonished afresh. Suffice it to say that I offered no further resistance. I handed over the pellets that were in my pocket, and Holmes proved to my satisfaction that they contained no opium. Then this extraordinary man explained how the effects I believed I had been experiencing from opium were entirely the product of my own imagination. Incredible as it seemed, eventually I had no choice but to believe him, once the evidence became incontrovertible. I then told him the whole story, omitting, of course, the name of my partner in the affair.

Before Holmes left me he asked me if I had ever seen anyone lurking about in the woods. I told him I had caught a glimpse of someone on several occasions. He asked me to describe who I had seen but I was able to tell him only that I believed it was a woman, and she habitually wore white.

Patient FJ
Recovery Diary 13

Okay, I'm not feeling so bad now. What's the point of being angry in this place?

Anger has always been a bugger for me. Naturally I've been told I must take responsibility for my own anger, and that everyone and everything 'making' me angry is simply a convenient external target onto which I project the rage I carry around inside me. It doesn't help much, especially as the people who tell you this kind of thing are invariably condescending pricks.

However, I seem to be calming down a bit since I've been here, so maybe something is working. Or maybe I simply haven't got the energy for it any more. It takes a lot of heat to keep a really rich, invigorating stew of indignation on the boil, and once the flames of your fury begin to subside all you're left with is a thin, simmering gruel of everyday resentment. The worst part is when you start to become reasonable and begin to see someone else's point of view, which is fatal. There are some people who can erupt with anger, let it all out, and then carry on as if nothing had happened, leaving everyone around them thoroughly rattled by the ferocity of their outburst, which has served only to relax and refresh them. These people are perfectly aware of what they're doing and are manipulative, calculating shits, and they're the ones I really admire.

What had enraged me about Sherlock Holmes showing up was that it introduced a new story which contradicted the one I'd just begun to get comfortable with.

I'd been desperate for an explanation of what was happening to me, and my conversation with Hatchjaw had given me something to clutch at. I was still in a terrifying, incomprehensible situation, but I'd begun to make some kind of sense of it. I thought I discerned a structure that appeared to regulate, if not explain, the world I'm in.

As a result I became relatively content. I was still scared and confused about the big picture, but I was under the impression I'd grasped the basic idea. It was all about dead writers, in rehab. As an explanation it's insane, but that doesn't matter. The important thing is that there are rules. You can begin to predict what will happen, within the parameters of your experience.

Then the rules are broken. Sherlock Holmes arrives. My story is blown out of the water. I have to be scared and confused all over again. And it makes me especially angry because there are aspects of the previous story that I'm very happy with, like the stuff about me being a hero. Of course, that was a new story, too, but it was a story I liked. It greatly improved my opinion of myself – and of Hatchjaw, who was revealed as a man of remarkable insight in coming up with such a perceptive analysis of my character.

Unfortunately, now I've given it a bit more thought, I realise his theory has got a couple of flaws. Firstly, there's no evidence to back it up. Secondly, it's a trite platitude lifted from a pop song. 'You've got to search for the hero inside yourself,' urged the alphabetically pivotal M People. Don't get me wrong, I'm all in favour of searching for the hero inside yourself. And if you can't find him, try luring the bastard out with alcohol and the prospect of a fight; that usually does the trick. But while M People were a great pop group they probably won't be troubling the selection committee for the chair of philosophy at any of the better English universities.

That aside, I was still pretty pleased with myself, and with the story, until the arrival of a fictional character undermined the whole happy narrative.

I was forced to confront afresh the dismal news that they're all just stories. Some of them offer comfort amid the dreadful chaos, and some provide explanations of it, but none of them can control it. For example, no matter how well I understand a scientific story about an active volcano, it's no more consoling than a story about a furious deity belching a fire that can only be quenched by chucking a few virgins in.

And our stories are in conflict, each struggling to survive at the expense of all the others, trying to eat them up. Ideas are animals. Nature, red in truth and claw.

Meanwhile, back in this story, I was pissed off. Especially when I found myself talking to someone I assumed to be Sherlock Holmes, and then discovered was only Dr Watson. Not only were fictional characters invalidating my narrative, I was being fobbed off with the second banana. But let me go back a bit, to the moment when my tranquillity was shattered by this unwelcome realisation.

I was in the Blue Room, drinking a cup of pretty good coffee. The room bore no visible trace of the recent fire, although I detected an aroma of bananas, which may have been produced by the paint in which it had been redecorated with remarkable promptness. I was feeling good about the ideas I'd exchanged with Hatchjaw, having decided, as I've said, that he was a highly astute judge of character and an exemplary physician. In the cosy glow of satisfaction that followed this agreeable assessment I began to wonder where Dorothy was.

The more I thought about her, and how enjoyable sex had been with her, and how her eyes gleamed when we were reunited after the fire, the more I wondered whether I should go and seek her out. Perhaps what held me back was a niggling sense of dissatisfaction. Why should I be the one who had to do the seeking out? Why wasn't she coming to find me? Absurd, I know. But I couldn't help it. I've never been able to help it, for as long as I can remember, ever since my infant sensibilities first became outraged by the fact that someone – almost certainly my mother – wasn't there when I wanted her. Over the years this angry wound has provided the toxin which has polluted an impressive number of my human interactions, plus a few with dogs, cats and other household pets that I felt weren't paying me enough attention.

And now I was at it again. I wasn't even in love with Dorothy, although I'd probably convince myself I was, if my craven neediness remained unsatisfied for long enough. However, I was very taken by her, and very turned on by her, and I enjoyed her company very much. Which is probably better than being in love, in the long run. But where was she? Would I have to swallow my pride and go to find her?

By now my mood had darkened, and I wasn't in the right frame of mind for what happened next. I should have paid more attention to a conversation I'd overheard about ten minutes earlier. I'd passed Wilkie Collins and Coleridge in the corridor, and as I stood aside for them I heard Collins gabbling excitedly about Sherlock Holmes. He was trying to explain what a detective was, and as they walked away Coleridge launched into a story about him and Wordsworth having once been spied on by the Home Office, and Collins interrupted him to say this was something else, something new. I didn't catch any more of what they said and I didn't give it a second thought.

At that point I didn't know that Hatchjaw had invited Sherlock Holmes to come and join our Mad Hatter's tea party. He'd mentioned that an outsider was arriving to investigate the fire, but I didn't put it all together until the moment when Hatchjaw walked in on me drinking my second cup of coffee, followed by someone wearing Edwardian clothes and a deerstalker hat. That was when I realised fictional characters had invaded my story.

As a result, I was a bit rude when Hatchjaw began to introduce me to the man in the hat, who stepped forward and held out his hand.

'You must be fucking joking,' I said.

They both stared at me. I slammed my coffee cup down on the table beside me and stood up. I turned on Hatchjaw. 'You cunt,' I said, 'what are you trying to do?'

'Please, Jim,' he said, 'try to control yourself.' He turned to the man in the hat, who had backed away. He'd turned pale and looked like he was trying to eat his moustache. Wait, I thought, Sherlock Holmes doesn't have a moustache.

That shows how far gone I was. I was making a judgment based on my recollections of images of a person who didn't exist in the first place. But real or not, the man in the hat had a round, bland face, totally unlike the popular pictures of Sherlock Holmes or the actors who have played him in countless dramatizations.

'Wait,' I said to Hatchjaw, 'is this Sherlock Holmes or not?'

The man in the hat stepped forward and spoke with a certain wounded dignity, while keeping a wary eye on me. 'I am not Sherlock Holmes, sir,' he said. 'I am his friend, Dr John Watson.' He held out his hand again.

I'm ashamed to say I turned on my heel and walked out.

That was one reason why I was so pissed off when I wrote that earlier entry. The other was because of what I learned when I bumped into Paddy as I was weaving my way back to my room. I felt a bit guilty when I saw him. He'd been pretty impressive in the fire, and I hadn't said anything to him about it. In fact, I hadn't made any attempt to find him at all. Which was what always happened: I only ever sought him out when I needed something from him.

'Hello, Jim,' he said, 'how are you feeling?'

'Terrible.'

'What's up?'

'To be honest, Paddy,' I said, flopping down on one of the upholstered benches that were placed at regular intervals along the corridor, 'I really don't know how much more of this I can take. Whatever this is.'

Paddy sat down beside me. 'I know. Tell me about it. It's insane.'

'Yes, and just when I thought I was getting used to the stark, raving madness of it, and that it couldn't get any more demented, I find myself talking to someone who doesn't exist. Well, only in books, anyway.'

'Ah. I take it you've met Holmes or Watson, then?'

'Watson. Allegedly. Why, have you met Holmes? Is he

here?'

'Apparently, but I've only met Watson, too.'

'What happened?'

'Nothing much. He asked me to tell him about the fire, so I gave him my version of events to the best of my ability. That was it. He seemed like a perfectly nice bloke. Just like in the books, in fact. What about you, what did you tell him?'

'I'm afraid I told him to fuck off.'

Paddy laughed and clapped me on the shoulder. 'You silver-tongued devil! That's the Jim we know and love.'

'No, it was stupid.'

'But very much you. Which is good. It means you're probably okay.' He turned to me and looked at me closely. 'Is that right? Are you okay? No ill-effects from the fire? No burns or anything?'

'Nope, I was lucky.'

'What about the smoke?'

'No. I don't think I breathed in very much of it. Why do you ask?'

'Hemingway was worried about you.'

'Hemingway? Why?'

'He was worried he didn't get you out quickly enough.'

'Wait. Hemingway said that he got me out?'

Paddy nodded. 'Yes. He's turned it into quite a little story. All about a modest, unpretentious man who rescues someone he has reason to dislike, but whose life he saves because he simply can't help being such a damned hero.'

'Fuck!' I jumped up and looked around wildly.

'Where is he?'

'Jim, steady.'

I slapped the wall with the flat of my hand and immediately regretted it. 'Shit!' I shouted as a hot, stinging pain surged up my arm. 'I was the one who rescued him! He fucking knows I did!'

Paddy was standing up now. He put an arm around my shoulder. 'Jim, stop. Okay? Just stop, mate.'

I stared at him, breathing deeply. 'But…but…' I choked and couldn't get the words out. I felt tears pricking my eyes. It was all so unfair.

'Sit down, Jim.'

I allowed Paddy to guide me back to the bench as I fought back my tears. 'Sorry,' I said as I sat down next to him again, 'I'm being a dick. I'm sorry.'

'You're not being a dick. And I know what it's like. We all do.'

I looked at him suspiciously. 'Who?'

'Us. Writers. You know that. We've talked about this before.'

'Have we? Yes, I expect so. But it really…' I trailed off. I felt my heart beating hard and tasted a familiar sourness at the back of my throat. It was the rotten taste of jealousy, and hatred, and rage against being hurt. I was, literally, full of bile. I swallowed hard and sat back, trying to get my breathing under control.

'You have to let it go, Jim,' Paddy said quietly. 'In the end, so what? Listen, half the people he's told the story to actually saw what really happened and know he's full of shit. And everyone else knows he's a windbag, so they probably don't believe him. And if anyone does…so fucking what? Is it really so important? Given all the other stuff we've got to think about at the moment? Don't let these things get to you. That's always been the trouble with you. You're too sensitive.'

I turned to look at him. He seemed completely sincere. I couldn't think of a single word to say. I groped for his hand, and grasped it for a few moments in a clumsy sort of handshake. Then I stood up and walked away.

I wrote the earlier, pissed-off diary entry as soon as I got back to my room, and it's now about two hours since then. I should probably go and try to find Hatchjaw, and poor, shocked Dr Watson, and apologise to them. And I should go and find Paddy, too.

He was right, of course. I've spent half my life consumed with jealousy and resentment, mostly – but not exclusively – of other writers. But what did it really matter if Paddy based a character in one of his books on me, or if I suspected that someone had stolen an idea of mine, or got some kind of credit that I thought I deserved more than they did? I was probably wrong. And Paddy was a good writer. A better one than me, if I faced the truth. What's more, he was a good friend, which was an even harder truth to face.

It was only when I got back here, to my room, that I fully processed what Paddy had told me. Not about letting it all go, because we had, in fact, talked about that before. But what had taken me completely by surprise, and shocked me to the core, was the suggestion that I was sensitive. I don't think he was just being kind in saying that to me: I think he genuinely believes that about me. Instead of seeing me as a selfish, solipsistic, overgrown baby who doesn't give a toss about anyone's feelings but his own, he really does believe I'm fundamentally a good person. Because that's what he is.

I should tell him that.

I'll definitely tell him when I see him.

I should probably go and find him, and do it now.

But first I'm going to do what I should have done ages ago.

Which is to go and find Dorothy.

I am an idiot.

Patient C
Recovery Diary 19

I feel heartsick, but not for myself. And I have a cough, which is a small price to pay in the circumstances. I shudder to think what might have happened. But why waste time on that kind of speculation, like a child imagining horrors? Instead, I will rejoice that we are all safe, and no one was injured very seriously. I have some charming little bruises here and there, and a scrape on my knee, and I must put up with the nuisance of washing my hair more than once to dispel the lingering smell of smoke, but nothing more. In other words, I am my usual tranquil, philosophical self.

Nonetheless I am troubled when I think about my rescuer and her lover.

Oh yes, I am certain they are lovers, or will be very soon. But my intuition tells me they have already been in each other's arms, perhaps for the first time at the very moment the fire broke out. And if the conflagration began just as they were consummating their passion, who can say which fire burned more fiercely? Ah, the heat of that first encounter, when all restraint falls away, and the flesh yields with such delicious abandon…

Even in the smoke and confusion I could tell how matters stood between them. The signs are unmistakeable to one who is on the lookout for them: the glance that lingers for the fraction of a second longer than necessary; the catch in the voice; the impulse to reach out, to hold, to be close to your lover – these involuntary actions betray us. And when desire overwhelms us in waves it causes vibrations that travel outwards in a kind of radiance, and you can feel it even as you run from the heat and smoke of an actual fire which sweeps up behind you like a living nightmare; even as you stumble, and are helped to your feet by a compassionate stranger. (I have noticed that Americans often display a touching generosity that is the other side of the coin, as it were, to the mercenary impulses they bring, rather disagreeably, to some other matters.)

As for my deeper feelings, I believe the joys and sorrows of others affect me just as much as any passions of my own. Thus I feel a touch of sadness when I observe a couple who are embarking on a love affair in unsuitable circumstances. As to the question of whether they are suited to each other, I don't consider it. For what is love if not the magic that makes us compatible – to begin with, at any rate? But I am wise enough, I flatter myself, to know when the situation is not propitious to the happiness of lovers.

'But surely,' I hear you object, 'are we not always being told that love will find a way, and all that?'

Yes, that is what we are told by those wicked people who write novels and romances, but they are telling us fairy tales, as so many have done before them. Love flares up, like a shameless country fire which spits and shoots out glowing embers, and it casts dramatic shadows on the walls of a cosy bedroom, but just as abruptly it sinks down, and can be snuffed out by the slightest breeze.

She is not in the first flush of youth but she possesses a quiet allure, and her dark eyes seem to draw you in with a challenge to discover a mystery they hold. And while you could never call her figure voluptuous, unlike my friend Dr Bassett, who is abundantly furnished in front and behind, her shape is pleasing enough. At least she is not one of those fashionably starved skeletons you see these days. I believe she has an old soul, and understands the bittersweet joys that come our way far better than those perennially youthful types whose spirits turn out to be delicate and vindictive, making them dull company in the long run.

As for the man, he must have been a handsome fellow before the ravages of time and dissipation exacted their due. But even those ravages can lend attraction to a certain kind of man. How fortunate they are to evade – even temporarily – some of the more brutal consequences of youth's departure. Such a reprieve is far beyond the hopes of women, who must face the facts each day in the looking glass, relying on skill and artifice to disguise the toll taken by the years – until we reach an age when such efforts become absurd, and dignity compels us to say, 'Enough, take me as I am or not at all!'

Perhaps they can find happiness, even here, even now. And if that happiness is fleeting, or eludes them altogether? It's quite likely, to be blunt. That story, after all, is more common than the other kind, which despatches the happy couple into a future of uninterrupted bliss.

But every love story has its compensations, even those that end in lonely silences, pitiful sighs, raised voices, slammed doors and floods of tears. And perhaps it's almost worth going through the storms and devastation of a broken heart just to experience the peaceful balm of recovery when it finally heals.

It's always the same: at first it seems impossible you could ever be happy again, and for a long time you reject any such suggestion with gloomy scorn. But one day you'll feel a stirring in your heart, which has been drained and shrivelled for so long. Something irrepressible and alive is expanding – a velvet caterpillar unrolling itself – a releasing, an opening, silky and effortless. You will discover with recaptured wonder that the view outside your window holds a simple beauty, and the sunlight pouring in through open glass doors onto the plain blue walls of an unremarkable room lifts your spirit inexplicably. All at once you want to move, to dance, or sing, or simply go for a walk and enjoy the warm air on a clear summer evening.

When you begin to recover in this way, and all the pleasures you were convinced you'd never feel again come rushing in to fill you up, you look back on the heartache you went through and almost bless it for the delight brought by your restoration.

Almost, but not quite.

So, I wish my new friend every joy, and may her lover bring her happiness for as long as it can be found. Our time may be short, even here. Who knows?

1 INT. MRS PARKER'S ROOM — DAY

Dorothy sits at a small table facing the window, writing in a notebook. The only other furniture in the little room is a single bed, an armchair, and a wardrobe.

There is a KNOCK at the door.

Dorothy pauses. A smile softens her concentration.

                    DOROTHY
          It's open, Jim!

As the door opens Dorothy hastily removes her GLASSES and hides then under her notebook. She turns to the door.
Jim enters. A handsome, mature man. Slightly stocky.

                    JIM
          How did you know it was me?

                  DOROTHY
          Call it an educated guess. Sit
          down.

Jim looks at the armchair. And the bed. And
Dorothy.

                DOROTHY (contd)
          Anywhere you like.

Jim sits on the bed. Dorothy raises an
eyebrow, waiting.

                    JIM
          Um, I was just passing. I
          thought it would be nice to
          pop in and see you.

                  DOROTHY
          Got a case of the blues?

                    JIM
          I'm feeling a bit glum, yes.

                  DOROTHY
                  (Drily)
          Poor baby.

JIM

(Hastily)

But that's not the only reason,
of course. I don't want you to
think I just came here because
I'm expecting you to cheer me
up.

DOROTHY

Perish the thought.

JIM

The truth is, I just had to
see you. I'm drawn here like a
moth to a flame. Or a
sleepwalker, in a drugged,
erotic trance, powerless to
resist your hypnotic allure.

DOROTHY

Keep going. I could grow to
like you when you're asleep.

JIM

Maybe I am, really. Perhaps
we're all... I don't know.
What's happening, Dorothy? Is
there any point to whatever it
is we're doing here, wherever
it is? I mean, who are we?

Dorothy stands up.

                    DOROTHY
        You've got all this the wrong
        way around, kid.

Dorothy closes the curtains. Faint sunlight
still seeps through them, warming the
darkened room.

                    JIM
        What do you mean?

Dorothy sits on the bed beside Jim.

                    DOROTHY
        I've always thought that if
        you want to indulge in post-
        coital *tristesse* you have to
        do the coital part first.

                    JIM
                (Laughing)
        I knew there was something I'd
        forgotten!

They kiss tenderly. They begin to undress
each other, taking their time, arousing each
other slowly. Their passion rises and they
clutch each other. Jim murmurs:

                    JIM (contd)
        I'm so glad I'm with you,
        Dorothy.

                    DOROTHY
        Likewise. Now come here...

She pulls Jim down onto her. They begin to
make love.

                                        CUT TO:

2. MONTAGE:

A steam train hurtles into a tunnel, puffing
smoke...
A flower unfolds in slow-motion...
A volcano erupts...

                    DOROTHY (V/O)
        Hey, cut it out!

                                    CUT BACK TO:

3. INT. MRS PARKER'S ROOM — CONTINUOUS

In the darkened room Jim raises his head and
looks down at Dorothy. They are both laughing.

                    JIM
                (mock innocent)
        What?

                    DOROTHY
        The clichés! I thought we were
        both writing this.

                    JIM
        We are.

                    DOROTHY
        Oh yeah? And how come you get
        described as 'handsome' and I
        don't get described as
        anything?

                    JIM
        Sorry. I'm a pig.

                    DOROTHY
        Pigs don't talk this much. And
        I'm taking over the script
        from here.

Dorothy grabs Jim's head and pulls his mouth
down onto hers.

                              CROSSFADE TO:
4. INT. MRS PARKER'S ROOM — LATER

Dorothy and Jim lie in each others, arms amid
tangled sheets. The sunlight from outside is
lower and fainter.

DOROTHY

So, about that *tristesse*...

JIM

Oddly enough, it seems to have
gone now.

DOROTHY

Maybe it wasn't an existential
crisis after all. More of a
biological one.

JIM

Maybe. But while we're on the
subject, let me ask you a
question.

DOROTHY

Is it a deep question, or just a
flesh wound?

JIM

Both, in a way. Tell me: if I
hadn't shown up here first, would
you have come to find me
eventually?

DOROTHY
(Laughing)
Vanity, thy name is Jim!

She raises herself up on one elbow so she can
look at him.

> JIM
> Sorry, I shouldn't have asked.

> DOROTHY
> No, I like that you asked. I
> like that you don't try to
> pretend.

> JIM
> I feel I don't have to, with you.
> I feel we know each other well
> enough, which is a bit crazy, but
> I do.

She leans over and kisses him on the nose.

> DOROTHY
> Me too. But about your
> question...

> JIM
> Never mind, I don't want to
> know.

> DOROTHY
> Yes you do. And I'll tell you.
> But only if you answer a
> question of mine.

JIM

Okay, it's a deal. Shoot.

DOROTHY

Would you have come to find me if
there were someone else here
who'd caught your eye? Someone
younger and prettier than me,
maybe?

JIM

(Beat)

Well, it hasn't happened, so I
don't know. It's hypothetical,
isn't it?

DOROTHY

So was your question. It didn't
happen, so I don't know.

They gaze at each other in silence. Slowly
they both smile, sharing their amusement —
and affection.

JIM

Well played. Perhaps we'd better
agree to call it a draw.

DOROTHY

Sure. Unless you're ready for
another round. Are you?

Her hand creeps under the sheets. After a moment Jim rolls closer to her. Their bodies entwine and they kiss and caress each other as they begin to make love again.

FADE TO BLACK

Patient FJ
Recovery Diary 14

It was late when I got back to my room. The view from my window was bathed in a limpid glow from the low sun; the air was still and clear, and birds were singing their last songs of the day. I was knackered.

But not too knackered to beat myself up about what I'd just done.

Some time ago (how long?) I'd left this room with the intention of getting out of here and finding Paula. Not only had I failed to do that, I'd just spent the afternoon in bed with another woman.

I was now entering a minefield that was sown with ordnance which I myself had devised and concealed. The siren voice that lured me on was recognisably mine, and the lyrics to its seductive song, of my own composition, went roughly as follows: 'Yeah, you can have two women, because you cherish them in different ways, and hey, monogamy is not man's natural state, whoa, whoa, yeah, yeah.'

I'd heard the song many times, and I bore a multitude of scars from all the previous excursions I'd made, cavorting to its tune, into that same minefield for yet another picnic amid the ruins of myself.

A type of addictive behaviour, for sure. I knew what I was doing, I knew how bad it was for me and for others, and I knew how it would end, but I couldn't stop doing it. Every addict knows the feeling. In the agonised moment when you're struggling with temptation, there in front of you – the bottle, the syringe, the dangerous sex – and trying to decide what to do, you know perfectly well that you've already made your choice.

I was the protagonist of an ancient myth, who prepares to undertake a prolonged wrestling match with a huge, powerful serpent, knowing all along it will crush him eventually no matter what he does. The prospect was immensely wearisome to me. However, I knew from experience that weariness could be my ally, and I should embrace it. In other words, stop thinking and go to sleep.

I lay down on my bed.

It seems I'm not going to get any rest yet. An announcement just came through the loudspeaker in my room. As it happens, I didn't actually know there was a loudspeaker in my room, and it scared the living shit out of me until I realised what was happening. But when I got over the shock I recognised the disembodied voice coming from the corner of the ceiling. It belonged to Hatchjaw and it was asking everyone to come to the Blue Room immediately.

The End of My Adventures with
Sherlock Holmes
by Dr John Watson

This is the last time I shall write about Sherlock Holmes. The man I considered to be my friend and mentor for so many years has finally trespassed on my goodwill once too often. A veil has been lifted from my eyes, and, much as it saddens me, I consider our relationship to be at an end. With a heavy heart I will now relate how this unfortunate severance came about.

My attempts to gain the confidence of the patients had proved singularly unsuccessful. Indeed, I was met with indifference at best and, in one case, a hostility so violent, and expressed in terms of such unrestrained profanity, that it can only be explained by the severity of the mental disorder from which the poor man is clearly suffering.

However, I had gleaned useful information from my inspection of the premises, my conversations with Dr Hatchjaw, and our encounter with his superior. I had formed a hypothesis which I believed went some way towards explaining the events that had taken place, and I confess I felt proud of what I had achieved.

Accordingly, when I next saw Holmes I was eager to share my findings with him. I did not have to wait long. No more than a few seconds had elapsed since my disagreeable encounter with the patient who spoke to me with such astonishing vulgarity when I saw Holmes approaching from the garden. As he entered through the French windows I stepped forward to meet him, intending to speak to him without Hatchjaw overhearing us.

'Holmes,' I said in a low voice, 'I believe I have unearthed some valuable clues.'

'Splendid,' said Holmes, 'let us hear them, my dear fellow.'

I did my best to indicate that I wished to speak to him in private, and at this point Dr Hatchjaw took the hint and walked off to the far end of the room, and made himself busy by rearranging some notices that were pinned to a cork board on the wall.

'I'm not entirely sure,' I said to Holmes, 'but I believe I know who was responsible for starting the fire, although it may have been accidental.'

Holmes raised an eyebrow and smiled. 'Have you discovered how and why the fire broke out, Watson, and the circumstances that led to its cause being concealed?'

'Not exactly,' I stammered, 'but I have penetrated a little way into the mystery.'

'Watson, you are an admirable fellow,' said Holmes, 'and you have done me a service by keeping Hatchjaw and others occupied while I got to the bottom of this little affair, which turns out to be relatively trivial, although not without a certain interest from a psychological point of view.' He patted me on the shoulder in a very familiar manner. 'Good work, Watson. By the by, have you noticed anyone loitering at the edge of the woods since we have arrived here?'

'Yes!' I cried, 'and I can't think why I didn't tell you immediately. Holmes, do you realise who is here? It's Moriarty!'

Instead of the shock or surprise I expected my words to cause, Holmes seemed, instead, to be merely perplexed. 'Surely,' he said, 'you mean Mycroft, don't you?'

'Good God,' I cried in confusion, 'do you mean to say that your brother is here as well?'

Holmes said nothing. He seemed to be pondering deeply. Finally his face cleared, and he chuckled. 'Fascinating,' he murmured. He took out his pocketbook and jotted down a brief memorandum while I stood gazing at him in stunned silence. He snapped the book shut, and smiled at me. 'An extraordinary phenomenon, and one to which I must give more thought in due course,' he said. 'And now, Watson, I think it's time for us to bring this matter to a conclusion.'

He looked over my shoulder and called out, 'Dr Hatchjaw? Will you kindly arrange for everyone in this establishment, including all the staff, to assemble in this room as soon as possible?'

'But Holmes,' I said in an urgent whisper, 'don't you want to hear what I've discovered?'

'Perhaps you can tell me of your adventures later, Watson,' he said with a laugh.

That was what did it. The man laughed in my face.

There have been occasions in the past when I felt that Holmes underestimated my capabilities, and when his impatience with me was only too apparent. But never before had it struck me that he was treating me with scorn. I use the word 'struck' advisedly, as I felt it like a physical blow. I was overwhelmed by a sense of futility and humiliation, which was slowly replaced by a cold, hard anger. Without a word I handed him his magnifying lens, and took his deerstalker cap from my head. I held it out to him. He raised an eyebrow. I thrust the cap against his chest so that he had to take it or let it fall to the ground. He took it with a puzzled frown and gave me a searching look. I turned and walked away.

I can write no more.

Patient FJ
Recovery Diary 15

The atmosphere in the Blue Room seemed tense. The
first person I saw was Dr Watson, looking monumentally
pissed off. A dozen other people were in the room, and
more were arriving all the time, but Watson's aura of
distress dragged at the attention like a nudist at a
funeral. He was slumped in a chair on the far side of the
room, trying not to scowl at a man standing by the
French windows who was wearing the deerstalker hat
that Watson had sported earlier. It suited him a lot better
than Watson. He was also wearing a cape, and he was
tall and thin, with a sallow face and an aquiline nose. I
took a wild guess he was Sherlock Holmes. At first
glance you might have thought he was bored, but
beneath his half-closed lids his eyes were alert as they
scanned the room, which was filling up quickly. I saw

Dottie come in through the door opposite me, and I waved at her. She flashed me a nice smile.

The last arrivals shuffled in. All the patients I'd seen in the canteen after the fire were in the room, plus the orderlies. All the chairs were occupied, with some people perched on the arms, and everyone else was standing against the walls. We were all facing Sherlock Holmes, who was now backlit by the setting sun outside the French windows. It was another lovely evening. Holmes looked around the room slowly and then stood with his head turned to one side, gently tapping a slender finger against his chin, apparently lost in thought. I got the feeling he wasn't unaware that the light behind him silhouetted his profile rather impressively. Hatchjaw stood beside him, looking nervous.

The last person to arrive was Dr Bassett. A path cleared for her. She walked up to Hatchjaw and stood in front of him, ignoring everyone else, including Holmes. She looked pale. 'You asked to see me,' she said.

Hatchjaw cleared his throat. 'Mr Holmes is going to tell us what he's discovered about the fire.'

'Very well,' she said. She moved to Hatchjaw's side and turned to face the room. Hatchjaw seemed surprised to find her standing so close beside him. Somehow she'd taken control of the situation. She folded her hands demurely in front of her and looked at Holmes with a polite smile.

Holmes inclined his head to her. 'Thank you, Dr Bassett.' He turned and addressed the room. 'And thank you, ladies and gentlemen, for coming to hear what I have to say. I won't detain you for long. Dr Hatchjaw asked me to investigate the recent fire, and I have done so. In the course of my enquiries some other interesting matters have come to my attention. I have discovered that a number of people in this establishment are engaged in deceptions of one kind or another.' He paused and looked around the room again. A surprising number of people seemed to have suddenly become very nervous. Wilkie Collins began to polish his glasses furiously with a gigantic handkerchief, and Hunter Thompson, sprawled sideways over a chair, pulled his hat further down over his shades.

'However,' Holmes continued, 'I will speak only of what is relevant to the fire, and say no more of these other matters than is strictly necessary.'

That seemed to lighten the atmosphere. People became noticeably more relaxed. At the back of the room someone farted very quietly.

'By the by,' Holmes said, 'I congratulate you all on a lucky escape. I understand that some minor injuries were incurred, but I commend those of you whose bravery and quick thinking prevented the consequences of the fire from being any worse.'

There were various noises of agreement. As I looked around the room I saw Hemingway staring at me. He raised his eyebrows. I shook my head pityingly. I heard a stifled snort of laughter and saw that it came from Paddy, who was also looking at Hemingway while being jabbed in the ribs by Dorothy. He caught my eye, and he and Dottie smiled at me. Hemingway glared at all three of us in turn. He was good at glaring.

'As to the cause of the fire,' Holmes continued, 'there is no great mystery. I have proved beyond doubt that it began when someone who was smoking at an open first-floor window on the east side of the building discarded a cigarette. I believe this person had observed certain events taking place below the window, and was determined to apprehend those who were involved. Rushing from the window, the cigarette was left smouldering in an ashtray. As a result the curtains caught fire.'

Holmes turned towards Hatchjaw and Bassett. 'I had very little difficulty in deducing all this. I have also identified the culprit, whom I am ready to name.'

Eudora Bassett's face was white and she was breathing heavily. She whirled around to face Hatchjaw. She took a deep breath, but just as she was about to speak a voice erupted from the other side of the room.

'Damn you, Holmes!'

Dr Watson was on his feet. His fists were clenched at his sides. 'You care for nothing and no one except yourself!' he said. 'My intellect may not be equal to yours, but by God, I am more than your moral equal. I would never treat you, or anyone, in the way you have treated me over these many, many years. I shall tolerate it no longer!' He turned and barged his way to the nearest door as people backed into each other, trying to get out of his way.

'Watson, please!' Holmes said. His voice sounded unsteady.

Watson paused but he didn't turn around. He was a only a few steps from the door. He seemed to consider something for a moment, then he shook his head briefly and continued towards the door.

'John!' Holmes cried.

Watson froze. He turned slowly and deliberately. He gazed at Holmes with cold fury. 'How dare you,' he whispered.

'Please, John,' Holmes said quietly.

'How dare you!' roared Watson with such force that his voice cracked. 'How dare you utter my name?! How dare you presume to an intimacy from which you have recoiled for so long? Hypocrite!'

'No, I assure you—'

'Yes! Even now there is calculation in your monstrous presumption! I see it, Holmes! I know you too well! Monstrous! Monstrous!'

'I am sincere, John.'

'Sincere? Only in your heartless curiosity are you sincere! Only in your cold, scientific inspection of me, and every other human soul, are you sincere. You treat me like a cur when it suits you, and then expect – no, demand – that I lick your hand when you wish me to fawn upon you, if no other admirer is available to reflect your vanity to you. Why, you show more affection and respect to those damned street urchins of yours! Those grubby boys whose lives you trifle with whenever you send them on an errand, running heedlessly into danger to collect scraps of intelligence for you. God knows what bonds of depravity bind them to you!'

Holmes's eyes widened. 'What do you imply?'

'I imply nothing. How could I?' Watson gave a short laugh: it was a thin, bitter sound. 'Never fear, Holmes, I don't suspect you of unnatural practices. Dear God, even that would be, at least, a sign of humanity, however foul and filthy. But any kind of passion is beyond you. Man, woman or child, you feel nothing for us. You turn away. Even from Irene Adler you—'

'Stop!' Holmes held up a warning hand. I saw that it trembled very slightly. 'I implore you to go no further. You must believe me. I have feelings.'

'The feelings of a fiend! Of a madman, torturing the living creatures in his power, simply for his own instruction and entertainment! Otherwise you never would have taken me on that excursion to Stoke Moran, and exposed me to such unutterable terror!'

'Ah, yes,' Holmes nodded. 'The speckled band.'

'The speckled balderdash! A serpent, Holmes, give it it's name! A loathsome serpent!' Watson shook his head in disbelief, his features contorted in a grimace of the most extreme distaste. 'How could you? You knew of my revulsion for such creatures. You knew that they, of all things, provoke in me an uncontrollable horror.'

'But I wasn't sure, you see—' Holmes began, but Watson cut him off:

'How can you say that? I had spoken to you many times of my encounters with those creatures in Afghanistan; how they paralysed me with fear; how they unmanned me entirely, and the deep and bitter shame of my cowardice.'

'No, what I mean, Watson,' Holmes said with a note of pleading in his voice, 'was that I wasn't certain it would be a snake until it actually appeared.'

'No! No, Holmes. That will not do. Afterwards, when

you described your process of deduction, you told me, very clearly, that once you had seen the bell rope, and the bed bolted to the floor, "The idea of a snake instantly occurred to me." Those are your words. They are engraved on my heart. Proof that you exposed me deliberately. Proof that the profound effect upon my constitution of merely glimpsing such a reptile was something you positively relished observing. As if I were nothing more than a collection of nerves and cells, with no more interest to you than a specimen in a jar. My intense suffering meant nothing to you. I believe my abhorrence actually amused you!'

Watson paused, shaking his head again. He seemed almost awestruck by what he was putting into words, as if by articulating his feelings he had finally revealed them to himself as much as to anyone else.

Holmes spoke in a low, modulated voice. 'You misunderstand me, Watson.'

Watson raised his arm swiftly and pointed at Holmes. His hand was steady. 'You cannot deny it! Your bloodless intellect betrays you even now!' He dropped his arm to his side. 'I despise you,' he said. 'All is at an end between us.' He wheeled around smartly, military fashion, and marched to the door. This time he had no need to shoulder his way through the bystanders, who had already cleared his path.

But when he reached the door he couldn't get it open. He grappled with the handle and pushed against the door to no avail, and then he just stood there, breathing heavily as the back of his neck turned crimson.

In the silence a tiny figure trotted forward. It was

Colette. She smiled up at Watson with a hint of sauciness and made a gentle cooing noise. She turned the door handle and pulled it towards her. The door opened inwards. There was a pause. Watson bowed to her stiffly, and emitted what sounded like a sob. Then he marched out.

Everyone turned to look at Holmes.

'Watson!' he called sharply. He gazed fiercely at the open doorway. As the seconds passed his face seemed to sag. He opened his mouth but no words emerged. I noticed he had very bad teeth. A spasm of what looked like pain contorted his features for an instant, and he swallowed hard several times, his sharp Adam's apple jumping up and down in his long, thin throat. 'Watson, please!' he croaked finally. He seemed utterly at a loss. Then his whole body twitched, as if he'd had an electric shock, or some drug had hit his system. He sprang forward, strode to the door, and out of the room.

All eyes turned to Hatchjaw and Bassett. 'I'm very sorry, everyone,' Hatchjaw said, peering at the empty doorway, 'but I'm not quite sure what to...' He trailed off, and looked helplessly at Dr Bassett.

'You fool,' she said quietly.

'Look, I'm sorry,' Hatchjaw said, 'but I did what I thought was best.'

'You thought it best to humiliate me in front of everyone?'

'No, no, that wasn't my intention at all. You don't understand.'

'Really, Wallace? And what don't I understand?'

'It's nothing personal, Eudora. Please don't get

emotional.'

Oh dear God, I thought. What was happening was so horribly familiar to me, and what was about to happen was so agonisingly inevitable, and the precision with which Hatchjaw was fucking it all up was so unerring, that I would have left the room if I'd been nearer the door, coward that I am.

'Very well, Wallace,' Bassett said. She was still speaking very quietly. 'I'll try to keep my emotions under control. And when you say I don't understand, you may be right. Because I certainly don't understand how you can dare to treat me like this.'

'Look, I simply wanted to be sure about how the fire started.'

'Why?'

'Well, because...I wanted to...' Hatchjaw swallowed. He spread his hands, as if showing her the room. 'To stop it happening again. It's important! For the patients.'

'Fuck the patients.'

Hatchjaw looked around at the rest of us with a ghastly smile. His skin was now a sickly shade of grey, accentuated by the dark stubble that rose up to his cheekbones. 'Eudora, you don't mean that.'

'Yes, I do. What are you trying to prove? That I shouldn't smoke? I know that. I know you're right. There. I said it. You're right. You're always right. But how are you going to make all this go away?'

'All what go away? What are you saying?'

'I want to know what's important to you, Wallace. Once and for all. Do you really care more about this horrible exercise in...in self-righteous...sadism, this brutal kangaroo court, than you do about me and my feelings?'

'Look, Eudora, let's just think about this.' Hatchjaw dropped his voice and tried to shift around to place himself between Bassett and the rest of us.

She ignored his efforts to make their confrontation more private. 'Tell me,' she said evenly. 'What do you care about most?'

'Well, I care about you, Eudora, of course I do.' Hatchjaw took a breath. 'But—'

'Stop.'

'What?'

'There's always a "but", isn't there?'

'No, I'm just saying…' He trailed off again. Something in her expression seemed to have stopped him.

'If only you hadn't said that word again, Wallace,' she said, very softly. 'That one little word. It's never going to change, is it?' She sighed and shook her head. 'Oh God,' she whispered wearily, 'I can't go on with this.' She made an odd, fluttering gesture towards Hatchjaw, as if she were warding him off, then she walked towards the door.

'Wait,' Hatchjaw said, 'where are you going?'

She stopped, but she didn't look back at him. 'I don't know.'

'What about our work?'

Bassett looked around. She seemed to become aware of the rest of us for the first time. 'I don't know,' she said again. 'I'm sorry, everyone. I did my best. But I can't carry on. I really can't. It's all over, and that's all I can say. Sorry.' With that she walked out of the room.

Hatchjaw didn't say anything or make a move to follow her. Very slowly he bowed his head. He swayed slightly and I thought he might fall over but he didn't. He just stood there, looking down at the floor. A tear ran down his nose and splashed onto the carpet, where it was absorbed quickly.

There was some movement among the people near Hatchjaw and I saw that Mary Seacole was making her way towards him, gently shoving people out of her path. But before she could reach him Hatchjaw turned, opened the French windows, and stepped outside. He was framed for an instant by the dying sunset, then he walked away.

Even as we squinted at the open French windows the last streak of sunlight sank behind the treetops. All the colour and vitality drained out of the room and a thin, grey gloom surrounded us.

Everything changed. The atmosphere was inert, no longer charged. A subtraction had taken place. Nobody spoke or moved. A terrible sadness settled over us. Whatever had sustained us against the horror and despair of our situation was no longer working. We had no comfort. We were dead. Or worse, perhaps. There was nothing we could do. Everything was ending and there was nothing ahead of us but emptiness.

Even though we remained motionless it felt as if we had already begun to move away from each other. Finally people began to stir. They shuffled around, taking a few aimless steps in one direction or another. Paddy, who was standing close to the French windows, slipped through them. I felt the urge to go outside, too.

As I moved to the windows I saw that others were heading the same way. It seemed that none of us wanted to stay inside, even though I was sure that nobody had any more idea than I did as to where they were going.

A mist was rising. As people emerged from the French windows it seemed as if they were wading into a shallow, pale sea. I stood on the lawn, looking back at the house, without a thought in my head, except that I wanted to see Dorothy. It was a basic need for some kind of comfort, I suppose. The usual thing. If someone sleeps with me I tend to assume they've signed up for the job of full-time nanny that I seem to expect from a relationship, or so I've been told by more than one woman. True or not, I wanted to find her. Had she already come out? It was getting darker and the mist seemed to be thickening. It was becoming quite hard to see people.

Then I caught sight of her. She was standing beside the French windows, peering around. I hoped she was looking for me.

'Dottie,' I called.

She smiled and walked briskly towards me. 'Hello, kid,' she said, taking my arm as she reached me. 'What shall we do?'

'I don't know. I suppose we could leave. Whatever that means.'

She shivered. 'It's getting chilly. Maybe I should get something else to wear.' She disengaged her arm from mine.

'Are you going back inside?'

'Only for a moment. Wait for me. Then we'll figure out what the hell to do with ourselves. Okay? Don't move, buster.' She planted a quick, warm kiss on my cheek, and trotted back towards the house.

'Wait, I don't think—'

'Jim, is that you?'

I turned to see Paddy looming out of the mist.

'Oh, hello, Fartface,' I said. 'Just hold on a moment.' I turned back to speak to Dottie. But I couldn't see her. I assumed she'd gone back inside the house, although I could hardly see it at all now, the mist was so thick.

'Fine woman,' Paddy said in my ear.

'Yes,' I said, 'I'm just going to wait for her, and then …' I stopped.

'Then what?'

'I don't know. What do you think?'

'Fuck knows.' Paddy looked around, squinting into the gloom.

'We don't even know which direction to go in, do we?'

'Well, the trees, are that way.' Paddy jerked his thumb over his shoulder, 'and I don't fancy that. From what I remember, the woods seemed pretty thick all along that side of the grounds. But I think there's a driveway at the front of the house. Or there was the last time I looked. I tried walking all the way around the whole building a few days ago. Or maybe it was longer ago than that. But it's much bigger than I thought. Bloody massive. In fact, I got a bit lost. How about you, have you gone around the whole place?'

'No. I tried it but I got lost, too. Which way is the

front drive from here?'

'If you follow this side of the house all the way to the end of the wall, it's around the corner at the end. I think.' Paddy peered around. 'Is that right? I've lost my bearings a bit. Hang on.'

Paddy began to walk away from me. 'We just have to follow the wall. Wherever that is.' He stopped. 'Maybe it's actually this way.' He changed course and moved off at a different angle. After few a steps I could hardly see him.

'Hang on a minute, Paddy. I want to wait for Dottie.'

'I'm not going. I'm just checking it out.'

He began to move away from me again. I felt an absurd sense of panic. I didn't want to lose sight of him. 'Okay,' I said, 'I'll come with you.'

But he'd gone. Swallowed up by what was now more of a fog than a mist. I decided to go and wait for Dottie by the French windows. I turned back towards the house. But it wasn't there. Nothing. I couldn't see further than a few yards in front of my face. I turned around in a full circle. Or maybe less than a full circle. Or maybe two full circles. I had no way of telling. I'd lost all sense of direction.

I was in the middle of a soft, white dome. I took a few steps in what I thought might be the direction of the house. As I moved, the dome of fog moved with me, keeping me always at its centre. I stopped. This was absurd. Absurd and scary. But I couldn't just stand there. I began to walk carefully in the direction I thought Paddy had taken, squinting so hard into the fog that it made my eyes ache. There was no way of knowing who or what was going to loom out of that impenetrable white wall, and my imagination quickly slipped its moorings. Odd shapes assembled themselves for an instant and then receded back into the murk. When the objects I saw turned out to be real, it took a while to recognise them. A glistening beached whale slowly transformed itself into a hedge covered in dew. A rowing boat gradually admitted it was a bench. I kept glimpsing what I was sure were groups of people just as they retreated beyond my field of vision. Strange noises drifted into my woolly white dome. I thought I heard voices whispering and chuckling. Churning water. Faint, peculiar clanking sounds. At one point I became convinced that a squad of soldiers, possibly Roman legionaries, was conducting manoeuvres somewhere out there.

I was approaching a high, dark wall. Good, it was the house. No, wait. It was a wall of trees. It was the woods. I'd been walking in exactly the opposite direction to the one I thought I'd taken. I stopped.

As I gazed into the trees I saw a figure moving among them. Or was it just another tree? No, it was definitely moving. Moving towards me. My blood began to pound as I saw it was the person I'd caught sight of before. The fog seemed to clear in an area surrounding her, or maybe it was just that she stepped forward. It was Paula.

I felt that I was falling into a chasm inside myself. I was dizzy, unable to move. Unable to breathe. She just stood there, about ten yards away, looking at me.

She smiled. It was the same smile she gave me all those years ago when I saw her on the steps outside the party, the moment she always claimed not to remember. And I understood why. That smile was simply who she was. Later, when we were together, she used to smile at me differently: she smiled because I was me, and it was personal, about me and her. But this was her first smile again, an expression of her essential happiness, offered to the world.

I thought my heart would burst.

Her face changed, and the smile became my smile, the one she saved just for me. She'd seen me. Her lips parted and dimples appeared in her cheeks. She held out her hand. She nodded encouragingly. She seemed happy, truly happy, but there was something else there as well. An awareness that everything could change. Not worry, or regret, but an acceptance that we have no way of knowing what happens next.

I took a step towards her. She half-turned away from me, keeping her eyes on mine, and began to walk slowly away, keeping to the edge of the trees, looking at me over her shoulder, still smiling. She wanted me to follow her. But something was wrong. I was walking towards her but I couldn't seem to keep up. She stopped, and waited for me. She was still smiling but I thought I saw a hint of something else in her eyes now. Concern for me, perhaps. I continued to walk, and now I seemed to be overcoming my difficulty. Slowly, the distance between us diminished. She held out her hand again.

I took her hand. It was warm and real. As we gazed at each other I felt a tremendous love for her swelling inside me. After a moment she began to pull me, very gently, towards her, and at the same time she stepped back. She was leading me away, into the forest. I felt myself moving with her, following her. Her eyes sparkled and now her smile was a simple smile of joy, of delight.

But then I saw something off to my left, about fifteen feet away, at the very limit of visibility in the fog. It was an odd, humped shape that I knew was human, even though it was motionless and looked more like a boulder. It was Hatchjaw. He was crouching, like an animal. A beast waiting only for the end. He turned his head and I saw his face. He was gazing at me from a great depth, a pit of utter misery. His pain was so intense that I felt it like an ache in my own blood. There seemed to be nothing left of him but what could be pitied, or comforted, and I didn't know how to do that. But I wanted to tell him I'd been where he was and I knew what was happening to him.

I realised I was no longer holding Paula's hand. I had taken a step towards Hatchjaw without making any conscious decision to do so.

I caught a movement out of the corner of my eye. Paula. A slight breeze had sprung up, just a breath, enough to move her hair. I felt a lurch of shock. She hadn't moved but she was further away. Something had happened to the distance between us again. And now her smile was different. Not sad, exactly, but wistful. Quizzical. Her hand was still extended, waiting for mine.

I hesitated.

As I looked at Paula her face was radiant. I knew that whatever I chose to do, she wanted me to know that it would be all right. I felt a great strength of purpose filling me, and I knew it came from her. She had somehow nourished me with it.

I glanced at Hatchjaw again. I felt I was able to pass on to him some of the strength I had taken from Paula, like a lifeline. I looked up and saw that Paula was now even further away. But still I could join her, if I chose to.

Again, I hesitated...

'Shit, what a mess.'

'Must have been going hell of a speed. Bust the barrier, end up down here. What's it like that side?'

'Not good. She's GCS 10, max. Better confirm second ambulance. And might need Helimed. Let's have a look. Yeah, more like GCS 5. Best put Helimed on standby, tell 'em chase the fire crew.'

'Yeah, I'm on it... Control? This is four-oh-eight. Control?'

'Go ahead, four-oh-eight.'

'Now on the scene of that high speed RTC. We've got entrapment, two casualties: thirty-year-old female GCS 5; fifty-year-old male, GCS 15. Please confirm second ambulance, request confirmation fire crew in transit, also please request Helimed on standby. Over.'

'Roger, four-oh-eight, second ambulance on the way, fire crew despatched, ETA four minutes. Will request Helimed to stand by. But don't hold your breath, Mark. They've got two other requests backed up. Over.'

'Do your best, mate. This is pretty ugly, but we may be lucky with the male if we can get him out. Over and out.'
'Roger and out.'

'Mark? Quick, we got a problem.'

'Oh, fuck. Is that smoke?'

'Yup. I'm coming over that side. Let's try and get the guy out. Get the spinal board close as you can.'

'Okay, but this door won't open more. Hang on. No, far as it'll go. Amit? Maybe we should wait for the cutters.'

'Don't think so, mate. This angle, the fuel could be going anywhere. Yeah, smell it? We need to move fast. Let's just try and get him through as is. Hang on. Okay, I got his legs, ready when you are.'

'Wait, wait. Just cutting the belt. Okay, ready. And… whoa! It's all right, mate. We're getting you out. You've had an accident. Okay? Can you hear me?'

'We need to move fast, Mark.'

'I know, but he's... Hold on... No mate, tell me in a minute, okay? You need to let go of her hand, mate. Come on, let go of her hand, and I'm just going to... Shit!'

'What is it?'

'He's just fucking walloped me! And he won't let go of her hand. Hang on, he's really kicking off in here.... Sir, we're trying to help you...no, we need to move you... yes, we'll get her out as soon as we can...no, please don't do that!'

'What's happening?'

'Jesus! Try to get him off me, Amit. He doesn't want to come out... Yes, I can hear you, sir. We'll get her out in a minute, now please...let go! Sorry, mate, I'll have to...'

'What the hell is he doing?'

'Okay, quick decision. He says he's not coming out unless we move her first. And he's kicking off every time I bloody touch him. Could be trouble if he's got a spinal.'

'Oh fuck. She's hardly got a chance.'

'Got to call it.'

'That fire could go any minute. Where's the bloody fire crew?'

'No sign.'

'He's got a much better chance than her. Not sure she's even with us now. And he's easier access, too. We should get him out.'

'He's going to fight every inch. Fuck knows how long it's going to take, and what if we're risking a spinal? At least she's passive.'

'Okay, let's do it. Just hope we can get her door open.'

'Okay, I'll just tell him... Sir? We'll do what you say... yes, we'll get her out first. So please let go of her hand... that's it, great, we'll get you out in a minute. Sit tight.'

Patient DP
Recovery Diary 17

I liked Jim well enough, and we'd had a fine time in the sack. I guessed he was no saint but I was willing to bet he wasn't as much of a sinner as he thought he was. However, men don't want to believe they're simply poor little lambs who've gone astray; they have to be the big bad wolf or nothing. Likewise, when a man gets an urge to be virtuous he tends to take it up in a big way, especially if he hasn't tried it before, and you can guarantee he'll cause more trouble than he ever did when he was wicked. Men are bad enough at the best of times, but God help us if they try to be good.

When I saw Jim again I feared the worst.

I'd been back to my room to collect the remains of a fur stole that's saved several generations of moths from starvation. I came tripping gaily out of the house and walked straight into a wall of fog, with visibility down to around ten yards. That's five yards further than I can usually see, as I refuse to wear my glasses in front of a man until I've known him for at least a week, or three fucks, whichever comes first (me, if I'm lucky).

I decided to stay put, and hope Jim would find me.

Soon I began to get the bugs. Everything was blank and white and silent, as if I'd fallen into a cave deep down in the snow. After a while the whiteness began to fade. Slowly the cave turned gray. Night was falling. I pressed my back against the wall, feeling the cold brickwork through my dress and the fur wrap. I had a jittery feeling the whole house would vanish suddenly and I'd be alone in the fog, forever.

With fraying nerves I peered myopically at every point of the compass, and a few that weren't even there for good measure. I couldn't focus on anything, because there was nothing to focus on. I began to suspect my eyes were moving independently and were in danger of parting company altogether, like quarrelsome lovers, rushing in different directions and then coming back to cross each other. A growing sense of giddy helplessness made me press myself even harder against the wall.

Now I was trembling. Chilly fingers of panic began to pluck teasingly at my stretched nerves in a sadistic prelude to the inevitable onslaught. I allowed thoughts I'd stoutly kept at bay to invade what's left of my disordered mind. I was dead. Jim wasn't real. I'd imagined it all - everything that had happened in the house, and all the people in it. I tried to argue with myself but my heart wasn't in it. I felt a scream building up inside me and I knew I couldn't stop it coming out. I consoled myself with the thought that if I wasn't alone, and anyone else was around, a good loud scream might fetch them. I was just about to let rip when a figure lurched out of the darkness. It was Jim.

'Thank God I've found you,' he said. 'We need to talk.'

'All in good time.' I put my arms around him and devoted myself to hugging him, and making a thorough job of it. He hugged right back, but he broke off before I'd quite finished with him. He leaned back and gazed into my eyes.

That was when I knew I was in trouble. He had that look men get, like a cross between a puppy and a fireman, when they think they've discovered their better self, and they're eager to give him a workout. There's no stopping them when they get like that, and the problem with a man on a crusade is that he always wants you to come along too. Jim definitely had something on his mind, but what he said next surprised me.

'Dottie, I'm not in love with you.'

'Is that all?' I laughed, and kissed him on the nose.

'I mean, I...I really like you, but...'

'Don't you worry your pretty little head about it,' I said, and reached around to give his ass a friendly squeeze. 'I don't give a damn. Anything else?'

I wondered who the woman was. There are a number of reasons why a man will suddenly tell you, out of the blue, that he doesn't love you, but it's usually because there's someone else he loves instead. Maybe it's someone he always loved, or maybe someone he's just found to love, or maybe he's just looking for someone to love instead of you. Sometimes he feels bad about the way he's treating you and thinks announcing that he doesn't love you will get him off the hook. On very rare occasions a man may tell a woman he doesn't love her for noble, selfless reasons, and those occasions are found exclusively in books and movies, children, and are what we call fiction, although you may hear some grown-up people using other words.

I was pretty sure that in Jim's case it was the usual thing, and there was another woman in the picture, and he was feeling bad about her, and about me, and wanted to make a confession of sorts. It was probably a result of the new-found virtue with which he was all aglow, and which was making me so apprehensive. All of this passed swiftly through my mind as I waited to see if he was going to tell me any more about why he didn't love me, but he didn't seem inclined to elaborate. Instead he just smiled sheepishly. 'Thanks,' he said. 'You're a terrific woman, you know that?'

'Yes, and get to the point.'

'There's something we've got to do.'

There it was: that little word, 'we'. I raised an eyebrow – one of my best, painted that very morning. I had to admit that whatever had got Jim fired up was making him quite attractive. Even though I was still recovering from giving myself a bad scare, and I was worried about what Jim was going to drag me into, I felt a familiar stirring in my loins, and I leaned towards him, parting my lips invitingly. But the invitation went unheeded, and

Jim turned his head to one side, frowning.

'Wallace!' he called out, 'where are you?'

Hatchjaw's voice rumbled from the darkness beside us. 'I'm still here.'

'Why not go on inside?' Jim said to the unseen presence, 'and I'll be right there.'

'All right,' Hatchjaw said, and he set off towards the house. Leastways, although I couldn't see anything, I was aware of an absence in the space from which Hatchjaw's dejected voice had emanated, and I figured he was heading for the old homestead.

Jim turned his attention back to me and gazed at me earnestly. I had a sneaking suspicion we were getting to the part where the shining knight on a white steed outlines the job description for the trusty squire, also known as the lucky kid who totes the spare armour and shovels up the horseshit.

'Look, Dottie,' Jim said, 'I don't know what the hell is going on any more than you do. At least, I'm assuming you haven't got a clue where we are or what's happened to us, have you?'

I gave my tousled locks a slow and sorry shake. He had the decency, finally, to move in for a kiss, and a pretty juicy one at that.

After we'd untangled our tongues he said, 'I'm pretty sure nobody here really knows what this is all about, and that includes Hatchjaw and Bassett. Which is the worrying part. Up until quite recently I was under the impression they knew the score but weren't telling us for some reason. But judging by the state that Hatchjaw is in, I think they're just as bewildered as we are.'

'They must know something,' I said. 'They're the doctors. Or the headshrinkers, or whatever the hell they are. If they've just been dumped here like the rest of us, why are they in charge? Why have they been looking after us?'

'Because they're good people.'

I chewed that over for a while without extracting much nourishment from it. 'And that's the only reason?'

'I think so. I think they found themselves with a job to do, and they did it to the best of their ability. They rose to the challenge because that's who they are.'

It was true. I'd never doubted they were good people who meant well, and I hadn't questioned the assumption that they were there to take care of us. You get a feeling about certain types: they're the grown-ups. 'I guess you're right,' I said, 'and I haven't been giving them very much credit for it, either. That was selfish, wasn't it?'

Jim smiled. He reached out and stroked my hair. I liked that.

'Not really,' he said. 'You've had your own problems to deal with, like the rest of us. But so have they, that's the thing. And speaking of being in love, you know they're crazy about each other, don't you?'

There was no doubt about that, and I'd seen it right away, but I hadn't given it any real thought. Maybe it was too much like thinking about your parents being in love, and visualising the inevitable consequence, referred to so romantically by Dr Freud as the primal scene. 'She's got her work cut out, though,' I said, 'because I imagine he's a hard man to love.'

Jim sighed. 'Tell me about it.'

'You recognise the type, do you?'

'He's a dickhead.'

'Get off the fence, why don't you?'

Jim laughed. 'Sorry. I mean, he's not just a dickhead, obviously. I had an extraordinary conversation with him after the fire, and he's a remarkable man in many ways. And very kind, as we've said. Actually, compassionate is the right word. That's what they both are. But if you want to talk about being your own worst enemy, Jesus, I've never seen a man sabotage himself so thoroughly.'

I recalled the events we'd witnessed earlier in the Blue Room. 'Yes, it was pretty painful in there,' I said. 'Whatever those two had going with each other, it felt like we were watching him stuff it in a sack and drown it.'

'That was just the last act. It's been going on for a while, as far as I can tell.'

'And you want to set things right with them? Is that what this is all about?'

'Yes.'

'Why?'

'Why not?'

'You've got me. I guess it gives us something to do, at any rate.'

'I get the feeling it's the *only* thing we can do. But perhaps that's just me. I think I've just had some kind of...I don't know. Change. I thought I wanted to leave this place. I even saw...a reason. To leave. A very good reason. But then I spotted Hatchjaw. I've never seen anyone in such utter despair. It was like he was feral, suffering from some kind of...elemental...agony. And I know about that pain. Not as much as him, but enough to understand that what makes it such a torment is knowing it's all your own stupid fault. Someone offers you their absolute, unconditional love, someone you'd be insane not to see is perfect for you, and that's what you do: you go insane, and ruin it. And that's what makes it agonising. You know perfectly well you're destroying a chance of real happiness, and you can't stop yourself from doing it. God, it's awful. And I can't leave him like that. Not because I'm noble in any way, Christ, my instinct is to run a mile from anyone who needs help, but I simply can't do it. I can't physically do it. I've got to stay and try to help him. Does that sound ridiculous?'

It was my turn to stroke his hair. 'No,' I said. 'It's not ridiculous at all.'

'Then what is it?'

'It's human.'

He heaved a deep sigh. 'Oh, God. Maybe you're right.'

'Is that so bad?'

'I don't know. I suppose I'll find out.'

'What are you going to do?'

'Try to talk some sense into Hatchjaw.'

'But that's only half the story, right?'

He gave me a rueful smile. 'I'm afraid so. But I have no right to ask you to do anything. I don't even know if you feel the same way as me.'

'Try me.'

'All right. Are you scared?'

Little did he know. I was still on the very edge of

panic. A suffocating dread was clinging to me like a damp overcoat I couldn't take off. If he hadn't been there I probably would have been trying to bludgeon my brains out against the wall. But I just nodded and said, 'I'm terrified.'

'Me too. But I've got a feeling that by leaving now, I'll be going nowhere. Literally. There won't be anything out there. Maybe just this fog, for ever. And all I'll have with me out there in that...nothingness, that nullity, is a terrible knowledge that I could have helped someone and I didn't. So I'm not being altruistic. I'm actually being a coward. I can't face that prospect. Can you? Or maybe it's different for you, I don't know. Tell me.'

'It's no different. And maybe you're right, and by staying and doing something, even if it doesn't work, even if it just passes the time...'

'Exactly!' He pulled me towards him and we nestled together companionably. 'Even if we achieve absolutely nothing,' he mumbled into my hair, 'at least we're taking action. We're not giving up. We're saying we're... I don't know, we're...'

'We're not dead yet.'

'Yes!' He laughed and gave me a squeeze, and I gave it back with interest. 'That's it. We're not dead, because maybe, just maybe, we can change something.'

'They've been telling us the only person you can change is yourself.'

'I must have changed myself, then, because now I want to help those two to be happy, even if I can't be happy myself, and if you knew me you'd realise what a big change that is.'

'Okay, but don't go joining the Salvation Army.'

'Don't worry, I'm not a candidate for sainthood quite yet.'

'Feel like proving it?'

'What, now?'

'Not if you'd only be doing it out of politeness.'

'No, no, I'd love to, it's just...'

A familiar tension in his voice expressed the eternal struggle between a good intention and a good fuck. I shouldn't have tempted him, poor boy, especially as he was quite right. If we wanted to pour balm on troubled waters we needed to get pouring right away, and not be stingy with the helpings. I gave him a playful shove. 'Nah, get out of here. What manner of steel-shelled, scale-covered monster do you think I am? Let's go to work. You want me to go find Bassett and pitch her some girl talk while you slap Hatchjaw around?'

'That would be brilliant. The only thing is, we don't know where she is.'

'I think I do.'

'She might be somewhere in the fog out there.' He waved his arm at the surrounding murk.

'You're not listening.'

'What?'

I grabbed his face and made him look at me. 'I'm pretty sure she's in her room.'

'How do you know?'

'When she walked out on us she went through the door leading back into the house, didn't she?'

'Yes, but she might have come out again. Everyone else has.'

'Trust me, she's still inside.'

'Okay, if you say so.'

'Now you're learning.'

'Do you know where her room is?'

'Sure thing. I've been in there for a few cosy little chats.'

'What about?'

'Me, of course. You know the routine: her on a chair with a notepad, me on a couch with a tale of woe, an aching womb, and a box of tissues to hand. The usual thing.'

'I hope it helped.'

'God knows. It was nice, anyway. She's a jolly good stick, as you British say.'

'Actually, I've never heard anyone say that except Americans imagining what British people say. Why do you always get that so wrong? Even pretty good American writers have a tin ear for British idiom.'

'Spank me.'

'Shut up.' He patted my rump, then became business-like. 'Right, let's meet in the Blue Room at…' He peered at his wrist for a moment, seeming reluctant to accept the fact that he wasn't going to find a watch there. 'Okay,' he said, 'let's just say I'll keep Hatchjaw in there, and you'll try to turn up with Eudora in about two hours. Not before, though, if you can manage it, and not too much later, either.'

'Your wish is my command.'

'Then come here, you.'

He gave me another damn good kiss. When we came up for air he stepped back and looked around, frowning.

A wisp of hair drifted across my face. Something had changed in the quality of the darkness around us. I raised my head. 'Is it just me,' I said, 'or is that the moon up there?'

'Exactly what I was thinking. Oh, it's gone again.'

'But there's a breeze. I think the fog is clearing a little.'

'Perfect. That's going to make it easier. Okay, good luck.'

To my surprise he turned and began to walk away from the house. 'Where are you going?' I said. 'I thought you were going to talk to Hatchjaw.'

He kept moving but turned and walked slowly backwards, keeping his eyes fixed on mine. 'There's something I need to do first.'

'Which is?'

'I don't want to tell you.'

'Why not?'

'In case it doesn't work. Call it plan B. See you later.'

Then he was swallowed up by the fog.

Patient FJ
Recovery Diary whatever

It took me about an hour. By the time I headed back to the house the fog was clearing, but it still lingered at ground level and I had to step carefully. I'd already had a painful encounter with a small stone ornament that revealed itself, when I peered at it while rubbing my shin, to be a rude little statue of a satyr, grasping his oversized phallus in both hands and looking very pleased with himself.

The dark bulk of the house loomed up ahead of me. A faint light was coming from the Blue Room, and I prayed that Hatchjaw was still waiting for me in there.

I thought about Dorothy as I picked my way towards the French windows. She was a remarkable woman. When I told her I didn't love her she seemed to realise I was simply trying to keep things straight between us. I'd decided not to say anything about seeing Paula, and Dorothy clearly had no idea there was another woman in the picture, or what had prompted me to be so honest with her, even though my declaration must have come to her out of the blue. I almost wished I did love her.

When I stepped into the room I couldn't see Hatchjaw. I had a sudden feeling of hollowness. Something was about to collapse inside me. Never before had I invested so much importance in any enterprise whose goal wasn't my own gratification, and now I'd failed. I felt tears pricking my eyes. Then I saw him. He was sitting in an armchair, tucked into the corner of the room. He was hunched over a low coffee table, and when he raised his head and looked in my direction I got the feeling he wasn't really seeing me. As I walked towards him his gaze began to focus, and he shuddered, like someone waking from a bad dream. His flame was burning low.

'Hello, Wallace,' I said.

He nodded slowly but didn't say anything. There was another chair on his side of the table so I shoved it closer to him and sat down. 'Listen,' I said, 'don't give up, okay?'

'Why not?'

'Love,' I said, without knowing why.

Hatchjaw winced and seemed to shrink away from me, as if the word were contaminated. I hadn't intended to blurt it out like that; in fact I'd prepared a little speech I'd been rather pleased with until that moment, when the reality of Hatchjaw's pain dragged me into the present, and out of an imaginary future in which a few well-crafted words of modest wisdom – which were now exposed to me as almost indecently silly and contrived – would heal his troubled spirit. I tried again. 'I mean, love is the one thing that can save us, in the end, isn't it?'

'Save us from what?'

'Death?'

I hadn't planned to say that, either. Hatchjaw gazed at me. He slowly raised his thick, hairy eyebrows in a polite but scornful request for me to explain myself. He knew as well as I did that I had no idea what I was talking about.

'Oh, fuck, I don't know,' I said. 'Forget that. But what about Dr Bassett? Eudora? Isn't she worth fighting for?'

'It seems I can only fight with her.'

'All right. And how do you feel about that?'

'Are you serious?'

I laughed. 'Yes, I know. It's ridiculous. But come on, let me have a go at being the therapist. How hard can it be? All I have to do is remain awake and inscrutable, and then after 50 minutes I say your hour is over and we've made some progress, and tell you to pay the receptionist and make another appointment. Isn't that how it works?'

Hatchjaw made a slight movement with one corner of his mouth. It wasn't actually a smile, more like a message that he would have tried to smile if he'd hadn't been otherwise engaged, suffering unspeakable torment in the deepest pit of hell.

'Look,' I said, 'I'm not pretending I know how to do this. But I genuinely want to help, or try to, and the only thing I can think of doing is getting you to talk to me, because it could be marginally better than sitting here and not talking to me.'

Hatchjaw looked down at the table. After a long silence he spoke quietly. 'Thank you. That's kind of you.'

'Not really. I'm probably just projecting. Dumping the responsibility on you, to succeed where I've failed so often and so spectacularly. I got it all wrong, so I want you to get it right for me. A bit like my impulse to continue buying good wines even after I'd stopped drinking, because I got a kick out of watching my guests enjoy them. Vicarious gratification.'

Hatchjaw raised his head and gave me a sidelong glance. 'Why is it,' he said thoughtfully, 'that you find it so hard to accept gratitude? Have you always been aware of a tension between your need for approval and your discomfort when you actually get it?'

'Whoa, hold on. Who's the therapist here?'

Hatchjaw nodded. 'All right. Why not? You're an intelligent man, Jim, and you've probably acquired a fair bit of wisdom in these matters, these affairs of the heart...' He stopped. He seemed to be gulping for air. After a moment he coughed a couple of times and continued. 'So perhaps it will do me good to talk to you, even though I don't think it will change the situation.'

'Never mind that. Why did you suddenly get wobbly when you mentioned your heart just then? You looked like you were about to cry.'

Hatchjaw turned to face me full on. He narrowed his eyes. 'Very good. Picking up on the subtext, the unconscious signals. I must have reacted like that because it's the phrase Eudora and I always use. Or used. Affairs of the heart. When we wanted to make a distinction between our professional relationship and our...other one.' He broke off and slumped forward, resting his elbows on the coffee table and burying his face in his hands.

I decided to say nothing for a while and let him sit there, breathing deeply. He didn't seem to be in any more distress than he was before, just tired of having to deal with it. And it gave me a chance to reappraise my tactics. My plan had been to deliver a withering critique of Hatchjaw's foolishness in throwing away the love of a good woman, and an expert analysis, informed by years of experience, of all the ways he was fucking everything up. I now saw that this approach was a terrible idea. What right did I have to lecture Hatchjaw about all the things he was doing wrong? None at all. This realisation was what had prompted me, on the spur of the moment, to take on the role of therapist or counsellor. If nothing else, I'd been on the receiving end of their ministrations often enough to impersonate one reasonably convincingly.

But now I'd assumed the part, I found it was starting to take me over. My thoughts were changing even as I was thinking them. I felt a wise, lofty compassion for Hatchjaw and his problems. Yes, I would certainly do my best to help this man – my patient – but perhaps not in the way he expected. He needed to understand the nature of his unhappiness. He was an addict, just like the rest of us, and his addiction was Eudora Bassett. After all, love is simply another irrational compulsion that drives an individual to behave foolishly and sometimes destructively.

Wait, where was this glib drivel coming from? It seemed to have arrived in my mind wholesale, along with the impersonation, as if I'd hired a psychiatrist's outfit from a costume shop – a Freudian dress coat, cigar, spectacles and beard, perhaps – and picked up a set of lazy, second-rate ideas to go with it. That was quite enough of that, thank you. My best chance of helping Hatchjaw was to be myself, not to dick around with this kind of armchair psychology. You'll never understand an armchair. Sorry.

And another thing: if love was no more than another kind of addiction, did I really want to cure Hatchjaw of his addiction to Bassett, even if such a thing were possible?

I realised that Hatchjaw had raised his head, and was looking at me expectantly.

'Sorry,' I said, 'are you ready?'

'Yes.'

'What should we do?'

'Ask me questions. Open questions.'

'Okay. Should I ask you about your feelings?'

Hatchjaw shrugged. 'If you want.'

'Right. So, tell me about your feelings.'

'I'm not very good at talking about my feelings.'

'Oh. That's not going to work then, is it?'

'Yes, it is. You've just got to be more specific.'

I thought for a moment. I thought about what it feels like to be in love, and feel you're losing the person you love. I thought about seeing Paula, little more than an hour ago. She seemed very real, but even if what I saw was no more than a vision, I still experienced all the old, familiar sensations. Seeing her, or even an image of her, provoked a physical reaction in me. There was no denying that kind of visceral truth: it was as real as slamming a car door on your hand.

'All right,' I said to Hatchjaw, 'tell me what you feel when you see her. When she walks into the room. What happens to you?'

Hatchjaw's gaze drifted away from mine and he stared into space, absent-mindedly pinching the stubbly flesh above his upper lip with his thumb and forefinger. Finally he turned back to me. 'I'd like to get into a bag, if that's all right with you.'

'Sorry, what did you say?'

'A bag. I'd like to do this in a bag.'

'What does that mean? Is that jargon?'

'No, it's a bag.' He reached under the coffee table and pulled out what looked like a folded black bed-sheet. As he shook it open I saw it was more like a duvet cover. A large bag, in fact.

'It's a resource we sometimes use,' Hatchjaw said, 'and it's actually very effective, even though it may seem a bit strange. It helps the patient feel secure and yet, at the same time, free; both seen and unseen; engaged with the world and yet protected from it. For many people it has resonances with enjoyable childhood experiences and it can be very useful to stimulate disinhibition.'

'You're going to get into that bag?'

'Yes. Would you like to try it?'

'I don't think there's room for both of us in there.'

'No, you can have your own.' Hatchjaw reached under the table again and produced another black bag. He offered it to me without unfolding it.

'Thanks, I'm all right,' I said. 'But you go ahead.'

Hatchjaw chucked the second bag back under the table. He pushed his chair back and climbed carefully into the bag he'd already opened up, hunkered down inside it and pulled the material over his head so it enclosed him entirely. He squirmed around inside the bag for a few moments, getting comfortable, then settled down.

I contemplated the bag. Even though I knew it contained nothing but Hatchjaw, there was something strangely mysterious about the dark, lumpy shape beside me, as if a sinister Santa Claus – the Anti-Santa – had left his black sack behind while he went off to do something unspeakable with elves.

I wondered if Hatchjaw was waiting for me to start. The longer I left it the harder it became to think of what to say. The bag was very still now. I couldn't even discern signs of breathing. It struck me that perhaps Hatchjaw had pulled off an extraordinary conjuring trick, and he was no longer there, and if I touched the bag it would collapse into an inky pool of fabric.

Just as I cleared my throat to ask if he was all right, the bag shifted and Hatchjaw's muffled voice emerged from it. 'I'll tell you how I feel when I see her,' he said, 'I feel awake. Not always in a good way. But undeniably present. And if I haven't seen her for a while, it feels as if a missing piece of a jigsaw falls into place. No, maybe that's not quite right. It's more that there's something missing when she's not there, but I'm not aware of that until she is there. Sorry, am I making any sense at all?'

'Oh, yes. But let me just ask you one thing.'

'Fire away.'

'Haven't you ever been in love before?'

Silence. I waited. When Hatchjaw finally replied I got the feeling, for some reason, that he was smiling. 'I don't know,' he said.

'What, you don't know if it was love or not?'

'No, I mean I can't remember anything before being here.'

Now it was my turn to be silent. This information gave me a queasy jolt of unease, which began turning to anger. 'Wait a minute,' I said. 'Are you telling me that you and Bassett just woke up here and decided you were doctors? I mean, have you had any training, or were you just making it all up as you went along?'

'Don't worry, I'm not bogus, or a charlatan. Any more than any psychologist is, I suppose.'

'How do you know, if you can't remember anything?'

'That's the weird part, I can remember all the things I learned before I found myself here. I can remember sessions with patients, although they all seem to be faceless. I have a store of expertise, and so has Eudora. More than me, in fact, which is why we both knew that she was the senior practitioner. The only thing I can't remember is who I am.' He paused, then went on in a quieter, more ruminative tone. 'But I think I must have been in love before. To return to the original question.'

'Why do you think you must have been in love

before?'

'I don't know. Something about the mixture of feelings.'

'What's the mixture?'

'Joy and pain, I think.'

'And that feels familiar?'

'The pain feels familiar.'

'Why do you think that is?'

'It's something to do with inevitability. Knowing the joy won't last.'

'Because?'

'Because…I know I'll screw it up.'

'There you go,' I said. 'You've definitely been in love before.'

Hatchjaw was silent for a few moments. I could now hear him breathing. I guessed he'd opened up the top of the bag a little to facilitate that process. This was confirmed when he finally spoke again, and his voice was less muffled.

'Yes,' Hatchjaw said, 'I have been in love before. And now I come to think about it I also realise I've been here before.'

'What, here in this room, in that bag?' I said, excited by the possibility that he'd remembered something about his past that would shed a bit of light on what we were all doing here.

'No, I don't mean that,' he said, 'I mean the point I've reached with Eudora. I've been at this point before.'

'Which is what?'

'The point where all I think about is how much I'm hurting her.'

'And yourself,' I said.

'What?'

'And yourself. Every time you hurt Eudora you hurt yourself.'

I heard Hatchjaw draw in a sharp breath. After what seemed like a very long time he expelled it. 'Fuck,' he said.

'What's up? Everything all right in there?'

Hatchjaw's head popped up out of the bag. 'Yes!' he said. His eyebrows danced up and down like a couple of thick socks being juggled. 'I get it!'

'That's nice. What do you get?'

'I have to stop hurting her. I've punished myself enough.'

I laughed. 'That's a good way of putting it.'

'It's more than that,' Hatchjaw said excitedly, 'it's the truth. I've always understood it as an idea, but for some reason I've only just experienced the truth of it.'

Hatchjaw really did seem to be undergoing a kind of epiphany. His face shone with sudden comprehension, although it could also have been perspiration, as it must have been hot in there. Whatever it was, there was no denying his earnestness, and it overrode the comic potential of the situation. It turns out that a man talking passionately about love with his head poking out of a bag doesn't always have to be funny.

'It's the Buddhist thing, isn't it?' Hatchjaw said. 'That we're all interdependent, and my happiness is inextricably linked to your happiness, and that by hurting you I hurt myself. It's not so hard to grasp, is it?'

'No. But easy to forget.'

'Very true! But it stands to reason that if we're all interconnected like this, and that your pain is my pain, then it's even more true for people who are in love, because they're more interconnected than anybody. People in love are hypersensitive to each other. That's one of the signs, isn't it?'

'Or the symptoms.'

Hatchjaw ignored that and continued, his eyes shining. 'But it's taken me so long to really understand it,' he said, 'and it's so simple. Maybe it was too simple for me. But it's definitely true; it's why I always feel so sick and miserable after I've argued with Eudora, and why I always wish I hadn't been so insistent on proving my point, if it means I had to punish and dominate her in order to do it. I'm just hurting myself. The more anguish I cause her, the more I inflict pain on myself. Which is just masochism. Maybe that's the problem, maybe I'm a masochist. Do you think I am? No, don't tell me. Tell me I'm being ridiculous, and to pull myself together, and we'll see if I enjoy it.'

He chuckled, and I joined in.

Hatchjaw's merriment subsided. As it did so, his face sagged and his eyebrows descended until their weight seemed to be pushing his eyes, no longer shining, back into their cavernous recesses.

His euphoria had left him as abruptly as it had arrived. 'All too late now,' he said.

I thought he was about to sink back down into the bag but his head remained visible, even if it now suggested a man drowning rather than a chrysalis emerging, as it had when he first popped up.

'All too late,' he repeated in a gloomy monotone.

'Not necessarily, Wallace,' said a voice from behind us.

I looked around to see Dr Bassett and Dorothy standing in the doorway.

Patient DP
Recovery Diary 18

Thank God Eudora spoke when she did. We'd been standing unobserved in the doorway of the Blue Room for several moments. She seemed to have herself under control but I was trying like hell not to laugh, and losing the battle. When Hatchjaw intoned, 'All too late,' for the second time, in that lugubrious voice, I began to snort like a camel with a fly up its nose. Then Eudora piped up and I was able to convert my convulsions into a reasonably convincing coughing fit. Not that it mattered, as I don't think Hatchjaw even noticed me once he'd seen Eudora.

I had no idea why his head was poking out of a black sack, like a talking plum on top of a pudding. However, as I seemed to be the only person present who found it particularly unusual I figured maybe it was normal practice in these circles, and I was deplorably unsophisticated. I stifled my girlish giggles, buttoned my lip, and followed Eudora into the room.

It had been a little over two hours since I'd parted from Jim in the garden and marched back to the house with a determined step, stout of heart and frozen of tit. It was time to face the sad fact that my fur wrap had nothing left to offer me after its decades of generous hospitality to the moths of Manhattan; accordingly, my first stop was my room, to pick up yet more clothing that had seen better days, and a few better nights. To be frank, I was also postponing the moment when the breezy confidence with which I'd assured Jim that Dr Bassett was still on the premises would be put to the test. In truth, it wasn't much more than a hunch. Still, a woman's hunch about what another woman will do in a crisis, based on what she herself would do in similar circumstances, is more reliable than many things in life.

I knocked on Dr Bassett's door almost before I reached it, not wishing to dither.

After a few long moments during which my vital signs took a vacation I heard a cautious voice that sounded strained, and surprisingly close, as if the speaker were standing just behind the door, perhaps clutching a blunt instrument.

'Who's that?' the voice said.

'It's Dorothy. And yes, I'm alone, Eudora.'

She opened the door and stepped aside. She was empty-handed but I wouldn't have tangled with her. Eudora Bassett did not look like a woman in the mood to be trifled with.

I slipped in and sat down while she locked the door behind us, then she sat opposite me in a comfortable armchair that was the elderly spouse of the one I occupied. We had spent many hours talking together in those old chairs, with me doing most of the talking. At first I'd found her hard to get along with, partly because she didn't seem to have much of a sense of humor. I like to keep the conversational tone light, and in the past some people were kind enough to say I was a wit. I wasn't so sure about that. I knew some very smart writers back in the old Algonquin days, and they could be damned witty, but they worked hard at it. It's tough being a fully fledged wit. Hell, it's tough just being a halfwit. And in the end most of those men were just a bunch of loudmouths.

Anyhow, for a long time I thought Eudora simply wasn't on the same wavelength as me, and I felt pretty flat about it. The very first time I came to her room for what they called Individual Therapy I remember her asking me, near the end of the conversation, 'Dorothy, why do you dislike yourself so much?'

'It's a rotten job, Doc,' I said, 'but somebody's got to do it, and I've had plenty of practice.' That would have gotten a smile where I came from, if not a laugh, but Eudora just nodded thoughtfully. Then she told me something I wasn't ready to hear just then, about self-deprecating humour being a way to deflect the pain of rejection.

Some time later, after I saw the truth of what she was saying, I began to realise how difficult it must be for her if patients tried to turn everything into a joke. She didn't want to come across as a sourpuss, but she couldn't make light of their troubles, even if they did so themselves. Your own problems are like your family – you're allowed to mock them but everybody else had better watch their step. We penitent drunks get grouchy when other people ridicule our spellbinding melodramas.

After a while I understood Eudora a lot better, and I like to think we became close, and maybe even friends. I certainly unburdened myself to her, and if there's one thing I'm sure of it's that she is a good woman. Talking to her had helped me more than I can say, and now, as she settled into her chair opposite me, I wanted to return the favour. I was going to help her, by God, whether she liked it or not.

'What can I do for you, Dottie?' she said.

'Talk to me, Eudora.'

At first she didn't seem too comfortable with the idea but I told her she had to do it, even if it was just to please me. I said I wanted to repay the debt of gratitude I owed her. She said I didn't owe her anything but she seemed touched by the sentiment, which was the general idea. She agreed to give it her best shot, and after a couple of false starts, while she got used to the novelty of the proposition, she talked to me. And once she started there was no stopping her.

It didn't take me long to discover she was lonely, being something of an expert in the condition myself, and knowing that it is God's own torment. Eudora said she liked listening to other people's problems, and that when they trust you they reveal remarkable things about themselves, which she felt privileged to hear. But it seemed obvious to me that she was starved of decent company, despite – make that because of – the parade of garrulous drunks, dope fiends and loonies who sat in her room all day, pouring their woes into her sympathetic ear. What could be more lonely than to spend your days hearing about the lives, loves and lousy livers of others without making a squeak about your own? Who listens to the listener?

Why, the loving soulmate, that's who.

Which brought us to the subject of Dr Hatchjaw, or Wallace, as she insisted I call him, although the name makes me think of a circus elephant for some reason. Probably a memory from my childhood, but this wasn't the time to paddle in that particular swamp. Instead I asked Eudora to talk about what was going on between her and the man with the sweet smile and the gorilla's eyebrows. I told her I knew it was a Love Affair, but that's the title of a very long book that runs to several volumes and a multitude of sins.

It didn't surprise me to hear that Wallace was a hard man to house-train. Eudora didn't put it like that, but I knew what she meant. Intimacy was the word she used, and she wasn't just talking about a roll in the hay. After a hard day's toil at the nuthouse a woman doesn't necessarily want a man to pounce on her with hot breath and smouldering eye and tear her clothes off – a bath might be nice first – and while amorous passion is appreciated, sometimes what she really needs is to sit down, put her aching feet up, and shoot the breeze with a friendly man who loves her.

But that was too simple for a guy like Hatchjaw. I knew the type. He arrives for a romantic assignation with a furrowed brow and the cares of the world on his shoulders. A little gentle prompting reveals that most of them are your fault. Further conversation will feature a more detailed explanation of all the things you're doing wrong. After which, if you're lucky, he may unwind and show a little tolerance for your childish foibles, and maybe display an interest in your womanly charms, too. By which time you're not really in the mood, thanks, buddy.

That's a somewhat one-sided picture. The discussion I had with Eudora about Hatchjaw, and men in general, was a little more highbrow than the impression I may be giving. We contemplated every detail of life's rich tapestry, then we unpicked the stitching and unravelled it, deploring the shoddy workmanship. In the process I played up the hard-boiled, wisecracking act for Eudora's amusement, and eventually we got to laughing a good deal about the whole comic opera, with many a hearty giggle about the myriad ways that life can find to drive us crazy.

Eudora's problems were made especially poignant by Wallace being that dangerous item, a good man, and a smart one into the bargain. Smart enough to know when he was screwing everything up with her, and good enough to feel terrible about it. However, he was at a loss to know how to fix things. And so was she, it seems. She said she was just as trapped by needs and compulsions as he was. It takes two to tango, was her view, and if you love someone, and you want it to last, you need to give each other some help to learn the steps.

Just as I concluded that we'd reviewed the battle lines in the sex war to our complete satisfaction, and seen the funny side of it along the way, I noticed a flicker of unease cross Eudora's pleasant countenance. I asked her what was up.

'There is a complication in my relationship with Wallace,' she said.

I assured her that there's no such animal as a love affair without complications, as long as one of the parties, at least, is still breathing.

She smiled. 'I suspect you're right. But since you've been kind enough to give me the opportunity to unburden myself I thought I'd better mention it. I feel I owe it to you.'

'You don't owe me a thing,' I said, repeating her own line back to her, 'but let me guess. A third party?'

'That's right.'

'So, one of you has been seeing someone else. You or him?'

'Both of us.'

I whistled softly. 'You've *both* been seeing other people?'

'Not exactly.'

'What do you mean?'

'It's the same person.'

After I recovered from my surprise I asked the obvious question. 'Male or female?'

She hesitated for a tiny moment. 'Female,' she said.

I paused to mull things over. I confess I was somewhat shocked. I may have a tough exterior but there's still a nice little Jewish girl somewhere beneath all the gristle. I'm always mildly ruffled to be reminded that for some people it's not enough to make the beast with two backs: they like to include extra backs in the equation, and other body parts too, from a selection of contributors. Not that I disapprove – God knows, I had plenty of friends who deviated from the standard model, including some who sat around our table at the Club. But I didn't go in for that kind of thing myself. Booze can loosen any inhibition, and I've found myself in a woman's arms a few times, and sometimes been aroused by it. But nothing much happened, and I've never been part of a real sex triangle, although I've turned a few down. A lot of men get a big kick from the idea of being in bed with more than one woman, although many of them would run like hell if the women agreed, and expected them to live up to their side of the bargain. Predictably, the men who suggest these things tend to have in mind the addition of an extra woman – rather than another man – to the proceedings, and there's nothing like the suggestion that you're not up to the job all by yourself to make a woman feel practically irresistible.

The fact is, most men I know have their hands full keeping one woman satisfied, and that seems about right to me.

Having done enough mulling I asked Eudora to tell me more.

'It happened fairly soon after Wallace and I arrived,' she began, but I cut her off.

'Arrived? From where?'

In all the natural excitement of dissecting another woman's love life I'd only just realised that these were ideal circumstances in which to interrogate Eudora about a few other important questions, like what the hell we were doing here. But before I could ask any of them she held up a warning hand and shook her head.

'There's not a lot I can tell you, I'm afraid. Wallace and I simply found ourselves here, like the rest of you. We knew who we were, and what our job was, but we don't know what happened to us, or what this place really is. We've largely avoided spending too long on those questions by immersing ourselves in our work. Which may be one of the problems. Whenever we have time together there always seems to be a long list of things to think about before we can think about ourselves.'

'Who makes the list?'

She smiled. 'Yes, it's Wallace, of course. And naturally, several items on the list are matters that just happen to be my responsibility, and are problems that can only be solved by me doing what he wants, the way he wants it done.'

'But he's not officially the boss, is he?'

'No, that's the interesting thing. He was the one who decided, right from the start, that I was his superior. At first I thought perhaps he got an erotic thrill from that, and giving me the higher professional status was part of the game. But I think it's more subtle. Wallace is one of nature's correctors. But here's the question: is it more gratifying to correct someone from a position of authority, or as the apparent inferior in a power relationship you can constantly subvert?'

'I get the picture. It's an old trick, isn't it? Bossing someone around by pretending to be helpful.'

Eudora laughed. 'Absolutely,' she said. 'We'd probably call it passive-aggressive manipulation, but I like your description better. It comes down to the same thing, in the end. It's all about people trying to control other people. And if you want to see a dedicated control freak at the top of his game I can tell you that Wallace Hatchjaw is world class, bless him.'

Eudora sketched in the rest of the background. She and Wallace began their affair almost immediately. Neither of them knew whether they'd known each other before they got here, but something about the naturalness with which they fell into bed together made them both suspect they had, and that they'd been lovers. Eudora said it was like picking up a book you'd been reading and had laid aside for a while.

Pretty soon their work began to overwhelm them, and it threw a king-sized wet blanket over their love life. And then someone arrived who seemed ideally qualified to be their assistant. She wasn't a patient, she just showed up 'out of the blue', as Eudora put it. She was the answer to their prayers, and at first she really did seem like an angel. 'But not for long,' Eudora said. 'Because whoever she was, she was no angel. Not Alice.'

'What was she like?' I said.

She sighed. 'What was Alice like? Like a drug. A terrible drug.'

Alice. The way Eudora went on to describe her she sounded like a ringer for the serpent in the Garden of Eden, but with fewer moral scruples.

'And yet,' Eudora said, 'I can't condemn her. In a strange way she was very innocent, which is what made her so dangerous. She didn't seem to be aware of the harm she could cause simply by being so...irresistible.'

'What was she, some kind of sex bomb?'

'It was more than that. And less. It certainly wasn't only about sex, anyway. Although I knew, almost from the start, that she was going to seduce Wallace.'

'But it takes two to tango, as you said yourself.'

'Yes, I know. But with Alice...' She trailed off and looked at me helplessly. 'I'm not so sure. She was a force of nature and neither of us could resist her. She seduced me, too. In every sense. I was terribly upset about her and Wallace, really devastated. Oh, we had our problems but I knew I loved him. And we were a comfort to each other, despite the bickering and everything else. I think you've discovered for yourself that we all welcome a bit of comfort in this place, haven't you?'

I don't know how she knew about that, but I didn't mind. I allowed myself a small, fond smile as I thought about Jim, and Eudora gave a little chuckle and leaned over to pat my hand. We didn't need to say anything else about it.

'Anyway,' Eudora continued, 'it wasn't long before I found myself in her bed. And as Wallace was already there, things got a bit weird for a while. I could hardy believe what I was doing, and I'm still trying to work out exactly what came over us. It was as if Alice was a missing piece of something. For both of us. Something we needed, or thought we needed, perhaps. I realised afterwards that she reminded me of my—' She stopped abruptly, frowning. Then she said, 'My childhood.'

She seemed upset. I handed her the box of tissues that always stood on a small table beside the chairs. She plucked one out, and as she raised it to her eyes she stopped and smiled. 'You're getting the hang of this, aren't you?' She wiped her eyes, gave her nose a good blow, and sat up straighter.

'What was that about your childhood?' I said.

'Let's just leave it at that. Long story. But it was the same for Wallace, he says. Alice was like a person he'd always been waiting for. That was very hurtful to hear from my lover, as you can imagine, but once I was enmeshed in the relationship as well, I understood. I won't go into any more of the details, because it was sordid, frankly. It still feels sordid. She did whatever she wanted with us. But at a certain point I saw that if we didn't take action we were lost. That may sound dramatic but it's true. I mean lost in every sense. Morally lost. Spiritually lost. Wallace and I both realised we had to save ourselves. It was a great struggle, and it cost us dearly, but we did it.'

'What did you do?'

'We got rid of her. I got rid of her.'

'How?'

Eudora gazed at me levelly for a long time. 'I can't tell you.'

309

And I didn't want to know, if that was the way it was. Some things are best left alone. I didn't doubt that whatever she'd done, she'd been right to do it.

'That's quite a story,' I said. 'But at least it has a happy ending for you and Wallace, if you managed to do what you needed to.'

She smiled a sad smile. 'Not really. It isn't over, you see. She's back.'

That stopped me in my tracks. 'Back?' I said. 'Back where?' I think I actually looked quickly around the room as I said it.

'Outside. We've seen her. At least, we've seen someone – or something – that we think is her, in some shape or form. She stands at the edge of the woods, in the trees, looking at the house.'

'Well, if she gets lonely she can always talk to my mom.'

Eudora sat up even straighter. 'Have you seen your mother out there?'

'It's probably nothing. Just a couple of times, I thought I saw her, or someone who looks like her, right there at the edge of the woods. But it could be my imagination; it's only happened at dusk, or in the mist at dawn, so I can't be sure.'

Eudora frowned. 'How strange. Us too. She's only there at dawn or dusk, when we can't really be sure it's her. But it's *someone*. I'm sure of that.'

We both glanced involuntarily at the window. The curtains weren't quite closed, showing a strip of fathomless black between them. It was the middle of the night. I remembered that Jim was downstairs with

Wallace.

'Eudora,' I said, 'do you still love him?'

'Yes.'

'He's downstairs talking to Jim. We're sure he still loves you, too.'

A strange expression crossed her face. There was a happiness in it, but also a kind of pain, and tiredness. 'I don't know if I can face this, Dottie,' she said quietly.

'Look,' I said, leaning forward and taking both her hands, 'now's the time to face it, or not at all. Especially if she's back – or whatever it is. You've still got a chance of happiness with the man you love. But you'll have to fight for it. And do it now.' I gave her hands a little shake. 'Besides,' I said, 'what the hell else are you going to do?'

She squeezed my hands. 'You're right.'

We both stood up.

Patient MS
Recovery Diary 12

My feelings were of desolation, deep and bitter. My equanimity was shattered by a sense of sudden exile, so painful to one who has struggled all her life to be accepted in a place she wished to call her home; and my heart ached with regret that I was unable to offer my help to those two unhappy souls who so needed it.

The obstacles I faced were quite unlike any I had met with before. I had no personal adversary with whom to do battle, and no cruel prejudices to overcome, such as those I encountered in my long and unwearied application at the War Office to secure an appointment in the Crimea. On those occasions I knew that certain people, with whose official gravity and repose I had interfered, shrank from accepting my aid because my blood flowed beneath a somewhat duskier skin than theirs. But here I had met with nothing but kindness and unaffected good feeling, and now I was cast out from my refuge, and parted from all who shared it with me. I was lost in a terrible fog.

I sought her, I confess. Oh, for a word from those lips!

I knew now with certainty that I had seen her twice or thrice at the edge of the forest. But how to find her? I almost laughed to think of ignorant voices, who knew her only from the newspaper accounts, crying out that I had only to seek the light of her lamp! I wonder what lively imagination had created that figure. She carried a lamp no more frequently than any of us. However, I had seen her eyes by lamplight many a time, and had taken sweet comfort from their tender looks.

What comfort could I, in my turn, now give those two doctors who had shown me such kindness? Tears streamed down my foolish cheeks. If my determination alone could have healed their troubled spirits they would have been happy in an instant. But my services as a nurse would not suffice to cure the sickness that ailed them. I thought that if I could find my friend she would advise me, but the dense fog hemmed me in on every side and I despaired of ever seeing that loving face again.

It was in this moment of darkness that the gentlemen found me, and described a plan that might allow us to repay the blessings we owed to our medical benefactors.

Patient FJ
Blah Diary Blah

What a star. Dorothy showed up at just the right moment with Eudora, and also had the decency not to laugh at the sight of Hatchjaw in his sack, despite the effort it must have cost her. I could have kissed her. As there wasn't any reason not to, I did. She felt nice and warm in my arms.

The act of springing up to embrace Dottie also meant I could vacate the chair next to Hatchjaw, into which I ushered Eudora while Wallace scrambled out of the sack, brushed himself down, and resumed his seat. Dottie and I hauled a couple of other chairs into position on the other side of the coffee table and sat down. All set.

Eudora and Wallace looked at each other. She summoned

up a smile, which he returned sheepishly. Neither of them seemed able to think of what to say. They both understood this was a critical moment, and they knew they shouldn't start raking over their past, but they couldn't ignore it, either. You can't make a new start from nowhere.

Hatchjaw leaned forward hesitantly. Eudora's hands twitched in her lap, as if they wanted to reach out to him, but then Hatchjaw checked himself and sat back. The wariness with which they were treating each other made me think of characters in a fairy tale who go on a long journey together and then reveal themselves to be not quite what they had seemed – the milkmaid who turns out to be a princess, perhaps, and who finds herself unexpectedly in the presence of an exotic beast who was previously disguised as the village idiot.

Finally Hatchjaw broke the silence. 'I'm sorry, Eudora.'

She shook her head. 'Let's not be sorry.'

That seemed to disappoint him, as if he resented not being allowed to apologise. He nodded slowly. 'All right,' he said, 'but I don't know what else to say.'

'Say you love me.'

Hatchjaw looked startled. 'I do,' he said, turning fully towards her. 'I definitely do love you...'

Oh Christ, I thought, please don't say it.

I was sure he was about to do exactly what had upset Eudora so much when they were last in this room. He was going to say 'but', and then qualify his declaration in a way that would make it worse than worthless.

I could tell Dorothy was thinking the same thing, and

so was Eudora. We all looked at Hatchjaw, willing him not to say it. We knew it would ruin everything. And so, miraculously, did he.

'I do love you…more than I can say,' he whispered.

Eudora took his hand. 'That's all I want to hear. As long as I know you love me, and you know that I love you, Wallace, we can deal with everything else.'

'I know. And I can change, Eudora. I have changed.'

'So have I.'

'I can give things up. All the things that annoy you. I know I can.'

'That's very sweet. And I can give things up, too, Wallace. But for now let's just start by saying we love each other.'

'Yes, let's get our priorities straight. I've only got one, really, which is you. You're my priority.'

'Thank you. And you're mine.'

This is going well, I thought.

Eudora moved forward in her chair and leaned towards Hatchjaw. 'We should tell each other more often, though, shouldn't we?' she said. 'It's easy to forget how simple and how important it is. Other things get in the way.'

'And other people.'

Eudora nodded grimly. 'Yes, other people, too.'

'Actually, I've got a theory about that.' Hatchjaw bounced around in his seat so he could talk to me and Dorothy as well. He seemed excited.

'About other people?' I said. 'What about them?'

'I mean about Alice.'

Eudora stiffened. She tried to take her hand from

Hatchjaw's but he held on to it and waggled his eyebrows at her. 'We've got to talk about her at some point,' he said.

Eudora sighed. 'I suppose so.' She bowed her head for a moment then looked up at him and smiled. 'Yes, you're right, Wallace. We need to face what happened.'

Hatchjaw released her hand, which she returned demurely to her lap. She gave him another encouraging smile. 'What's your theory?'

Hatchjaw took a deep breath. 'Well, it's just an idea, really. But didn't you always feel there was something a bit... I don't know...changeable about her?'

'She could certainly be volatile,' Eudora agreed. 'Very moody.'

'But more than that. I used to find that she even looked different at different times. Didn't you?'

Eudora nodded slowly. 'Maybe.'

'Definitely. And I think she actually looked different depending on how I was feeling. Almost like a kind of emotional chameleon effect.'

'I know what you mean. Although that's pretty subjective.'

'But there's something else. It was Sherlock Holmes who pointed it out to me, just before we had...the meeting.'

I heard Dorothy shift in her seat beside me. 'That jerk,' she muttered.

Eudora smiled at her and rolled her eyes. Both women laughed.

'Yes, I know,' Hatchjaw said. 'But he pointed out that at some time or another everyone in this place has seen a person – a figure – at the edge of the woods, and that everyone has seen a different person. It even happened to him, as well. And who they saw depended on who they wanted to see – or didn't want to see.'

Eudora held up a hand to stop him. 'Wait a minute. What are you saying? Are you saying that Alice...isn't ...'

'Yes,' Hatchjaw said. 'I'm saying Alice isn't real.'

'Really,' Eudora objected, 'that's a bit much.'

A voice came from the other side of the room: 'Yes, Wallace. A bit much. To say Alice isn't real.'

Someone was standing in the French windows. I felt the breath leave my body. I probably would have had a heart attack if I hadn't already been dead.

It wasn't Paula. That was what was so shocking. She didn't even look particularly like her, which made it worse, somehow. If the resemblance had been stronger it would have been less uncanny. But despite not looking like her, the person in the doorway reminded me of Paula so powerfully that I was overwhelmed by a desperate yearning for her.

Then I understood. It was the yearning itself that reminded me of Paula, not the woman who now walked towards us and stopped a few feet from the table, hand on hip, regarding us with amusement. She had a lovely smile.

She was petite, about the same size as Paula, and she had short, dark hair, but there the physical resemblance ended, except that she had large, brown eyes. But this woman's face was more angular than Paula's, almost elfin, with a sharpness about the nose and chin that prevented her from being really pretty in any conventional way. And yet she was gorgeous. She had an extraordinary vivacity, a magnetic allure, and I found her utterly compelling.

What am I talking about? I was in love with her.

Love at first sight. The familiar phrases spring to mind, and are insufficient. A spark between us. A special connection. True, but they don't cover it, do they?

It's more like a kind of instant recognition that takes place. To do with chemicals, neurons, body language, pheromones, I don't know. But there's a jolt, like seeing a famous person in the flesh. And the recognition flows both ways, and what I'm recognising, and what I know the other person is also recognising, is our ability to unsettle each other. To ruin each other.

I see a woman. We exchange a look. All bets are off. In a flash, something has shifted, deep beneath the surface, tectonically. The frankness of that glance is a mighty force: it whisks away the light blanket of restraint and good behaviour that's kept you out of trouble for a while, and leaves you exposed: naked and foolish, eager to journey into the unknown with this stranger. And, of course, the voyage is going to be dangerous. But because you've had that moment of mutual recognition, it means you're both undertaking an expedition into uncharted territory with a fellow explorer you've never met before, but about whom you know some very personal secrets. The look that passes between you in an instant says: I know who you really are. I know how it will feel to hold you. I know how you'll laugh, and how you'll cry. I know how you'll come.

It's always different and yet always the same: something inside me responds to something inside you, and that process takes place at an animal level. And it's not always about sexual attraction, or attraction at all. Sometimes it's a violent repulsion. I've met certain men with whom I've almost had a fist fight within seconds. Some of those men went on to become close friends, when we'd found a way to deal with what we provoked in each other. And sometimes that didn't happen, and we fought, physically or not, either there and then, or over a period of days, months, or years, hating each other with an enduring, visceral loathing, because the other side of 'I know who you are,' is, 'Who the fuck do you think you are?'

And now Alice has that effect on me. The old, familiar demon springs up, chortling with hellish glee, goading me to risk everything yet again. Why not put on this blindfold, Jim, and go out to play in the traffic? Spin the chambers of this revolver and put it to your head? Drink the bottle without the label, just to see what happens?

And all because a woman is smiling at me.

And at everyone else, I realise. I glance at Dorothy and the other two, and with a dreadful shock I see Alice has the same effect on all of us. The erotic charge between me and her, which I thought was entirely exclusive to us, is also vibrating between her and

Dorothy, who is gazing at her with an expression of wistful longing. And Alice is returning that look, and the looks that Eudora and Hatchjaw are giving her.

What the hell is happening? No more than three seconds have passed, at most, since this woman walked into the room, and in that time I've fallen in love, been convinced the feeling is mutual, discovered that the other people in the room are also in love with her, realised she's not only aware of it but is encouraging it, and is somehow returning their adoration, and now bitter jealousy is twisting my guts. This is insane. Get a grip.

Hatchjaw broke the silence. 'Alice,' he croaked, 'we didn't expect you.'

She threw back her head and laughed. It was a rich, rippling sound that made me think of honey and cream. 'Of course you didn't, darling.'

She walked to the table and slipped around it in a sinuous movement, like a dancer, and stood beside Hatchjaw. She stroked his head and then tugged gently at the tight little curls of hair just above his collar. Exactly as Paula used to do to me. My heart lurched.

Alice bent down so her head was close to Hatchjaw's. 'How could you expect me,' she crooned softly, 'after what you did to me?'

'What do you mean?' Hatchjaw tried to turn his face up to look at her, but her grip tightened on his hair. 'What? What did we do?'

She laughed again. 'Are we going to play a game, Wallace?'

'It's all right, Alice,' Eudora said in a very low voice, 'he didn't know.'

Alice released Hatchjaw's hair and smoothed it down as she turned to face Eudora, who, I noticed, had tears in her eyes. 'Really, Eudora, darling? I find that hard to believe.'

'It's true,' Eudora whispered.

Alice stepped nimbly over Hatchjaw's legs and slipped into the space between his chair and Eudora's. She gazed down at her for a moment, then gently took her head and pressed it to her midriff, cradling it and stroking Eudora's hair, more sensually than the playful way she'd touched Hatchjaw. 'Poor baby,' she said, pulling Eudora's head even closer to her belly and swaying her hips.

The effect was arousing, and Alice knew it. As I shifted in my seat I saw she was gazing at me over Eudora's head, a smile playing on her lips. Then she turned her gaze to Dorothy and the quality of her smile changed slightly, and became somehow more womanly, although it still expressed amusement at a shared joke. And it was still erotic.

I tore my eyes away and glanced at Dorothy. She was enraptured by Alice.

Eudora struggled free from Alice's embrace. 'Stop,' she said, dabbing at her eyes. 'I'm sorry, Alice, truly sorry for what I did, but this must stop now.'

'Yes, you're right, of course,' Alice said, smoothing down her dress. It was made of a deep, dusky red material that clung to her body, and she ran her hands down the fabric slowly, caressing herself. 'We must pull ourselves together.'

She threw a dazzling smile at me and Dorothy. 'What will the others think?'

Caught in the searchlight of her full attention, I was stunned into imbecility. 'Don't mind us,' I said brightly.

'Oh, but I do mind,' she said, looking at me from beneath lowered lashes. 'I don't want you to think that we're completely decadent and wicked. Although I expect Wallace and Eudora have told you all kinds of dreadful things about me. Have they?'

The last question was directed to Dorothy, who replied quietly, without the customary edge of amusement in her voice. 'I don't know if they were dreadful. Eudora told me what happened between the three of you, if that's what you mean. It seemed a shame to me, I guess.'

'Did she tell you they poisoned me?'

Hatchjaw sat up with a jolt and looked around sharply, as if he'd just snapped out of a dream. 'Alice, that was just a mistake over the medication. A misjudgement.'

Alice smiled at him indulgently. 'Really, Wallace? Why don't you ask Eudora?'

At this Eudora gripped the arms of her chair as if it were being tossed around in a stormy sea. 'Please,' she said, closing her eyes, 'let's just stop, can we?'

Hatchjaw leaned across Alice and peered at Eudora. 'But is it true?'

Dorothy and I exchanged a glance in which dread was enlivened by a glimmer of shameful excitement.

Eudora opened her eyes. 'It's not that simple.'

'But did you do it?' Hatchjaw persisted. 'Was it because of the…situation between us? I mean, what was behind it, Eudora?' It occurred to me that he was thrilled by the possibility that Eudora might have been driven to desperation by jealousy over him.

Eudora smiled wanly. 'It was more like a game that got out of hand. Tell him, Alice. You were at least partly responsible.'

'Actually, she's right, Wallace,' Alice said. She reached out and stroked Hatchjaw's cheek, which seemed to have a hypnotic effect on him. 'Or partly right, anyway.'

Eudora released her grip on the arms of the chair and sank back into it. 'Let's leave it at that, shall we? I can't take much more of this, to be honest.'

'That's all right, sweetheart,' Alice said. 'Don't get stressed about it. All this drama is a bit much, isn't it? I don't know about you but I could do with a bloody cigarette. Would you like one?'

Hatchjaw began to speak: 'She doesn't want one, because she's—'

'Yes, I would,' Eudora said. 'Thank you, Alice.'

Alice flicked open a small, elegant handbag that was hanging at her hip on a slender strap and began to rummage in it. Eudora and Wallace looked at each other in silence.

Hatchjaw took a deep breath. 'Eudora,' he began, 'I thought you said—'

'What? What did you think I said?'

'I thought you said you'd give up cigarettes.'

'And I thought you said you'd give up nagging me about smoking.'

'Actually,' Dorothy broke in, leaning forward beside

me, 'she didn't say specifically that she'd give up cigarettes, Wallace.' There was a sharpness in her voice that surprised me. I glanced at her and saw she was looking at Hatchjaw with a rather fierce expression.

'Well, that's what I thought she meant,' Hatchjaw said.

I sympathised with him. 'To be fair,' I said, 'that's what I assumed Eudora meant, too. That's what anyone would assume, really.'

I thought I was being extremely reasonable, but for some reason Dorothy turned on me. 'Oh, what a surprise,' she sneered, 'it seems both the men are making assumptions about what a woman means, when what she actually says is clear. Whaddya know?'

I was shocked by her tone, but when I looked around I saw that Eudora was nodding slowly, with a grim smile. Hatchjaw was frowning, as if he had something to say but was considering it carefully. He looked extremely glum. As for Alice, she was still peering into her handbag, apparently oblivious to the conversation, searching for the cigarettes. She was taking a very long time to find them, given the bag was so small.

'All right,' Hatchjaw said, 'it appears I misunderstood. However, like Jim, I thought it was a reasonable inference.'

'Give it a rest, Wallace,' Eudora said. 'I really don't want to talk about it.'

The dynamic in the room had changed completely and it scared me. I needed reassurance. I summoned up a conciliatory smile and turned to deliver it to Dorothy. She just glared at me.

'Oh shit,' Alice said, 'I don't seem to have any after all.'

Great. Now we were all thoroughly unsettled and miserable.

Eudora had flouted Hatchjaw's disapproval for nothing, and was left craving a cigarette she may not even have wanted before Alice suggested it. Dorothy and I found ourselves sourly at odds for no good reason, over something neither of us really cared about, thus lacking the passion for a worthwhile fight. And poor Hatchjaw was robbed of the opportunity to deploy the wounded reprimands he'd doubtless been preparing, and looked like a child deprived of a treat.

The only person who was happy was Alice.

'Never mind,' she said, smiling innocently at Eudora, 'it's probably for the best. I've been trying to give up, too. How's that been going with you?'

Eudora shot her a bitter look and turned away. She seemed defeated and confused. Alice looked around at the rest of us. 'Oh dear,' she said, 'I hope I didn't interrupt anything important. Did I?'

She was looking at me. I smiled at her.

'James,' she said, 'you look like the only one who isn't cross about something. Can I come and talk to you?'

I felt suddenly light-headed. I wondered how she knew my name. She slipped behind Hatchjaw, walked around the table in a few quick steps, and perched on the arm of my chair.

Her flank was touching my shoulder. I felt the blood thicken and throb in my veins. She crossed her legs, which brought her body even closer to mine, and leaned against me. I was breathing heavily. She slipped her arm around my neck and draped it over my shoulder. Out of the corner of my eye I saw Dorothy tense herself. But I didn't care. Or rather, I couldn't care, because I couldn't think. My mind had seized up.

Alice brought her head close to mine and I felt her hair brushing against the side of my face. 'Do you want to come with me, Jim?' she said. Her voice was low and husky but I knew the others could hear.

And I knew what Alice was doing. But I wanted her so much I was helpless.

I saw my arm press itself against her as I raised it and then slipped it around her hips. I knew what would happen next, and I couldn't stop it.

It was just as well that someone else did.

'Going somewhere, Jim?' Paddy said from the French windows.

I realised I was already on my feet, entwined with Alice, and we were only a few steps from the door, and the passage beyond it that would lead us, unerringly, to my bed. Eudora and Hatchjaw were staring at us, their faces white and pinched. Dorothy had turned away, refusing to look at me and what I had been about to do.

I let go of Alice and moved away from her. Her arm, which was still around my shoulder, dropped to her side. She was staring at Paddy, her face expressionless but her eyes glittering.

'I hope you don't mind if we join you,' Paddy said.

I could see the other patients, crowded behind him in

the darkness.

As my head began to clear, I felt a certain glow of pride. It was the last thing I ever imagined I'd do, but bugger me if I hadn't organised an intervention.

It had taken me more than an hour to round everyone up, and it would have been longer without Paddy's help. I'd called it Plan B when I said goodbye to Dorothy and strode off into the fog, but naturally I had no idea what I was doing. A familiar scenario, in which my confidence is matched only by my incompetence. Follow me, everyone, I know a shortcut through the quicksand.

But sometimes confidence is all you need, and I was convinced this was the most important thing I would ever do. Now I just had to convince everyone else. I was hoping I'd be able to pitch my case to a few of the friendlier inmates, and get a bit of practice on them, before tackling the patients I found less congenial.

Inevitably, the first person I encountered was Hemingway.

By the time I recognised the hulking shape ahead of me he'd already seen me and it was too late to retreat. I hauled my face into the approximation of a smile and strolled up to him, trying to pretend he wasn't the last person I wanted to see at that moment, or any moment, for that matter.

He squinted at me warily through narrowed eyes as I approached, as if I were a heavily armed guerrilla of uncertain allegiance emerging from a Catalonian forest, and continued to squint when I was inches from his face and it was perfectly clear who I was.

I smiled some more, and nodded affably at him. He crossed his arms and carried on with his masterclass in advanced squinting.

By now I was grinning at him like a masturbating chimp but it was obvious he wasn't going to compromise his virility by saying anything unless I spoke first.

'What about this fog?' I said.

'What about it?'

I resisted the temptation to talk at length about the weather just to annoy him. I had a mission. I adopted a friendly tone, making an effort not to speak through gritted teeth. 'Look,' I said, 'I think there's been some confusion about what happened in the fire. It seems neither of us are quite sure about who rescued whom.'

He narrowed his eyes even more, which I wouldn't have thought possible without closing them entirely, and tilted his head back so his chin was jutting out at me. Even the man's beard was assertive, as if demanding to know whether there were any other beards in the vicinity, and if they wanted to make something of it.

'Maybe you're not sure,' he said, 'but I am.'

'Well,' I said carefully, 'that may be the case. Perhaps we'll just have to accept that we both have a different perspective.'

He didn't reply. It was obvious what he thought of my different perspective, and where I could shove it. I tried to remind myself that the nobility of my purpose should raise me above the personal animosity between us, but he really was an insufferable prick. However, I knew I had a clear choice about what happened next.

I also had a problem. Giving up any degree of my pride and self-regard has always seemed to me like ripping out a selection of my favourite internal organs. Experimentally, I imagined myself bowing my head to Hemingway and admitting meekly that I was wrong, and offering him a sincere apology. Even thinking about it made me sick.

At that moment Hemingway sighed, and I thought I detected a softening in his features. Or maybe he was just getting a stiff neck from tilting his head back and looking down his nose at me. But I chose to take it as a conciliatory gesture, and I decided to make a concession.

'All right,' I said, 'let's leave it at that. It was a stressful situation, and it's possible I misunderstood what was happening.' There. Not just an olive branch, more like the whole bloody tree.

But no. He refused to say anything, the bastard.

I was about to turn on my heel and walk away when I heard Paddy's voice.

'What a heart-warming sight,' he said as he approached us, 'two brilliant minds, face-to-face in friendly discourse. Like stumbling upon Plato and Aristotle gossiping in the shrubbery. Master and pupil engaging in timeless dialectic.'

He stood between us with his arms folded, smiling broadly. What he'd said was rather clever. He'd clearly implied that I was in the position of being Hemingway's pupil, as Aristotle was Plato's. But in terms of character, who wouldn't prefer to be Aristotle? Plato was a miserable turd, and his views on art and artists are well known. And then there's the whole question of his behaviour towards Socrates: not showing up on the last day of his life and sending a feeble excuse about being ill, when he was obviously shitting a brick about being seen as an ally of the condemned man. You'd much rather go for a drink with Aristotle than Plato any day.

However, the comparison seemed to please Hemingway. Perhaps the suggestion that his status was technically superior to mine boosted his gigantic ego so much that it obscured any other considerations. Or perhaps he realised he couldn't reasonably object to it, and decided to be gracious about it. Either way, he nodded gruffly to Paddy, and the corners of his lips twitched upwards fractionally within the grubby foliage of his facial hair, in what he may have intended to be a smile.

I saw my chance. Paddy's arrival meant that I could now tell Hemingway everything I wanted him to know without actually talking to him. By explaining my plan to Paddy, with Hemingway as a bystander, it would be difficult for him to refuse to help me, even though I wasn't asking him to. I turned to Paddy:

'I've got an idea,' I said.

I was surprised by how readily Hemingway fell in with the plan. But not by his claim, after I'd finished outlining it, to have been thinking along very similar lines himself, and that he'd been about to broach the subject with me just before Paddy arrived. What a coincidence. However, his bluster didn't irritate me too much. Perhaps I was just getting used to him. But there was something else, too. When I began to talk about how much the two doctors were suffering, and what we all owed to them, his expression changed. He looked at me searchingly, without the hostile squint that I'd been finding such a disincentive to frank and friendly conversation.

'So this plan is going to help Dr Bassett?' he said.

'Both of them,' I replied. 'We need to help both of them get over themselves and face the fact they're in love with each other.'

Hemingway's countenance seemed to undergo a spasm of some kind, which he suppressed quickly. 'Then I guess they deserve to be happy,' he said, 'if anyone does.'

I got the impression he was making an effort to be manful about something, and then it dawned on me what it was. I should have guessed. She was an attractive doctor, and he was…well, he was Ernest Hemingway. He was in love with her himself, whatever he thought that meant. I realised I should probably reconsider everything that had happened between us in this light, and everything I felt about him. I still considered him utterly insufferable, but at least he was human. As human as the rest of us.

We found the others easily enough. None of them had strayed far from the house and everyone was eager to help. They were all dispirited by the situation between Bassett and Hatchjaw, and some were in tears. Each one of them confessed they'd been haunted by the thought of what would happen if they abandoned the two doctors in such a wretched condition, and in every case they gave this as the reason they hadn't tried to leave.

We located every inmate. As the assembly grew, and people discussed the proposal, they shook their heads with wry surprise, or smote their brows, or found other ways to emphasise their astonishment that they hadn't thought of it themselves, and said how blindingly obvious it was once you considered it.

There were no dissenters. I think anyone who may have had doubts was probably swayed by the fact that Hemingway and I appeared to have settled our differences. Not that we were exchanging fond caresses, exactly, or tenderly picking lice out of each other's hair, but at least we seemed able to tolerate each other's company.

And now here they came. A few of them were nervous, but they all knew what was expected of them. Even those who had never experienced an intervention, or even heard of the idea, grasped it very quickly and found it impressively horrifying. The last thing an addict wants is to change, and being forced to confront the consequences of our behaviour is an appalling prospect precisely because we suspect it could work.

None of us believed Bassett and Hatchjaw were addicts, but I still thought of what we were doing as an intervention. We wanted them to change their behaviour, and we were going to confront them with the impact it had on us. We wanted to tell them they were no different from the rest of us, and deserved to be happy.

But that was before Alice arrived.

As Paddy stepped into the room he saw her and stopped in his tracks. Then he staggered forward as Mary Seacole collided with him. Everyone else had begun to file in behind her, and now they all came to a halt in a series of minor pile-ups. But even as Paddy recovered from the impact of Mary's considerable bulk he didn't take his eyes off Alice for an instant.

'Hello, lovely Patrick,' Alice said.

Paddy stood stock still. His mouth was slack.

It was Dorothy who came to the rescue. 'Come on in, Pat!' she said very loudly, as if he were deaf. 'You appear to know Alice already, so don't stand there like a petrified fish, keeping everyone else outside in the cold.'

Paddy seemed to pull himself together. 'Alice,' he said. He nodded to her and walked across the room, averting his eyes as she pouted at him. He took up position with his back against the far wall and then became intensely interested in his shoes.

By this time Mary Seacole had walked into the room and come to a dead stop, just like Paddy. She seemed stunned by the sight of Alice, and gazed at her fearfully.

In an instant, Alice was transformed. She switched off the sultry pout she'd used on Paddy and beamed at Mary like a mother seeing her child after a long absence. The effect was astonishing. Mary heaved a great, shuddering sigh and her face began to collapse into a mess of grief and yearning.

But then a strange thing happened.

Coleridge appeared on one side of Mary, and Hemingway on the other. Both men stopped and did a kind of double take when they saw Alice, but then other people began to come in behind them. They flowed into the room around Mary like a tide around a rock, and as they did so, Mary pulled back from the brink of disintegration and began to glare at Alice. As this happened Coleridge and Hemingway broke free from their immobility, edged past Mary, and walked over to join Paddy.

The spell was broken. Alice seemed to lose her composure. She was trying to dazzle each new arrival with her attention, but as their number increased the power of her allure became visibly diluted. The effort of making whatever adjustments were necessary to captivate each individual was simply beyond her. There were too many of us.

As the room filled up I glanced over at Eudora and Hatchjaw. They were sitting very still and watching everything quietly. They didn't appear particularly troubled by what was happening. In fact, they looked relieved.

Alice was no longer concerned with the rest of us. She fixed Wallace and Eudora with a steady, piercing gaze, which she maintained as she wove her way swiftly across the room until she was standing in front of them. I understood she was now trying to isolate the two doctors from the rest of us.

She looked down at them. 'You know what these stupid people are doing, don't you?' she said. Her voice sounded thinner and had lost some of its richness.

Eudora raised her eyebrows. 'Not exactly,' she said, 'but I imagine they want to tell us something. It looks like a kind of intervention to me.'

'They don't care about you,' Alice hissed. 'You know what they're like.' She turned to Hatchjaw. 'You know, don't you, Wallace? They're selfish brutes who abuse your good nature.' She reached out and stroked his hair once more, and her voice regained some of its smooth, creamy texture. 'You're so kind to them, and they just want more and more from you. I wish you'd let me look after you,' she whispered, turning back to Eudora, 'both of you. We're so good together, the three of us.'

'Leave them alone!' cried an angry, high-pitched voice very close to me. It took me a moment to realise it was mine. I cleared my throat.

Everyone turned to look at me, including Alice, whose eyes met mine with such intensity that I felt it almost like a physical blow. They seemed to expand in her small, heart-shaped face until I was unable to see anyone else in the room. I consciously tried to lower the pitch of my voice as I spoke. 'It's true that we've got something to say. And we're going to say it whether you like it or not.'

'You're a fool,' Alice said.

She had a point. I hadn't thought all this through, and having said we were going to say something, I now didn't know what else to say. Luckily my narrative instincts, combined with a natural inability to keep my mouth shut, took over.

I tried to look past Alice and address Eudora. 'We were all outside,' I said, which was pretty obvious but I had to start somewhere, 'and none of us wanted to leave. We were all so upset by what's happened with you two. We need you to know how much you both mean to us.'

Alice shifted slightly, obscuring my view of the doctors. 'You mean you want to project all your problems onto them, as usual,' she said, 'and they're such good people they can't refuse to help you. You're vampires, all of you. Take responsibility for your own lives, and let these poor people have theirs.'

'I don't want a life of my own,' Hatchjaw said.

Alice whirled around to face him. 'What are you talking about? Of course you do.'

Hatchjaw ignored her. He looked around the room at the rest of us, nodding slowly, as if he were drinking in some kind of nourishment from us.

Eudora was now back in my sightline. She smiled at me. 'Thank you, Jim.'

Alice turned on her. 'Don't thank him, for fuck's sake! He's trying to drag you back into the bloody nightmare!' She spread her arms, attempting to encompass both the doctors in a kind of embrace. 'You can walk away from all this,' she cried, 'and just come with me!'

'Lady,' drawled a voice from the corner, 'you want to talk about vampires, take a look in the mirror.' We all turned to see Hunter Thompson leaning against the wall. 'Or maybe don't look in the mirror,' he continued, the cigarette holder clamped between his teeth waggling up and down as he spoke, 'because you may not see anything.'

'Aha!' Coleridge cried, clapping his hands together and making everyone jump. 'Well said!' He turned to Thompson, presenting his portly little belly to him, and began to declaim: 'Why stares she with unsettled eye?

Can she the bodiless dead espy?'

'Christabel,' said Thompson. His cigarette holder shot up as he grinned.

He was right: Coleridge was quoting from his own poem, which is at least partly a vampire story. I've always been rather ashamed by how much I like it, as it's dreadful Gothic hokum. But despite its silliness the poem exerts a powerful fascination. Especially as a lot of it is, essentially, steamy lesbian erotica. God bless literature.

'Oh, be quiet, all of you!' Alice said.

'Why should we?' Dorothy said from beside me. I looked at her, and although she barely returned my glance I sensed that the bond between us had been restored.

Alice turned on her. 'Because they don't need to hear all this from you,' she spat. 'Can't you see it's your needy, whining demands on them that are driving them apart?'

'Not from where I'm standing,' Paddy said, jerking his chin at the two doctors.

Alice whirled around to see that Eudora and Wallace were holding hands. She swooped towards them. 'Can't the three of us be happy again?' she said.

Eudora shook her head. She winced for a moment and I saw that Hatchjaw was clutching her hand so tightly it was white.

Colette's husky voice broke in. 'It is lovely. They want only each other.' She gave a throaty chuckle that subsided into the soft rattle of an old smoker's cough.

Alice turned on her. 'Keep out of this! All of you!' She

looked around the room with a scowl.

Something had happened to Alice in the last few moments. Her face was no longer animated by the elfin, gamine quality that had made it so vivacious, and now her features seemed merely sharp and pointed. In fact her whole body had changed. The litheness had left it, and instead of being sinuous and supple she now appeared thin and bony. She seemed smaller and, disturbingly, older.

'We don't want them to keep out of it, Alice,' said Eudora from behind her. 'That's what you could never understand, could you? That it's about other people.'

Alice balled her fists and held them against her sides. She was shaking. 'You don't know what you want!' She flung the words over her shoulder, still scanning the room, looking at us wildly now, as if searching for some sign of weakness in our faces, or anything she could use for leverage.

My God, I thought, she's just a shrill, nasty little woman.

'Alice, we're sorry,' Eudora said. 'We can't help you.'

The sadness in her voice startled me. Once again, the atmosphere in the room had changed. Now the doctors seemed like parents, heartbroken by a terrible duty.

I thought of my own parents, whose failed efforts to conceal their disappointment in me eventually made me feel so terrible that I cleared off as soon as I could. It was only later that I discovered, as all adults do, through practising such strategies themselves, that these efforts were bogus, and their brave smiles and pained reassurances were intended to be penetrated, so they could let me know how badly I'd let them down, and how angry they felt, without risking the unpleasantness that any direct expression of emotion might cause. A typical English family, really. Don't make a scene, it's not nice.

But there was none of this calculation in Eudora's voice, or in Hatchjaw's haunted expression of regret. They cared about Alice, as much as they cared about us, and whatever else she may have been, she was a person who was suffering, tormented by the self-inflicted unhappiness unique to our species.

It was this realisation that stripped Alice of the last vestiges of allure and glamour with which she'd been able to mesmerise us, and she seemed to resign herself to its loss at this moment, too. The last of her energy drained away before our eyes.

I think everyone in the room had come to the same understanding about Alice. She was, undoubtedly, the mysterious figure each of us had glimpsed periodically at the edge of the woods. Our own imaginations had lent her the resemblances we thought we saw in her. We had attributed great power to her, and now we all realised that any power she had, depended entirely on our own belief in it. However, by some means or other she had induced us to invest that belief in her – and that, after all, is a kind of power in itself.

But even if that power or ability was now diminished, and with it the enchantment she cast over us, that didn't make her any less strange or disturbing. And while she may have been as damaged and troubled as the rest of us, she was different, in a way that had once awed us and now repulsed us.

She didn't belong here. Alice now knew this with as much certainty as the rest of us. She stared around the room, no longer attempting to hold our gaze and compel our engagement, but as if she simply wanted to fix us in her mind. Then she turned and walked slowly but steadily to the French windows and stepped out of the room without a backwards glance.

As I gazed after her I saw with a shock that beyond the windows it was beginning to get light. Dawn was approaching through the lingering mist, into which Alice faded, her shape seeming to remain for a moment, delineated by its wisps, before all corporeal trace of her was dispelled, and the vapour that held her form began to drift away.

Something seemed to clear within the room as well. Despite the mystery of our presence there, nothing now felt mysterious, and everything seemed blessedly ordinary. I was seeing everyone plainly. We were patients in a rehab facility: the usual collection of noble jackasses, fascinating in the infinite variety of our dreams, dull in the familiar stubbornness of our folly. And the doctors were simply two exemplary people who wanted to help us. The fact that they also loved each other passionately was both wonderful and cheering, a strange and unexpected aspect of the healing we all craved.

They were still holding hands, and now they looked around at us, smiling.

'Thank you for doing this,' Eudora said.

'No need for that,' Dorothy said, 'we haven't done

anything.'

'Yes you have,' Hatchjaw said, 'just by being here. You've reminded us what's important. There's nothing more to do.'

'Are you sure?' I said.

'Positive,' Eudora said. She really did look happy.

Paddy laughed, pushing himself away from the wall. 'You mean there's no need for all the speeches we've prepared so carefully?'

'No,' Hatchjaw said, 'but if you've put a lot of work into them please go ahead, and we'll gladly listen. Especially if you might find it therapeutic.'

'Oh, shut up, Wallace,' Eudora said fondly.

'All right,' he said, and laughed. 'Perhaps I will. But I may have to take up smoking again.'

I looked around the room. No one seemed disappointed that they wouldn't now be required to talk publicly about how they felt, and many people looked relieved. I was pretty sure everyone felt as tired as I did. Tired but happy.

Hemingway stretched, and yawned ostentatiously, setting off the usual contagion.

'Yes,' Eudora said, 'perhaps we should all try to get some rest.'

People began to move. It was time to go to bed.

I was aware of Dorothy, close beside me, and was suddenly uneasy. I wanted to go to bed by myself but how could I tell her that without hurting her feelings? Before I could think of anything to say she took my hands:

'Jim, I'm dead beat. I don't know if I have the energy for any gymnastics in the sack right now, much as I like it. Sweetheart, how about we take a rain check?'

I felt a stab of indignation. It was absurd but I couldn't help it. I was being rejected.

Dorothy smiled. 'Sorry, did I beat you to it?'

I laughed. We opened our arms to each other, and fitted our bodies together comfortably. We kissed with gentle deliberation. After a few moments we disengaged. Dorothy gazed into my eyes and I gazed back. Whatever we saw there seemed to amuse us equally and there was nothing for it but to kiss again. Eventually we released each other and both took a step back, rather formally, as if obeying some unseen cue. She gave me a final smile, full of affection but with a hint of wistfulness.

'Sleep well, Jim.'

'You too, Dottie.'

We turned away from each other and went our separate ways.

Everyone was leaving. No one was talking now, but the silence felt natural and companionable as people made their way to the various exits. I glanced over to see what Eudora and Wallace were doing, but they'd gone.

I reached the door and walked out without looking back, heading for my room. I felt weary, but in a very pleasant way.

I looked forward to getting some sleep.

Transcript

Memorial service for James Foster at St Mary's Church, Nether Stowey

Eulogy by Felicity Pickering (previously Felicity Foster, James's first wife)

Good afternoon, everyone. It's wonderful to see so many people here, and it was very moving to hear the messages and tributes from those who couldn't make it. I thought Angela read them out very beautifully. And I'd like to take this opportunity to thank her personally for conducting such a lovely service. I had no idea Jim had got involved with the Quakers, and Paula tells me she was in the dark, too. So, one more intriguing little secret – but probably not the last one, even now – from a man who inspired love, loyalty and limitless exasperation in equal measure.

(*Laughter*)

If I wanted to be cynical I could say – with no offence to Angela at all – that perhaps Jim had been attending Quaker meetings to research something he was writing. But it's also quite possible that he was very sincere, and had developed some kind of spiritual belief. And, of course, both those possibilities could be true. We're all complex, contradictory creatures, but Jim took positive relish in those contradictions, and his delight in the contrariness of human nature, especially his own, was a vital part of who he was.

And I may as well say it, because it's what we're all thinking: *what would Jim have made of this?* I know it's a cliché to say that someone would have enjoyed their own funeral, and it's a pity they're missing it, and then to go on to say that in a way, you know, they *are* here... which Jim would have called sanctimonious drivel. Many years ago, when we were married, we once discussed funeral plans in a vague, speculative way. Jim said he had only one request; it was that if anyone dared to read out that terrible poem saying that death is nothing at all, and he was only in the next room, to kindly beat them to death with a shovel immediately, so they could come and join him in the next room.

(*Laughter*)

Whatever else you thought of Jim you have to admit he could be very funny when he wanted to. When I think of the early years of our marriage, nearly all I can remember is laughing with him. It's that playfulness which I will miss so much...sorry. Damn, I swore to myself I wasn't going to do this.

(*Pause*)

Sorry. That's better. Right. Phew. I may have vowed not to cry but you notice I brought a handkerchief up here with me.

(*Laughter*)

Jim would have had something to say about that. Something about the unconscious, I expect, or some infuriating generalisation about women that would still make me laugh.

Anyway, the reason I wish Jim was here is not only because *he* would enjoy it but because *we* would enjoy it. Hearing what he had to say about it, getting his take on it, that distinctive voice, that mixture of scepticism and something else – dare I say tenderness? I will, and it's taken a long time for me to be able to use an affectionate word like that about him. Those of you who knew us well, and witnessed the break-up and its aftermath, will know that I used a lot of words about him in those days and none of them were affectionate. But I just needed time for the wound to heal. Time, and the love of a good man. Without Adam, who is the kindest and most understanding man in the world, our reconciliation wouldn't have happened. Oh God, look, I'm making him blush.

(*Laughter*)

I'm sorry, darling, but it's true. And I will always, always be grateful that you, Adam, are such an extraordinary man that you were able to make us all friends, and we've all had such a good time together in the last few years: us and Jim and Paula. I know, I know – how frightfully modern and middle-class, but it's a damn sight better than staying angry and bitter, isn't it? Sorry, I'll get back on track, and I won't go on for much longer.

Graham Greene famously said that a writer must have a chip of ice in his heart. Jim told me he had a slightly different version of that idea, and sorry about the language but these are his words, not mine; he said that as well as a chip of ice a certain type of writer also needs a smear of shit on his soul. I don't know if that's true, but Jim insisted that a writer like him needed that smear of shit to keep him in the world, and prevent him from disappearing, as he put it, up his own fundament. It was like a vaccination, he said. He also said that great writers didn't need that reminder, because they're always in the world, but he didn't consider himself a great writer, and claimed he was liable to take himself too seriously if he wasn't careful. I don't know if he was a great writer or not, and people will have their own opinions about that. But I do believe he had great talent – for writing, and perhaps more especially for life. In the end that may have been his greatest gift: the ability to enjoy life to the full.

Which is what made Jim so attractive. No matter where he was or who he was with, he was determined to find something to enjoy. And if someone is so clearly enjoying life in your company it makes you feel attractive and special yourself. So you want to be around a person like that. That quality, in a successful, good-looking man, can be very hard to resist. I know that a lot of women, including some of the women here, didn't exactly make a heroic effort to do so.

(*Laughter*)

When Jim was teaching the Creative Writing classes that he pretended to despise so heartily, and said he was only doing for the money, he would tell his students that character is defined through action: that if you want to know what a character is really like, throw a crisis at them and see how they deal with it. That seems to be true in life as much as it does in a book or screenplay. In many ways James's entire life was a process of testing that idea, and plunging himself into one crisis after another to define, and perhaps to forge his own character. And over the years I noticed that however much he mocked the ambitions of his students, and made merciless fun of them in private (in a highly entertaining fashion, as you can imagine), he was always ready to help them. He was very generous with his time, and patient, and encouraged them wholeheartedly, and I know for a fact that many of them felt extremely grateful to him and were inspired by him. And yet if you'd judged him only on what he said to you about his classes, and those students, you wouldn't have known that. So if you want to judge him, judge him on the number of people who have come here today to remember him, and the way we all feel about him. All the other stuff was played for laughs, and it got plenty of them.

But there was much more to Jim than that. He was an extraordinary man. We all know that, and that's why what he did at the end didn't surprise us. I bet he thought it would, but it didn't, because we knew what he could be, behind all the faults that he could see more clearly than anyone else. And what he could be was the unique man we will all miss so much. In the end, the best possible tribute I can pay to Jim is that it was a pleasure to know him. And I feel lucky to have had that truly exhilarating pleasure. Thank you.

Transcript

Memorial service for James Foster at St Mary's Church, Nether Stowey

Eulogy by Paula Foster (James's second wife)

Hello everyone. Thank you so much for coming. James had so many friends, and I don't even know a few of the people here, who knew him before I met him, but it's wonderful to see you and I hope I get a chance to meet you all later.

There are also two very special people here who some of you may not have met, although you probably know about them. Amit and Mark, the paramedics who were the first to arrive after the crash. They're at the back there. Sorry, guys, I don't want to embarrass you, but everyone is so grateful to you. Thank you so much for being here.

I am standing here today with a strange mixture of feelings. I am sad, of course, so very sad to have lost James. And at the same time I feel proud, and also grateful. James saved my life, and he sacrificed his own life to do it. That is the simple truth. Amit and Mark are quite clear about it: James refused to be taken from the car until they got me out, even though they thought there was a much better chance that James would survive, and I think James knew that. But still he insisted. And this is what makes me feel that I am lucky, or perhaps I should say blessed, because as I am grieving, and missing James so desperately, I have those other feelings to comfort me.

What Felicity said was true: we're not really surprised. I know I'm not, anyway. I'm not saying James was a saint, because we all know he was far from it. Even with me he could be angry and cruel. But he was also very, very kind. I think he was kind to a lot of people, in his own way, but I think I saw it more than anyone else. Maybe because I am from a different world, not a literary type like most of you, and also, of course, from a different country. And I think James could relax with me because of that. We all know he had a very competitive streak, and he was always ready to have an argument, especially with other writers, although I could always see the affection behind it.

But with me he was almost too kind. Of course, there was the age difference, and he was very protective of me. And sometimes it was actually frustrating for me, to be honest, that he simply refused to see anything bad in me. It was unrealistic, but it made him so happy to believe I was a completely good person. But I can be just as horrible as anyone else, I can assure you! Maybe even as horrible as a writer!

(*Laughter*)

I had a dream about James two nights ago. I know it's very boring to hear about other people's dreams, so I'll keep it short. For the last few days I've been uneasy, wondering if James really understood how much I loved him. I know it's common, when we lose someone close to us, to say, 'Oh, I wish I'd told them I loved them,' but nonetheless I felt it very powerfully, and it made me unhappy. Then, in my dream, I was at the edge of a kind of forest, and I saw James, quite close to me. I wanted very much for him to come with me, away from that place: to come back to life, I guess. But then he looked at me and I knew it was all right to let him go. I could see that he knew very well how much I loved him, and how much all of you loved him, too. And so I left him, and I was no longer worried. I felt a kind of happiness, and that is how I still feel.

Okay, it was just a dream, and it would be easy to say that the psychology of a dream like this is simple, and it's just wishful thinking. But the dream was very strong, it was exceptionally vivid: the smell of the trees in that forest, and the dampness of a kind of mist that was between us. And I tell you about all this simply because I'm convinced that deep down James knew how all of us felt, and that he loved us, too, all of us. I'm sure of it.

So, while it's only natural for us to mourn our loss, let's not be unhappy. James may have been a complicated person but some things about him were quite simple. If I learned anything from him, it's that there is nothing wrong with wanting to be happy, especially if we can make other people happy too. That's very simple, isn't it? And yet so often we forget how important it is. James made me happy, and I hope he made you happy too, and I hope the memories we have of him and the love we feel for him will continue to make us happy.

Thank you once again for coming.

FJ
Final diary entry

Sorry.

I've gone too far. Putting those words into Paula's mouth was shameless even by my standards. At least Felicity is still alive and can defend herself. In fact, if I keep any of this material I may delete the previous section altogether. Writing the script for your own memorial service is too much of an indulgence, and now it's time to stop.

But I did warn you, right at the start, that I would be making it all up. Fair play.

I've been told not to write any more, or advised not to, which amounts to the same thing. We're encouraged to get involved in activities here, and they had no objection to me keeping a diary, but when Dr Beedsly found out what I was actually writing he didn't like it at all. According to him, I'm using fiction to avoid the truth about my condition, and the 'fantasy' I've been writing is a form of denial. He said I'm trying to control the narrative, which I thought was pretty funny, but he didn't.

'I'm a writer,' I said. 'Controlling the narrative is my job description.'

'Not in here,' he said. 'Recovering Substance Abuser is your job description here. Tell me, do you feel that what you've been writing is helping with that job?'

'It's helping me process my experience.'

'Process it, or avoid it, do you think? You may be an old hand at this, James, but it doesn't mean you can take a shortcut. My perception is that what you've been doing means we're still stuck at step one. What do you feel about that?'

'Oh, come on. I accept I'm powerless. I really do.'

'I think we need to do some more work on that, James.'

Hello twelve-step, my old friend.

I asked if he wanted me to destroy everything I've written. No, he said, just don't write any more of it. He also suggested that I begin my inventory (Hello, step four) by rounding off this diary with a brief summary of the facts. The truth, in other words.

Almost everything I've written so far is a fabrication,

distortion or exaggeration, including the swashbuckling, Rabelaisian persona I created for myself. I'm less entertaining in real life. Whatever that is. I've been distracting myself by writing a story, but now I may have to find out.

Is Beedsly right? I think I wanted to get busted for the diary, which is why I left it on the table in the Blue Room where I knew he was just about to sit down at coffee break. I made sure I left it open, too, to help him overcome any qualms about patient confidentiality he may have had. I was pretty sure he wouldn't have any, though, as he's a bit of a starfucker beneath the lofty, Olympian compassion, and he's rather proud of the writers, rockers and ravers who frequent this joint. It's got a good reputation among recovery cognoscenti and it's quite fashionable in a shabby chic way.

And Beedsly is good, no doubt about it. He's charismatic, and he's devised his own version of the twelve-step approach that appeals to intelligent, creative types more than the standard model, because in small, subtle ways it flatters them. So does he, and when he gazes at you with his heavy-lidded brown eyes, magnified behind his rimless glasses, his attention is like a warm bath. He makes you believe he's truly fascinated by your unique story, rather than being bored shitless by it, having doubtless heard the same one countless times. It's always the same one.

So, I apologise if I've misled you. It's been fun.

It's all fun and games until someone dies in a car crash.

Paula and I had been to lunch with Felicity and Adam. I was driving us home, and with my impeccable sense of timing I chose the worst possible moment to tell Paula I wanted to talk about our relationship. When has that announcement ever been anything other than a prelude to bad news? Nobody says, 'Darling, I think we should talk about our relationship because it's all going so terrifically well.' If it's going well, you don't need to talk about it, in the same way that a doctor doesn't need to talk to you about your test results if there's nothing wrong.

We were 20 minutes from home, and Paula was nearly asleep. I was doing about 80 along a straight stretch of motorway. I cleared my throat, and then delivered the fateful phrase like a stillborn child. Paula sat bolt upright. I glanced at her and saw she was staring at me with a wild look in her eyes. I hadn't drunk anything, of course, but she'd had some wine with lunch. Quite a lot of wine, I guess. And some champagne beforehand.

'What do you mean?' she said, a catch in her voice.

I realised how stupid I'd been. 'It's okay,' I said, 'it can wait until we're home.'

'James, what is it?' she cried, and threw her arm around my neck, pulling herself towards me with perhaps more strength than she'd intended, causing me to turn the wheel involuntarily. An ear-splitting klaxon wailed from a truck we were overtaking. I was level with the driver's cab and I glimpsed his white, angry face, contorted by the obscenities he mouthed at me. Paula's fingers were woven into the curls at the back of my neck and she tugged at them, trying to kiss me. As her lips brushed my cheek I lost control of the car.

If you had to choose, is it better to be loved by someone you don't love, or to love someone who doesn't love you back? It's probably a meaningless question but it's the kind of thing that ran around my mind as I recovered, furious that my body insisted on healing itself, despite being very badly burned. It seemed horribly cruel, to be in increasingly good shape for the annihilation awaiting me. I was like a prisoner on death row receiving the best medical attention to make sure I was healthy enough to be killed. And so it turned out. When I was well enough, grief destroyed me.

The really terrible thing about grief is that it's so fucking boring.

It's like having a chronic illness: all you can think of is your own sickness; it dominates your life, it fills the screen, it demands your attention at every moment, and leaves you no escape from yourself. Eventually the sheer tedium of being so utterly self-absorbed becomes unbearable. And when life becomes unbearable for an addict there's only one thing to do.

I took refuge from grief in the old, familiar fortress of self-pity, from whose ramparts the addict pours boiling recrimination on everyone and everything except himself (save a few accidental splashes). I was convinced I had a legitimate excuse for once, as I was in genuine pain and my suffering was intolerable. Which is exactly how you feel every time, of course. Justification, that's the name of the game.

And when the wearisome hullaballoo abated, I found myself here.

I wonder if I would want to be the person I wrote about: the man who died to save his wife. The sinner who is finally redeemed by an unselfish act. Everyone loves that story.

Did it work? I hope the way I constructed the character didn't seem too contrived. What I was aiming for was a gradual shift in perception, with a growing appreciation of the protagonist's depth and complexity. Slowly the reader would realise that the man I introduced myself as at the beginning of this account was a mask, and that beneath the assumed mantle of the cynical, curmudgeonly misanthrope a noble heart was awakening. I may have gone a bit over the top by the end, with the stuff at the memorial service, but I don't care. It's all an exercise in wishful thinking and there's no reason to hold back.

And yet.

The stupid thing is that I really was trying to be that man. I didn't want to break up with Paula. I was doing what I thought was best, for her. I was trying to be unselfish and noble. I may not have sacrificed my life for her, as I do in the story, but I wanted to sacrifice my happiness, because I thought she'd be happier without me.

What a fucking idiot.

Paula loved me, and I loved her. I loved her more than

I realised, and now she's gone I love her even more. What a mess.

The fantasy of cleaning up that mess is what I've been constructing.

Life is a mess, and dying can be messy, too. But the idea of death itself is orderly, and the experience of how it feels to be dead exists only in our imagination, and so it can be controlled. One of the things I wanted to achieve with my story was to rewrite the terrible mess of my relationship with Paula and the horrible way it ended. I wanted to make it like the love affair with Dorothy Parker that I created for myself: not without its challenges, of course, and not lacking in passion either – but essentially under control; the melancholy tinged with just enough wisdom to be agreeably bittersweet, the parting poignant but loving, and a result of mutual choice.

The kind of bullshit that only happens in stories. Save us from the truth, dear fiction, and give us the illusion of a greater truth so we can feel okay about ourselves.

Big day tomorrow. It's been two weeks, and now I'm allowed visitors. Not that you'd want visitors in the first week anyway, as the physical detox renders you pretty much unfit for human consumption. And then you have to spend a week of what I can only describe as muted despair, while you face what you've done, yet again, and the destruction you've wrought. It's a painful, lonely process but it wouldn't be improved by having company. No witnesses, thank you. But once you've got through it they open the doors to your nearest and dearest, if those two categories aren't mutually exclusive. They encourage your family to visit, but the only person I'm expecting to see is Paddy.

He's not dead, as you may have deduced. That was just another exercise in wishful thinking, although it's only a small part of me that's ever wished him dead, and that part was usually deranged in one way or another – by drink, drugs, jealousy, anger, love, or any of the things that you always seem to have had not quite enough of at one moment, and just a bit too much of the next.

I look forward to seeing him, as much as I look forward to seeing anyone. And I mean that in the nicest possible way. In the absence of the one person my heart yearns for, Paddy's company will occupy that absence in a way that won't actively drive me to madness and despair. That's as good as it's going to get.

Emptiness must be filled, and the world will have its way. The absence of one thing means the presence of everything else except that one thing. If you're lucky you can choose which parts of everything else you want to allow into your life. Paddy has never judged me and I know he just wants me to be happy. I count that as friendship, which is no small thing in an unfriendly world.

Now I'm going to sleep.

Dr Myles Beedsly

To: paddywhackhack@gmail.com

Re: Your visit

Dear Patrick,

Thank you for visiting James yesterday. As we agreed, I'm writing to let you know how he seems to be doing today, now that the dust has settled from yesterday's events.

First, let me say that James is very lucky: you are a true friend to him, and I can see you care about him deeply. I know he cares about you, too, and I hope that was confirmed in the hours you spent together, which were clearly emotionally draining for both of you. I feel privileged to have been present for some of that time. As you can imagine, in the many years that I have been doing my work I have witnessed all kinds of encounters and confrontations in these meetings, but I can honestly say the compassionate intelligence you showed James, and your commitment to his well-being, are of a kind I see only rarely.

James was pretty shaken by what you helped him to face, and by the realisation that he has a lot of very hard work ahead of him if he is to return to health and wholeness. Only someone who knows him as well as you do could have encouraged him to confront the seriousness of his illness with such forcefulness – which is the only way to penetrate the layers of denial James has built up to protect himself against the terrible pain he is in. Denial has an awesome power, and a mind as clever and creative as James's can make it almost impregnable, using apparent self-awareness to actually strengthen and entrench the denial itself. For all our talking, true change must happen in the heart.

On that subject, James's heart is tender, and it has received a kind of trauma from yesterday's events. My hope is that he will be jolted out of his self-deception and set on the road to recovery. But I must be truthful and tell you I can't be sure. Sometimes we see people make remarkable breakthroughs and we are then disappointed. There is still a long, hard road ahead for James. But on balance I am optimistic.

Thank you once again for coming all the way from London, and spending so long with your friend, and committing yourself with such passion and integrity to his recovery. Now it's up to him. I will let you know of any developments, and in the meantime I look forward to seeing you again next week. By the way, I am a great admirer of your writing.

With my very best wishes,

Myles Beedsly

FJ Diary

I awoke suddenly. It was dark and I had no idea where I was.

It'll come to me. Until one day it doesn't, which is what happened to my mother.

The snowflakes settle on the white sheet, and are absorbed by it, and there's a flare of white and then slowly everything gets dark.

If I could have a blowjob for every time I've woken up without a clue where I was I'd be on a tight schedule. Sometimes I've woken up and had the blowjob there and then, or even been woken up by it, which is a nice way to begin the process of finding out where you are and who you're with and what happened last night. It's usually nice, anyway, although I woke up once to find myself being expertly fellated by a head that felt, as I began to caress it encouragingly, a bit lumpy. I squinted down and saw a few strands of greasy grey hair plastered over a scabbed, flaky scalp. A flicker of memory. Dancing under Waterloo bridge. Homeless people. Then it all came back. It's amazing how much goodwill you can generate among a group of elderly derelicts if you arrive at their cardboard campfire with two bottles of vodka in the early hours of the morning, just when the party is flagging and some of the revellers are becoming downhearted in a way that's often expressed, in these social circles, through unpredictable outbursts of violence. You can really cheer them up. And now, as dawn chilled the air, one of them was showing their gratitude in the only way available to her. Or possibly him. God help me, I didn't want to know how much worse this could be. I swatted the scaly head away from my groin, staggered to my feet, nearly fell down again under the impact of a tremendous hammering headache and ran away.

I used to tell that story and think it was funny.

Very faintly, I heard a bird singing. I wondered what time it was. I tried to gather my thoughts and feelings together. Perhaps I could make something of them. Possibly a rudimentary person, or the semblance of one. Why not? In the beginning God simply took some mud, and breathed on it, and hey presto, a full-size, naked, jabbering sinner is up in your face, raring to go. Up with the lark.

But my thoughts were vague and disordered, and as

for feelings, they rippled through me swiftly like a shoal of fish streaking past, and I couldn't grasp any of them for long enough to know what they were. Everything was ominous and uncertain.

I tried to listen to the bird again, in case it had a message for me. But it had stopped singing.

Daylight was penetrating the curtains. At least it wasn't night. That was something.

Slowly an unfamiliar feeling stirred in me. Perhaps it was just a meaningless spasm of cells: a ghost, drifting through my machine, but it felt like something more definite, with a shape and a tiny, determined pulse. It could have been hope.

I opened the curtains. The fresh morning sun shone on the glistening grass, the trees, and the distant, rolling hills.

A movement caught my eye. Someone was standing at the edge of the woods. It was a woman. She waved at me. In an instant – in less than an instant – anything I may have been thinking and feeling, conscious or unconscious – my worries and fears, my aches and pains, my sadness and confusion – all of it was blown away by an explosion of joy as I saw it was Paula.

Happiness filled me up like helium in a balloon.

I knew she would come.

All she has for me is love. She never judged me, no matter what foul or filthy things I said or thought or did. That story about the blowjob, for example. She just accepted things like that. Even Paddy sometimes recoiled from my worst excesses, although I could see he tried not to. He more or less admitted that was the case, not long before he died, by way of a kind of confession. He said he hoped I'd forgive him if he'd sometimes held back, or thought any worse of me for my lack of restraint. He said he was quite jealous of my ability to surrender myself to all those impulses. I told him he hadn't missed much, except a lot of useless trouble. Not quite true, actually, but there was no need to tell him so at that stage.

But Paula loves me unconditionally and now she's waiting for me. When I reach her she'll put her hand in mine and lead me through the woods, glancing at me every now and then and giving me the smile that's for me alone. We'll emerge from the far side of the forest and climb the gentle hills and see what lies beyond them. At the crest of the final hill we'll stand and gaze at that unknown landscape. I'll put my arm around her slender waist and her hand will rest on my shoulder, her little fingers gently tugging at the curls on the back of my neck, and then we'll kiss, and then walk on.

Dr Myles Beedsly

To: paddywhackhack@gmail.com

Re: Unwelcome news

Dear Patrick,

I'm sorry to tell you my optimism was misplaced. James left the facility this morning. I've received information that he went into town to the supermarket, where he purchased alcohol. Worryingly, he was also seen near the steps on the far side of the pier, which is where some drug dealing goes on. I've been unable to find out where he went after that.

I've seen this before, and I must emphasise: if you should wonder whether you made a mistake in working with James on his problems in the way you did, dispel the idea instantly. Your work with James was an exemplary expression of friendship and I wish everyone who visited patients here was able to do what you did. It seems James was simply unable to face what's required of him to commit to the process of healing himself.

As you may know, we have a very strict policy here. If patients relapse during their stay they're forbidden to return here under any circumstances. This rule is drummed into them from the moment they arrive, so I'm sure James thought about what he was doing.

I've read his recovery diary. He left it out in such a way that it was clear he intended it to be read. I've photocopied and scanned the final entry he wrote and I attach it to this email. I'm not a literary critic but it seems to me that James was attempting, in some way, to write himself back into the fantasy he'd been using as a part of his denial. See what you make of what he's written. We supply the patients with notebooks in which to write their recovery diaries, and James appears to have taken a couple of fresh ones with him, suggesting he wishes to continue writing; that may be a reason not to expect the very worst, which one must always be prepared for.

If you know where James is, and you're able to contact him, please send him my very best wishes, and tell him I will never give up hope for his recovery. Naturally, I can't help feeling that what's happened is partly a failure on my part, even though I know from long experience that I am no more to blame than you or anyone else. Every decision is made by the patient alone. Nonetheless, I feel great concern for your friend's welfare, as I'm sure you do. Please keep me informed of any developments, or anything you think it's appropriate for me to know. I want to support James, and those who care for him, and I regret I'm unable to offer him further treatment here at present.

With my warmest regards,

Myles Beedsly

Patrick Warrendale
To: mylesbeedsly.healing@btinternet.com
Re: Unwelcome news

Myles,

Thanks for message. I'm sending this on haste as I think I know were Jim may has gone. I'll drive as is quicker that train at this point also Flick and maybe adam will come. You have my mobile number so please call me if you hear anything I will do same.

Best,

Paddy

Epilogue

From high above, the little churchyard looks as though it's full of freshly dug graves.

As you descend you realise the illusion is caused by the long shadows that stretch out on the grass from each gravestone. As you drop even lower you see that many of the inky shapes are truncated and irregular, cast by ancient memorials that are little more than mossy hummocks now.

But among them is a grave that's relatively recent – a matter of weeks since it was dug, by the look of the sparse growth covering it.

A man is sitting on the ground next to this grave. He is propped up against the headstone, which prevents him from toppling over. An empty bottle of vodka lies on the grass beside him. On his lap the pages of an open notebook flutter in an evening breeze. He takes no notice. His eyes are closed.

The day has been warm but the sun is setting and the air has held a chill for the last hour. It's only two miles to the sea and the Quantock stone cools quickly.

The man has lost his shoes somewhere, and his socks – if he was wearing any – and his bare feet are as pale as marble. His trousers are torn at one knee and he wears no jacket or coat, only a thin shirt. His body is losing heat very rapidly.

A man appears at the entrance to the churchyard. He runs along one side of the squat little church and then weaves through the headstones towards his friend. A woman follows him, trying to keep up, her light coat flapping like cumbersome wings. The man shouts over his shoulder and the woman slows down, but doesn't stop, as she struggles to extract a phone from her bag and make a call on the move.

Paddy reaches James's body. He encircles it with his arms, pressing his face against it. He calls something hopeful to the woman, who is gasping now as she continues to trot towards him while shouting into the phone, saying she doesn't know the postcode, it's the church, just come to the church, it's only a small place.

Paddy takes his jacket off and rolls it up into a pillow to support James's head as he eases him down onto the grass. Felicity reaches him, sobbing as she tries to catch her breath, asking if he's all right.

Paddy tells her James is bloody cold, and they try to think, their minds stumbling: should they try to wake him up? They can't remember what you're supposed to do.

Felicity says she thought you weren't meant to move them, isn't that right?

Paddy's thoughts come into focus: he tells her no, that's if people are injured, that's when you don't move them. But this is an overdose – so they should keep James awake.

Felicity asks about the risk of choking, choking on vomit, doesn't that happen? She wonders if they should do mouth-to-mouth.

Paddy says he thinks James is still breathing. He puts his cheek to James's mouth. He nods briefly to Felicity, then he begins to shake James gently, telling him to wake up, wake up, Jim, it's me, Paddy, and Flick is here, and we want you to wake up, you have to wake up. Come on, Jim, wake up.

James's head rolls from side to side. Paddy takes his face in his hands and leans in close to him. He tells James to listen. He tells him he must wake up. He says: we love you, Jim, we love you.

James's eyes open with a slow, deliberate lifting of his lids until he is looking steadily up at Paddy.

He opens his mouth. He expels a long, shallow breath. He doesn't inhale. His eyes begin to roll back into his head.

Felicity's hands fly to her mouth.

Paddy grabs James under his arms and hoists him back up into a sitting position but now James's eyes are closing. Paddy slaps his face, quite hard. He tells him not to go: don't leave us, don't you dare leave us.

Felicity drops to her knees, shedding a shoe. She gropes for James's hand and seizes it and shakes it and tells him that she needs him, everyone needs him so much, they love him, he mustn't leave them.

James becomes very still. Just as Paddy is about to slap him again James's eyes open once more. He seems to be trying to focus.

Paddy helps him with curses: fuck yes, that's it, don't go, you bastard.

James's eyes drift towards Felicity, then back to Paddy. His mouth moves. It forms the faintest trace of a smile.

Paddy grips his shoulders and shouts in his face: yes, that's it, Jim, laugh, you fucker, go on, stay alive.

James's head turns fractionally, to and fro. A shake of refusal, or something else? He draws in a shuddering breath and lets it out with a sigh. Then he's still.

Felicity gasps. She begs him to stay. Please stay with us, darling.

Silence.

In the distance the sound of a siren. Then another.

James seems to slump a little. His eyelids droop again.

Paddy cradles him, his lips close to James's ear. He tells him that it's up to him. He can make a choice. It's his call.

James's head drops forward. It's difficult to tell if he's nodding or falling.

From high above again, the ambulance and the two polices cars look oddly lurid in the stroboscopic pulses of their blue lights: too small and frivolous for their tasks. They stop beside the little church and disgorge their occupants, who swarm quickly through the churchyard.

In contrast, the trio they approach are a motionless composition, bathed in the last rays of the setting sun, like figures in a painting of a biblical event.

The professionals reach the scene and begin to do their work, focused on their actions, not thinking about the outcome, whatever it will be.

Acknowledgements

I would like to thank Scott Pack and Natalie Galustian for their valuable editorial advice through several drafts of this book, and for their patient encouragement. Thanks also to Wendy Lee, Sara Davies and Theresa Boden for their help and suggestions at different times, and to Jim Clayton for insights into how paramedic teams operate.

I'm indebted to numerous people who have written about the literary figures I've attempted to bring to life in my book. I've drawn information and inspiration from various biographies, commentaries and other works, and I've benefitted immensely from the scholarship and diligence of their authors.

Above all I'm grateful to the dead writers themselves. I hope their spirits will look kindly on my efforts, which are a labour of love.

Also by Paul Bassett Davies from Lightning Books

Please Do Not Ask for Mercy as a Refusal Often Offends

Detective Kilroy is assigned to investigate a horrible murder. He's a fine cop, from the brim of his hat to the soles of his brogues, but his inquiries, far from solving the mystery, lead him into a deeper one – and to Cynthia, an enigmatic woman with a secret that could overturn Kilroy's entire world.

But where is this world? It seems both familiar and uncanny, with electric cars, but no digital devices, and the audience for a public execution arriving by tram. Meanwhile, the seas are retreating, and the Church exerts an iron grip on society – and history. Power belongs to those who control the narrative.

Kilroy is forced to take sides between the Kafkaesque state that pays his wages, and the truth-seekers striving to destroy it, all the while becoming increasingly besotted with a woman who may only love him for his mind – in an alarmingly literal way.

Please Do Not Ask for Mercy as a Refusal Often Offends is a dystopian satire that manages to be funny and frightening in equal measure.

'Echoes of Douglas Adams at his more mischievous. Top marks for originality and subversive humour'
Maxim Jakubowski, *Crime Time*

'A detective investigating a murder unwittingly pulls back the curtain on his dystopian world in this thrilling sci-fi mystery. Davies knows how to keep the pages flying'
Publishers Weekly

'It questions power, propaganda and corruption, while maintaining emotional intelligence. It's also bloody funny'
International Times

Stone Heart Deep

When burned-out investigative journalist Adam Budd's estranged mother dies, he inherits her estate. This includes Stone Heart House, a huge, ramshackle mansion on a remote Scottish island. He visits the island to sort out her tangled affairs, and at first it seems like a charming haven of tranquillity. But after he witnesses a strange accident, he begins to develop suspicions about the inhabitants.

Why does everyone seem so eerily calm, even under stress? What is stopping Harriet, the lawyer helping him with his affairs, from leaving the island when she so clearly wants to? Is he making a big mistake by falling for her? And why have so many children gone missing?

Stone Heart Deep is a compelling and claustrophobic thriller with a remarkable twist, as if Iain Banks had rewritten *The Wicker Man*.

'A rattling good thriller. Shades of *The Wicker Man*. Once I'd started reading I could not put it down'
Iain Maitland, author of *Mr Todd's Reckoning*

'This brooding chiller is a gripping adventure'
Camden New Journal

'There are echoes of *The Wicker Man* as the outsider tries to get a grip on what is happening around him. I was engrossed in this compelling tale'
Yorkshire Times

If you have enjoyed *Dead Writers in Rehab*, do please help us spread the word – by putting a review online; by posting something on social media; or in the old-fashioned way by simply telling your friends or family about it.

Book publishing is a very competitive business these days, in a saturated market, and small independent publishers such as ourselves are often crowded out by the big houses. Support from readers like you can make all the difference to a book's success.

Many thanks.

Dan Hiscocks
Publisher
Lightning Books